Sacred Vow

Sacred Vow

C.G. Walters

a Dragon's Beard® book
DRAGON'S BEARD PUBLISHING
Micaville, NC

This is a work of fiction. All characters and events portrayed in this novel are either fictitious or used fictitiously.

Sacred Vow
Copyright © 2006 C.G. Walters
All rights reserved, including the right to reproduce this book, or portions thereof, in any form.

a Dragon's Beard® book
Published by Dragon's Beard Publishing
P.O. Box 200
Micaville, NC 28755

www.DragonsBeard.com
Dragon's Beard® is a registered trademark of Dragon's Beard Publishing, LLC

Library of Congress Control Number: 2006900006
Walters, C. G., 1956-Sacred Vow / C.G. Walters
    www.CGWalters.com
    "a Dragon's Beard® book"
    ISBN-10: 0-9774271-4-5 (pbk)
    ISBN-13: 978-0-9774271-4-7 (pbk)

Book design by arismandesign.com

1. Metaphysical-Fiction 2. Visionary-Fiction
First Trade Paperback edition: August 2006

Dragon's Beard Publishing is committed to protecting the environment and to the responsible use of natural resources. As a publisher, with paper a core part of our business, we are concerned about the future of the world's remaining endangered forests. We are committed to implementing policies that will facilitate the conservation of ancient and other endangered forests globally and will ensure that we are not contributing to the destruction of these irreplaceable natural treasures.

GPI is a non-profit program of Social and Environmental Entrepreneurs and is dedicated to increasing the use of environmentally preferable paper within the book industry. To date, 120 North American publishers have signed formal policies. GPI serves as bridge to assist publishers in the process of converting to recycled and ancient forest friendly papers. For more information, visit http://www.greenpressinitiative.org/

As good stewards of the environment, Dragon's Beard has committed to a three-to-five year initiative by implementing a company-wide policy that includes maximizing the use of recycled paper and phasing out the use of papers that may contain fibers from endangered forests.

*To the many cherished friends,
seen and unseen,
who helped bring this book
into existence*

Thank you to my dear wife, Kathy, for the casual conversation that inspired this book . . . and for reading all the many iterations that followed. Thank you for your support and belief, while the process took time, energy, and resources from everything else.

Much gratitude to Audrey and John for putting my first work into their handmade books and making me want to see more of my work in print; to Diana Donovan for the instruction and guidance to make the work suited for print.

Thanks to Roland for the conversations and sharing; to Jon for input and a flexible means to support the habit of writing; to the guys on the job (and every one of my friends) for tolerating my talking about little else. Thanks to Bruce and Paulina for the fellowship.

For your own Pu-erh tea, see Elaine at www.theteaclipper.com

Thank you, my dearest friends and support outside my own household, the back creek gang . . . my mentor, one who helps me see the possibilities and believe they are worth sharing, and my teacher. How I enjoy the "just good fun" and conversation that the four of us have together.

. . . And to you, too, Kitty—First Crone—for the teas, the conversations, and much more.

Eternally nearer than lovers entwined,
Our worlds, infinitely disparate,
In this one place.
Neither move
Without inciting the other,
Unperceived by senses
Save the intuitive.
Release your fear,
As the veil dissipates.
Nothing bizarre emerges,
For I have always been here

Dragon's Beard® Publishing

PO Box 200
Micaville, NC
28755
www.dragonsbeard.com

Publishing new works of fiction and non-fiction that focus on the mystical, metaphysical, and mythical insight within us all.

Contents

Introductions 1

The Journey 86

Going Home 205

Afterwords 270

Introductions

Prologue

Choice of the ritual location was dictated by nature just days before. Hundreds of people had roamed hill and field, dowsing for the place possessing the energy necessary for their purpose. The intended process could not take place on one of their customary ceremonial sites, but only the spot identified as radiating the strongest flow of earth energy at the anticipated time of the rite.

Three ley lines, channels of the land's energy, crossed a wooded hillside in a small patch of flat ground. Two ancient hardwood trees, one standing on either side of the rear of the opening, leaned forward before the rocky slope that bordered the backside of the level area. Their leaves filtered what little light could make its way from above.

Between the trees, at the base of the slope, there was a large greenish-gray stone. Its jagged face rose some twenty feet in the air. Three small streams, swollen with recent rains, flowed down the slope, marking the perimeter of the flat plot of land in front of the stone, before converging and flowing downward over a small waterfall. The stream-encircled ground was carpeted with a thick, soft moss.

Once the location had been identified and verified, the holy women who would use that place and its energy consecrated it. On the appointed evening, shortly after midnight, a ceremonial procession of The Nine—which consisted of the Crone Mother, leader of their mystic order, and eight more of the wisest women of their society—Katerina, understudy to the Crone Mother, and their considerable entourage made their way to the location. For several hours, from their village to the south, those who remained behind could see the winding line of torches, and hear the repetitive chants as the group made their way to the anointed site.

Once the group arrived, still in the dark of the night, attendants placed torches around the perimeter of the chosen site. Then they spread seating mats in a large circle on the ground for those who would perform the ritual, with the Crone Mother's back to the large boulder at the head of the flat ground. Katerina took her position, in the center of the circle, facing the Crone Mother. Once the members of the ceremony were seated, their retinue withdrew some distance from the site, in order not to disrupt the proceedings.

A time of silence then passed among those women remaining on the holy site, Katerina and The Nine. When no more sound of those traveling back down the hill could be heard, The Nine began a unified chant. Katerina remained silent, yielding to the trance induced by their voices. As planned, the light of dawn had just begun to make its way through the canopy of leaves.

Within a very short time, the chanting ended, but Katerina was not aware of the change. Where she had gone, The Nine could not follow, could not see what Katerina saw. Their task was now to assist Katerina in a search through her parallel lives, and to wait until she chose to return.

Hours passed as Katerina moved through the many complementary realities surrounding her—now made apparent to her by this expanded awareness—searching more than any of The Nine had anticipated as possible. The light of dawn, noon, and now late evening had filtered through the tree cover above the seated women.

Despite her travels, Katerina remained attuned to every mind and spirit involved in the ritual. She was well aware that several of the wise ones had long been wishing for her to conclude her efforts, worried not for themselves but for Katerina and the conceivable limits of her stamina. Katerina knew they would stay with her as long as she could convey assurance that she was not in any danger.

Being surrounded by the Council of Nine evoked such power and information that it was almost too much for her mortal body to endure. Each of The Nine was unequaled in her individual expertise. And all that power was being focused into a narrow beam, directly at Katerina. Fortunately, the most illuminated teachers in their culture had trained Katerina all her life for such a passage.

The collective life force of The Nine permeated every cell of Katerina's body, which resonated with an enhanced energy, supporting and shielding her from much of the impact of her transitions. Alone, she would not have been able to investigate so much, so quickly. Conversely, being assailed by their concentrated radiance was having a brutal impact on her physical form.

Katerina was always able to enter her parallel lives without the help of The Nine. In fact, she had entered into many parallel lives since being made aware of "him" a few months ago. In those unassisted visits, she could visit only one location per session, and then had to return home, resting for some extended period before traveling again. That process had proven to take far too long. It did, however, have its benefits.

Returning home between visits was necessary for Katerina's mind and spirit to filter the visited life back into the generally unperceivable background of her unconscious mind. Interim filtering wasn't happening today. This ritual was allowing Katerina to open up to alternate lives, giving each life predominance in her consciousness, just long enough to allow her to seek out what she needed to know, and then pull away from that place. Full disconnection from these lives would have to take place when she finally returned home at the end of the ritual. Today she pushed herself forward as she never had before. More than just her life and her world depended on the outcome.

Searching

No longer confined to material experience, Katerina crossed into the dimly lit room, invisible to its inhabitants. She had never visited this world before, never laid eyes on this person, yet Katerina's bond to the lean, gray-haired man seated at the wooden table was so intense and immediate that she barely managed to suppress the impulse to reach out and embrace him.

He rested a forearm on either side of the tattered book at which he stared, completely absorbed. In a few moments, he began to read aloud to himself, in a gentle voice.

"So long have we been sharing our experience, our becoming, that it no longer makes sense to imagine such a thing as either of us wholly divisible from the other . . . if it ever did make sense."

Slowly he sat upright, eyes staring in Katerina's direction, though completely unaware of her, staring *through* her formless presence and beyond her. A smile spread over his weathered face. Mesmerized, Katerina watched the man's bright eyes as he began to move his head to the left. The moment his attention came to rest, an undeniable serenity radiated from his face, drawing Katerina to turn and seek out its inspiration.

He was looking into the face of a woman sitting in a large, upholstered chair, motionless, silent, and eyes closed. Upon first recognition of that face, Katerina's intimacy with it involuntarily pulled her nearer. It was her own face on which Katerina was gazing, many years older, but indisputably *her* face. Katerina wanted to linger and rest her spirit, weary from all the traveling today, to just take in the simplicity of their life together in this place. But she knew that would be unwise.

Though only an observer, Katerina felt herself beginning to fuse into this life, making it her own. And this reality was progressively laying claim to her. Synthesis into the visited environment was a known problem with this manner of searching. She had been cautioned against becoming too tired and being seduced into idling.

She took one last look at her partner in this alternate life—at the partner of this parallel self. Katerina forced herself to continue the search elsewhere. This man was surely a manifestation of the one she sought, but this was not "him."

Then she released her hold on this life. The tangibility of another facet of reality dissolved around her, as it had so many times before that day.

When letting go of a visited life, Katerina often had a sense of rapid movement—somewhat unnerving. It was similar to the dream sensation of falling when on the brink of sleep. Except this movement went in all directions simultaneously, including inward.

As Katerina removed herself from this life of hers, she retained traces of it. Though she had visited the place for only moments, that reality had been thoroughly integrated into Katerina's definition of self, her emotions, and her mind. The same thing had happened with each parallel life that she had visited today. The resulting assimilation of parallel self-definitions was proving to be the hardest part of this task. Katerina could feel something similar to layers of simultaneous lifetime awarenesses building within her consciousness. With each new layer, Katerina's definition-of-self expanded, but the primary identity receded a little. The more the tether to her prime personality weakened, the more dangerous the next visit became.

These dangers to the visitant were why this ritual was so rarely performed. Only by forcing acknowledgment of her exceptional skills had Katerina been able to persuade The Nine to consent to, and assist in, her searches. With each passing in and out of these parallel lives, Katerina became progressively more understanding of the Crones' concerns.

Good fortune and bad awaited Katerina at the next location she tried to visit. For whatever reason, she was blocked from entering the environment. This meant the spirit of the very person she had come to visit denied her access—so she had been taught. The barrier was good because of the respite it afforded her, even momentarily. It was bad because this failed attempt was an opportunity lost and she had no time to waste. Katerina could feel her subconscious becoming overwhelmed. She would have to abandon the search very soon.

As though she had been slammed into a wall, Katerina rebounded. With no time to prepare, she entered into another parallel life. The quickness of the transfer had a severe impact on her already depleted energies.

Hazy images began to take form before her eyes. As in every other visit today, what Katerina saw and felt was as real to her as the life in the world of her physical form. These people, her lives in parallel realities, always existed right before her eyes. They were as real as any member of her order that she interacted with day in and day out. In this process, Katerina merely opened her awareness to the otherwise unacknowledged doorway between the infinite realities.

Memories that were hidden from her a moment before—memories belonging exclusively to this parallel life—began to introduce themselves into her consciousness. A flood of previously inaccessible senses, personal to this life, began to send their messages to her brain. Emotions without history for the traveling Katerina of a moment before began to structure in her mind the network of associations that gave them consequence. It was becoming almost impossible to fully open herself to yet another mind, another life, and still retain her distinction from them.

"Maintain the focus," she reminded herself. "Where is the Union?"

Psychically, she searched the structure in which she stood for evidence of his presence. She knew he had been in this room only a moment before. Scanning one room after another with her mind, her senses met him returning up the stairs from a lower floor.

Perceptive of subtle energies, he stopped, and turned his head as if trying to catch the sound or sight that had fleetingly stirred his attention. Though her presence was centered in another room, Katerina held her mental focus on him, just outside of his range of perception. There was something very special about this one, and she took time to enjoy that uniqueness.

But he is not the Union, her mind cried out.

"Suen?" he called.

"What is it, Yeetar?" his partner replied from a room at the back of the top floor.

Yeetar looked around, curious. It was obvious that he had perceived an unfamiliar intrusion into his world. He seemed to be reaching out with something more than his five senses, trying to locate her. So Katerina cautiously began to withdraw her presence.

Significant, she thought. But, still not the Union.

Katerina heard Yeetar reply, uncertainly, "Nothing, Suen," as the last of Katerina's foreign essence departed from his world.

Katerina knew she could not attempt another visit. Her need to return to the Motherworld was too great. As soon as she pulled herself back into the mortal form that was her own, every member of The Nine instantaneously received her request for termination of the rite. The gurgling song of the streams that surrounded the circle of Crones aided her return.

Though Katerina felt her spirit fully identify with the body of her home reality, her mind was overwhelmed with the competing identities she had integrated into her awareness during the searches. Still in the seated meditation posture, Katerina slumped forward, reaching her hands to the ground for reconnection, pressing her palms to the soft, living moss that covered the ground below her. Her breathing was deep and slow. With each inhalation, the scent of the evergreen forest strengthened her connection to this place, her primary home.

Surges of energy began to run through her muscles, making them twitch. Katerina strove to suppress these involuntary movements. Undoubtedly, out of need for its own survival, Katerina's conscious mind was feverishly sweeping through the queue of her recent experiences and vanquishing all contending identities to the subdued recesses of her subconscious.

Katerina had no way of telling how long the hand had been on her shoulder. Still unable to withdraw her concentration from the processes of recovery, she wasn't yet able to perceive whose hand it was. A minute later, still unaware of who stood above her, Katerina began to realize that sympathetic energy flowed into her through the supportive hand, assisting Katerina in her efforts to integrate.

She had not wanted anyone to know how much impact the ceremony had had on her. She had been bold in her claims of being able to handle the process.

"You have done well, dear heart, and we are glad you are back with us."

Katerina knew the voice. Head hanging down, eyes still closed, her sensory perception becoming exclusive to the world of her body, she replied, "I could not find him, Holiness. So many manifestations of him, but none of them were the Union."

"That is both auspicious and unfortunate. With so many connections, the bond between you and him is exceptionally strong. It does, however, complicate finding the appropriate manifestation when seeking him without some assistance on his part.

"You have been remarkable in your effort, Katerina. No one

would have asked so much of you. Care for yourself now, my child. This is a demanding task that you have undertaken."

"I am certain something is not as we expect this time," Katerina said.

"We may not understand why things are proceeding as they are, Katerina, but the Collective Consciousness cannot be wrong. We must carry out our practice as it has been handed down to us. The method has always served the need, and will again . . . in its own time."

"Yes, Mother. But when I received the visions, it seemed he was not within an order. Is it possible?"

"The images you saw must be coincidental, not indicative of his full person, Katerina."

"How can he refrain from replying?" Katerina asked, finally regaining enough strength to rise to her feet, though slowly. "Perhaps he cannot, or does not understand the Call."

The old Matriarch wrapped an arm around Katerina's back and helped the younger woman to steady her wobbly legs. Katerina looked into the concerned, almost teary eyes of her superior and said, "I truly feel that something is unique to this occurrence of the rift."

"I know you do, and I respect that belief. But you must accept that no matter the situation, the situation is perfection, as it has always been."

A tear rolled down the wrinkled cheek before the elder continued.

"I would not have had you suffer this burden, Katerina, if I had such power to decide. And I must accept that this charge is yours to bear, in your own way."

Despite the Matriarch's compassionate tone, Katerina took her words as a reprimand. "I will not fail my duties. Until I find the Union, I will search without cease."

Rubbing Katerina's back, the old woman said, "You have always surpassed your duties, dear girl, and are doing so now. You will not fail, cannot fail. It is we who must not fail you."

Tea Ceremony

In all of his fifty-three years, few pleasures consistently satisfied Ian Sarin like fully focusing on a hot cup of tea, especially in the familiar comfort of his home on a New England winter evening. At the end of workdays in the frighteningly specious world of logic—computer logic—Ian loved reentering this personal sanctuary, and making a ceremony out of preparing his tea. The simple motions brought Ian a serenity he couldn't explain. Of course, he occasionally made changes in the ritual. There were always new teas to try, and he periodically used a different teapot, cup, or other trimming. But the unhurried, predictable routine invariably took him from the intensity of his toil to the calmness of his center.

Ian would lean back in his favorite old chair, placing the hot teacup on the wide wooden armrest. The antique recliner had cracked red leather cushions. A dear couple in their nineties had given him the chair, for some reason unknown to him. It had belonged to the woman's grandfather. Like its former owners, that old chair was ever welcoming. Without fail, it soothed Ian to sit in it.

Whether it came immediately after work or followed drinks and dinner with friends, separation from his labor was never complete until Ian had the day's closing cup of tea. The rising steam from the cup celebrated a shift into the more genuine side of his life, of himself. Single, living alone, quietude was his guidepost.

Withdrawn from the activities of the day, Ian would focus on a favorite teapot or some other object within the room, absorbed in aimless wonder until he achieved something he called a sense of "presence" or expanded awareness. The tea's warmth and flavor never failed to lull him into the anticipated meditation. With palm and fingers wrapped around his cup, Ian would take his time and lingered over every sip, staring blankly, unintentionally, into the room before him . . . looking outward, peering inward.

One winter evening, while in this unmindful passage, Ian slipped into a path that he could not have previously imagined. At first, the experience appeared to be no more than some mild visual distortion, not unlike the onset of one of his occasional migraines. In this hyper-relaxed state, Ian ignored the blurring edges of the images. He knew that the best way to avoid the onslaught of the potential headache was to relax more deeply and allow the storm to flow through.

Without becoming attached to or analyzing the experience, Ian allowed the sensations to draw him where they would. A ghost image of an outdoor scene began to display itself before him. Surprised by the specificity of the evolving scene, Ian tensed up, straining to resist the unexplainable sensory imposition. This caused a mild nausea. Ian took the nausea to be added evidence that he was developing a migraine. So he again focused on relaxation.

He could not completely convince himself that the relaxation that ensued was solely due to the conscious effort he made, rather than the mere seduction of the experience. The infrequent migraines had never before provoked anything remotely suggestive of a hallucination.

With a distinct sense of motion, Ian felt himself transported from his New England home, winter outside, to the edge of a forest in spring—who knew where? The shift from ordinary consciousness to the extraordinary state of deep meditation was stronger and quicker than any previously experienced. It was so exhilarating it almost caused him to faint. As the two contrasting scenes before him continued to transpose, Ian's familiar room became the more ethereal of the two.

Then he felt an abrupt snap to his nervous system. Both the nausea and psychological elation disappeared. The result was even harder for Ian to remain detached from.

Ian became enchanted by what his senses were reporting, and even more so by the novelty of the transformation. His room had been redefined to a path within an evergreen forest. Yet he knew he was still sitting in his recliner. The smell of evergreen needles and pungent wild plants overwhelmed that of his ginger pu-erh tea. It was all so real that he could even feel the moisture of the lush forest environment. Odd, however, was the utter silence of the place.

Then Ian realized there was another person in this woodland scene. The woman seemed a little more imaginary than her surroundings and she had the radiance and movement usually reserved for dreams and fantasy. Rather than something separate, moving across the landscape, she flowed as part of the scene, from point to point. She made no abrupt movements or gestures. Ian wondered why she seemed so familiar, though he was certain that he had never seen her before.

Her hair was a deep, rich auburn, very long and braided into a single strand. The style of her clothes was unusual. She wore a long-sleeved, full-length gown. Over the dress was an open-sided tunic, not quite as long as the gown, loosely tied at the waist with a woven belt. Both garments appeared to be handmade from a thick but loosely woven natural fiber. The gown was off-white, probably the natural color of the fabric. The tunic was light green, heavily embroidered with symbols that Ian did not recognize. The ordered placement of the symbols, however, gave him the impression that her attire was a uniform of some sort. One thing he could not help but notice: the soft cloth of her clothing flowed as smoothly over her form as she moved through her environment.

Fully focused on the wildflowers that she was collecting and adding to her basket, the woman walked to Ian's right, completely unaware of him. She moved her lips as if talking to herself, or to the birds that flew about and perched near the ground on the lower branches of the trees. Then the woman finally noticed Ian. She stopped in surprise, but only for a second. Her eyes went wide and her mouth dropped open . . . just before she gave him a full, welcoming smile.

It was as if she knew who he was but had not expected to see him just then or there. She spread her arms and moved quickly toward him, laughing and talking as she came. To his dismay, Ian could hear nothing of what she said to him.

Ian had initially taken this lissome woman to be much younger than he. But as she drew nearer, he saw that she was about his age. She seemed much fuller of life than Ian had been in years, even though he considered himself quite youthful for his age. Her skin was smooth and fair in color, and it had a healthy, even glow. Equally beautiful to him were the soft lines around her eyes.

Ian was drawn to the woman; he sensed that some kind of intimacy existed between them. She apparently felt the same way, for she leaned over to kiss him without hesitation. Her scent was of delicate flowers over an exotic wood. Ian felt anticipation of her touch—much more than just a mere physical response of an unattached man being kissed by a lovely woman.

Ian's anticipation was denied. He never felt the touch of her lips. As she stood upright, returning slowly into focus, Ian could not take in enough of her striking face. Now he wondered why she wore that quizzical expression, head tilted and brow knitted. Perhaps she, too, could not understand what had happened to the sensation of the kiss.

Ian was even more overcome by the rapidly expanding emotion that he felt for this woman, from deep within—and, somehow, being near her gave him an almost exaggerated sense of satisfaction with himself. Ian was totally absorbed in his passionate response to her. I am truly blessed, he thought in almost perfect contentment.

It was about then that Ian's logical mind regained its ability for rationalizing and seized full control. I am sitting in my study, it proclaimed forcefully. This is an illusion!

Abruptly, the woman and her surroundings dematerialized, going from tangible form to ghost image to her absence, merely a blurred perception of Ian's study. His body and mind convulsed when the last traces of the illusion retreated into the precise forms of the study. A rush of confusing emotions was forcibly fused into his conscious perception of himself and his reality.

Gripping the arms of the recliner, Ian sat rigidly upright, distraught. As unnerving as the physical stimulation had been, the emotions that churned within him now were worse. For a brief moment during the woman's visit, he had possessed an incontestable sense of purpose and wholeness. Now he felt devoid. The sharp contrast wounded him deeply.

Had something precious slipped away? More than that, why did he feel so certain that this woman's departure meant a loss of more than he'd known he was missing from life? In his many years of meditation, guided imagery, and similar experiences, Ian had never felt such stirring sensations.

Now that the brunt of the experience had passed, his mind rapidly alternated between supreme elation at "meeting" this remarkable woman and a full rational denial of this little vision, or whatever one might call it. What had just transpired? For all the world, it had felt that in a matter of seconds the tangible world before Ian had completely redefined itself as he remained the only constant. But he was not ready to accept an explanation quite that extreme.

"What a powerful vision," Ian said to himself, confining the account to something within the comfort zone of his conscious mind.

Step by step, Ian retraced the experience. He had been enjoying the fragrant aroma of his ginger pu-erh tea while his eyes ran over the bamboo-like designs on his recently acquired, handmade ceramic teapot. Obviously, he had finished the tea and set the cup in his lap . . .

Perhaps," Ian thought, "I suddenly lost consciousness." No, he knew he had not slept or blacked out!

In fact, Ian reminded himself, the change started as he was looking at the teapot, just finishing his cup of tea. He had been thinking of nothing in particular, allowing himself to drift free from any thoughts. The next thing he knew, the relaxation was moving quickly into a mysterious domain.

The loss of that enchanting woman called Ian back. Despite the evidence to the contrary, he knew she was somehow real. And the emotions she had provoked in him were certainly so.

Quickly getting up from the chair, he walked across the room.

After taking a few steps, Ian turned and stared at the recliner as if it were some unknown object. Then, as if to reassure himself that he was indeed in his study, he slowly let his attention drift around the room. There was the makeshift stereo cabinet, a faux antique armoire—on which an untalented amateur had sought to express an imagined skill. His eyes fell to the worn pine floor and traced a path back to the side table, on which sat the muted green teapot with its bamboo design. Each familiar item was a comfort.

What had the woman in the forest been? He was certain it was not a dream! The experience had been far too lifelike.

Ian felt compelled to classify the experience as some sort of visual aberration, like a mirage. A mirage, however, is something caused by the environment external to the seer. But, what were the conditions that caused this aberration?

In the case of a vision, the controlling conditions are more defined within the seer, within his or her mind . . . or life. That put the weight of the explanation of this occurrence on him. What about Ian or his life had recently changed, allowing this peculiar experience to take place?

Ian consoled himself with the conclusion that *if* he had had some sort of vision, at least it was pleasant and non-threatening. Or rather, it had been pleasant until he "awoke" and found that his visitor was chimerical.

Continuing to tell himself that he was distressed over nothing, a mere reverie—though elaborate—Ian sat back down in the recliner. Could he recreate the experience at will?

Trying to relax, he reached over to touch the teapot. Such a short time had passed since Ian poured his first cup of tea that the pot was still hot.

He picked the teapot up and tilted the spout over his cup. Steam rose as the stream of hot tea fell into the cup. Ian half expected that something else might escape from the teapot. When the cup was full, he set the teapot down and settled back into his chair. For a short while, he tried to think of nothing, just stare without purpose at the teapot and cup.

Ian made every effort not to think of the woman in the forest and his experience with her, but he failed. He had no better success for the next couple of weeks. Almost all he could think about was related to his encounter with the woman in the forest. Over and over, Ian tried to determine exactly what had happened that night. He considered how it had happened, analyzed why it had happened, and how it was different from any vaguely similar experiences he had had previously.

Despite the fact that his visit that night was always on his mind, he spoke to no one about it. He didn't need *anyone else* questioning his mental stability.

During that time of assessment, Ian did not have tea in his study, or go through his tea ritual at all. Once in a while, he would sit in the study—but not in the recliner—and consider the scene of the event that occurred that night. He convinced himself that the vision was more interesting than disturbing. His response was to study it as an "experiential aberration," some anomaly of perception.

Such things as visions or visitations were not completely incomprehensible to him—in concept, anyway. Ian had done a little reading concerning metaphysical, indigenous, and East Asian beliefs, though he did not consider himself knowledgeable, not by any means. Now and again, he had attended a spiritual workshop or a retreat. Such diversions were interesting, and occasionally vital—along with art, music, and poetry—to balance out his left-brain-centric career. Before the woman's arrival, Ian had never experienced anything that threatened to cross the threshold between the expanded perception of deep meditation and the preternatural. Even though he had come to believe such things were possible, he had always been comfortable that there was generally a wide margin of safety between the possible and the probable.

All this analysis did little to placate Ian's ruffled logical mind, and offered absolutely no comfortable answers. The least of the rationally objectionable labels considered during his scrutinization was "vision"—"dream" remained *utterly* insufficient for what he had experienced—Trying to define the encounter as a mere hallucination, however, caused an upwelling of resistance within his depths. Though he struggled to avoid giving credence to the idea, Ian knew that he was not completely convinced that the experience had been merely visual.

From the moment he had first experienced the woman with the auburn hair, Ian had felt something new evolving in him. It seemed that much about him was transforming.

The change was physical. Certain parts of his body, internal and external, seemed to vibrate in response to some unexplainable stimuli outside the range of his conscious perceptions. The change was spiritual. He had acquired some deep undeniable connection to this woman that he could not rationally understand. The change was psychological, some kind of redefinition of self that he could not grasp consciously, as if his mind and feelings were opening or expanding. The redefinition included expanding his identity as a segmented awareness and bonding with something larger than himself . . .

None of this evolution greatly disturbed Ian. He did not personally know anyone knowledgeable about such things as visions. But from what he had read, he knew he was displaying normal symptoms after a numinous experience, which he also reminded himself was defined as any experience that defies explanation within the scope of one's current view of reality. For Ian, a personally experienced vision, as opposed to theoretical visions, qualified as such an experience.

Ian tried to respond to the sensory aspects of the vision as an adventure, a particular bit of good fortune. He hoped to repeat the experience once he understood more about what was going on. There was just one remnant of that evening that Ian was not comfortable with. In fact, he would have sought another vision the following day if not for the residual emotions he possessed . . . or that possessed him. Ian was compelled to understand these emotions before allowing the chance of another vision.

He could accept the possibility of a lingering emotional ecstasy resulting from any strong supersensual experience such as his vision . . . similar to a religious rapture. But the emotion that Ian was feeling was directly associated with a single element of the vision, with the woman in the forest. The total intimacy he felt with her was more than Ian had ever known with *any* person. And he could not believe such an impassioned connection could be instantaneous. Yet, he had to believe . . . or accept that the bond had existed even before he had the vision.

That unguarded assessment troubled Ian. His yearning to return to the woman of his vision had the remarkable force of an addiction. For that reason most of all, Ian resisted the urge to pursue another encounter. He was not willing to let anyone or anything have such power over his destiny.

About a month later, Ian had convinced himself that he was in charge of his own choices. Despite not feeling in control of every emotion, he let down his rational guard and began pursuing another experience with the woman of that unforgettable night. Speculating that the image had been a product of a combination of environmental factors in his study, Ian decided to duplicate the circumstances to the best of his memory.

His efforts did not produce a vision the next few times he had tea in the study. Perhaps, Ian thought, he was trying too hard. In time, however, the woman did reappear. This time they did not meet in the forest, but in his study.

The progression of her appearance was precisely the same as before. The items in his focus began to blur. Then a transparent outline of her figure emerged. As she began to take form, Ian noticed a growing tension within himself. He speculated it was the conflict between what he perceived and what his logical mind could accept. Forcing himself to relax, the queasiness he was feeling disappeared quickly.

She was wearing a much more formal-looking garment with a cowl, embroidered with many of the same symbols as the tunic she had worn before. When she fully materialized at the other end of the study, she raised both hands and gracefully pushed the hood back from her face, and down onto her shoulders. A feeling of joy swept over Ian as he saw her smiling face unveiled.

His pretense of scientific research fled the moment she arrived. In the brief instant before total abandonment into the moment, Ian took mental note of the genuineness that denied what he perceived as merely visual. Nor was Ian stirred to know why he felt what he did, but allowed himself to revel in it.

Ian was disappointed that the woman did not offer a kiss on this visit . . . and a visit was what it felt like to him. Instead, she slowly raised a palm in salutation. He got up from his chair and welcomed her to his home.

"It's so good to see you again, my friend," he said. "Come and have a seat with me."

She shook her head and pointed to her ear. Ian understood that she could hear no more of what he said than he had heard from her during their last visit. Turning to his recliner, he motioned to it with his hand. She declined, pressed her hands together as if in reverent thanks, and lowered her head slightly.

They stood, smiling and staring at each other. Ian did not know what she was feeling, but he was certain that their lack of dialogue did not limit their interaction. For his own part, Ian felt much communication was taking place, without the need of a single sound.

She glanced about the room, eventually gesturing as if to ask if it would be all right for her to have a look at a pottery piece that displayed stamped Celtic symbols.

"Sure," he said. "Make yourself at home." He rushed over to join her. "It's made by a potter who lives in the mountains where I go sometimes. I love the symbols that the artist has used."

His visitor stooped to look closely at the miniature monolith. She pointed to a symbol, a triskele, looked up at him, and made a comment he could not hear. Ian raised his hands to either side of his chest, palms upward, and shrugged his shoulders to indicate that he did not understand what she meant. Standing upright again, she pointed to a triskele on her garment.

"They are the same!" he said. Ian wondered if she was from a Celtic culture. He knew, however, that the triskele was not unique to the Celts.

Wishing to present the woman with a gift, Ian picked up a small candleholder that also bore the triskele design and offered it to her.

"Please, let me give you this."

She appeared grateful of his offer, but shook her head, declining politely.

"Please," he insisted.

After pausing for a moment—that Ian took to be considering how to respond—she slowly reached out a hand as if to touch the pot. Excited that she was accepting the gift, he further extended his arm. Without ever touching the pottery, her hand jerked away and her face took on a look of fright.

This movement caused Ian to quickly withdraw his outstretched hand and almost drop the candleholder. After recovering his composure, he noticed she was smiling again, but she had both hands up in front of her, palms out, signaling that he should not bring the pottery to her. She slowly pointed one hand to the place from where he had taken the pot. So, he put it back on the shelf.

With that bit of awkwardness, their visit began. Ian's visitor relaxed and returned her attention to his offered token, gracefully nodded in thanks again, and mouthed something, about the pottery—he assumed.

Ian silently watched her and his embarrassment evaporated. The gentle woman looked up and gave him another of her enchanting smiles. Showing her about the room, he talked and laughed as if she could hear him. She responded in kind. Happily, they carried on their silent exchange.

It became apparent to Ian that she did not want to touch anything in the room, or else could not. Several times she motioned to Ian to turn an item around, so she could see its backside.

At some point, Ian's new friend moved to have a look at a book in the bookcase. She took a couple of steps toward it—and then vanished into thin air. Ian was seized with a momentary distress, and then he was startled to find that he was again sitting in the recliner, teacup in hand. He could not understand how it was possible, but evidence suggested that he had never moved from the chair. From all appearances, Ian had been the only one in the room the whole time. But he felt certain that he knew otherwise.

Now that Ian had experienced another visit—or vision, because he interchangeably referred to the experiences by both terms, unable to conclude which they really were—he looked forward to enjoying another one. Ian planned not only to enjoy them but also to find some answers. Crafted after his experiences in computer testing, he would use a base environment of everything just like it had been the first (and second) teatime. He made the same type of tea, used the same teapot, and sat in the same chair. Everything was just the same as it had been previously.

After a couple of successful visits, he started to change one thing at a time. If changing something kept her away, Ian would return things to the way they had last been for the next tea, verify another success, and then see if he could cause a repeat failure. The first conclusion he drew was that even with the absolute replication of the first visit setup, success was not always guaranteed.

Katerina

Ian and his new friend had quite a few pleasurable visits over the six weeks that followed. With the exception of a couple of short periods when she did not show at all, he saw her one to several times every week. Her visits lasted only seconds on his watch, yet the activity that he could recall made Ian feel that they had been together upwards of several hours at a time.

He came to call the woman Katerina sometime after her second visit. Absentmindedly interrogating himself after he returned from their time together, trying to get some better idea about what exactly he was experiencing, Ian realized that at some point he had begun referring to her by that name. The certainty and familiarity with which he used the name amused him.

Ian started to search for the justification of this inadvertent christening. Surely, he had picked up something in the vision without realizing it, something that suggested her name. After considerable deliberation, he found no such clue. And yet he experienced discomfort when he *did not* refer to her as Katerina.

He was certain that he somehow *knew* her name. And even if it was not her name, what would it hurt to call her Katerina until he knew her name for sure? Using this name was much more soothing to him.

Ian next encountered Katerina as she was sitting in the grass under a tree of beautiful purple flowers. Comforting a dear, little girl, perhaps three years old, on her lap, Katerina acknowledged Ian's presence at about the moment he became aware of her.

When Katerina spoke to him, the child looked about as if she had no idea whom Katerina was addressing. But, the little girl did not seem disturbed by Katerina's response. Once the youth decided there was no one else with them, she laid her head back onto Katerina's breast and closed her eyes.

"You have a lovely daughter," Ian said.

Katerina shook her head, very slowly, in order not to disturb the child's rest. The caring look for him on Katerina's face gave comfort to the depth of Ian's soul. He had never imagined that there could be so much connection between two people merely through visual communication. No wonder the child was so contented in the company of such an empathic woman.

"She's not your daughter?" he asked.

Again, another slow denial, and then Katerina stroked the child's hair.

He looked about at the surroundings. They were in a sculptured garden, spanning in all directions as far as he could see. True, he could not see much more than fifty yards in any direction, but the paths that disappeared in every direction implied there was much more beyond.

When Ian's attention returned to her, Katerina was gazing intently at him. At first he was a little embarrassed with the attentiveness of her focus.

"You know. I suppose I should start by introducing myself, though it seems we are rather familiar already." He was starting to ramble, so he calmed himself before continuing, "My name is Ian Sarin. It has been a joy to meet you, dear lady." He bowed his head.

She nodded in acknowledgement, placed a hand on her chest opposite the head of the sleeping child, and spoke. It was obvious that she had introduced herself, but Ian did not catch her name.

"I am so sorry," he responded. "I have always been inept at lip-reading."

Then Ian started nervously rambling again, "You know, after we met the second time, I got the most assured idea that I already knew your name. I had no reason for it, but I just could not help believing that your name was Katerina. In fact, having become so certain of it, I was afraid that I would just call you . . ."

Noticing her smiling and nodding, Ian regained his focus, thinking he had missed something she was trying to convey.

"I am sorry. What did you say?"

Again, she placed a hand on her chest, but spoke with slow, exaggerated movements, slightly pausing between each syllable. She appeared to say I . . . am . . . Kat . . . er . . . ina.

What she said seemed obvious, but Ian distrusted his eyes. Surely, his own preconception of her name was making him imagine that he understood what she said. Still, he had to check.

"Katerina? Your name is Katerina?"

She nodded with enough enthusiasm that the little girl stirred to see what was happening.

"That's amazing," he said. "How could I have possibly guessed that?"

Katerina kissed the little girl's cheek, and tried to coax her head back to rest. Apparently, the little one had received all the comfort she required and was fully revitalized. Without any further indication of intent, the child jumped to her feet, looked quickly to one side, and started to talk excitedly.

Katerina nodded, and the girl rushed toward one of the many paths radiating from the clearing. Waving back to Katerina, the child barely missed running into Ian. She seemed no more aware of his presence than she had earlier.

He laughed at the transformation and watched the child disappear around a flowerbed. When he turned to look back at Katerina, Ian was surprised that she was now standing right in front of him, gazing into his eyes.

Katerina reached to touch him, but her hand remained barely suspended in front of the upper right side of his chest. "Hello," she mouthed. He was sure of that.

Reflexively, Ian reached to touch her face.

He was so engrossed in her eyes, that he did not really pay any attention to his hand. Anticipating the touch, his senses informed him that his hand had moved enough that it should now be reporting the feel of Katerina's skin.

Ian pulled his attention from her eyes and looked to where he expected himself to be touching her face, along her jaw line. The translucent distortion that he saw instead of his hand caused him to jerk backwards. He pulled his hand back, bringing it right in front of his eyes for a better look. Still Ian saw nothing but a fuzzy impression of a hand.

"What the . . . ?" he said, stepping back again.

Noticing that Katerina was waving her hand in front of his face, Ian let his attention follow *her* hand. She drew a single finger to her lips, gently suggesting quiet, calm. From her lips, his attention went back to her eyes; in the process he became as subdued as the child had been a moment before.

What difference does it make that my hand is not solid? he thought. Ian looked around himself and back to Katerina. It was an odd feeling to perceive himself as the only intangibility in the environment.

"Look where I am, what I am doing," he said out loud. "Why should I be so surprised just because I see something else unexpected?"

Though still not completely comfortable with the appearance of his hand, he was calmed. Being careful not to point with his finger, Ian asked for a tour. "Let's take a walk. Please tell me about this gorgeous garden."

They wandered about for quite a while, winding through

path after path. It was all much manicured, more like an arboretum or a study of wild flora than the garden of even a lavish estate. He didn't see any indication of a dwelling of any kind. Of course, since Ian could not hear anything during the visitations he could not rely on sound to tell him if they were close to any houses.

With the sights and the company, it did not take Ian long to completely forget about the distortion he saw instead of his hand. The couple talked like long-lost, dear friends, spending most of the time looking into each other's eyes as they talked and walked. He was surprised that neither of them stumbled, he especially, since he had no idea where they were going.

Though he did not ever feel the contact, Katerina reached out to touch or stroke Ian—or more precisely, his location—frequently. He was amazed how much intimacy could be conferred by the implication of such a motion. The gentleness with which Katerina carried out those gestures, the look in her eyes, almost satisfied any need for touch, to a degree that he had never known before.

When she was close enough, Ian "touched" Katerina. He had no physical sensation as a result of the effort, and he did not look for confirmation of that touch. He did not want the pleasure of his experience interrupted by what he suspected he would or would not see.

As Katerina continued with the tour of the endless garden, Ian's conscious mind started to push for answers to questions. Was he only a matter of his consciousness projecting to a location near Katerina when he was in her world? If so, what were the perceived sensations of his body in this place? He experienced fragrances, experienced movement as he walked.

And there was one odd sensation that was starting to disturb him. Ian's movement had a vague hint of being guided, as if he was in some confined space. He walked along with Katerina, but it didn't fully feel as if he was moving as a result of his own physical effort. The idea made no sense to him. Yet, it did explain why he never stumbled as he kept his eyes only on Katerina during their tour of the garden.

Two little children came barreling down the path. Their little faces lit up when they saw Katerina. They began chattering and waving, without slowing their pace. She replied with similar enthusiasm. Off they disappeared in the opposite direction, without any indication that they had seen Katerina's guest.

The interruption was good for Ian. It brought him back to the joy of his moment. He returned to the steady exchanges with Katerina, rather than dwelling on the pointless concerns of his conscious mind.

Shortly afterward, he and Katerina stepped into a clearing and the sky opened up over them. The flood of sunlight drew Ian's attention ahead and then upward, where he noticed a magnificent old-world building.

"What a remarkable place, Katerina! What is that?" Ian said, looking back and forth between Katerina and the structure, which stood about fifty feet away.

Moving in front of him, Katerina lifted her left hand toward the structure, as if to introduce it to him.

Overwhelmed by its unique beauty, Ian repeated, "What is it?"

She looked him right in the face and began to slowly pronounce something. Ian hated trying to lip-read. He found the slow, labored pronunciations to be more distracting than helpful. For all he knew, Ian caught nothing of what Katerina said, despite her efforts.

"Do you live here?" he guessed.

Yes, she nodded. Motioning for him to move forward, they headed for a large, ornate entrance. Katerina began telling him about it, at normal speed.

Her home was the archetypal French country cottage. It was neither small, nor very big. The exterior was extremely well crafted with stone, stucco, and heavy timbers. Quite a bit of the stone and exposed wood was carved, apparently by various craftspeople on different themes, at different times since the styles were so different. The cottage had to have been ancient. Unless her world was much different from his, he thought, not even the wealthy built homes of this size with such detail and artistry anymore.

Ian realized that he was acting as excitedly as one of Katerina's young friends. Moving this way and that, he tried to take in all the rich detail. Katerina moved toward whatever he showed an interest in and tried to tell him about what he was seeing. Nearer the main door, off to one side of the building, there was a sculpture that fascinated him. Katerina stopped to see what he was looking at.

A path led directly to the intriguing sculpture. She waited to see if he wished a closer look. Ian turned toward the house, concluding that he could see the statue well enough from where he was, and he did not want to delay their entry into the house. Katerina followed suit and turned to continue toward the door.

An instant later Ian changed his mind. "I'll be right back, Katerina. I am going to run over there for a quick look at the statue."

As he was behind her, Katerina did not see his change of direction. A few steps into his jog, a sense of internal strain, a visceral pull, started to get Ian's attention. Another couple of steps and he experienced a rush of faintness. Before he could take another step, Ian lunged back—against his recliner.

The return to his study was abrupt, but he recovered without complication. His little stroll toward the statue alone let him know he was correct in supposing he could not move far from Katerina when in her reality. Based on that experience and the children's unawareness of him, Ian concluded that in that place he was an apparition honed in on, and seen only by Katerina.

Katerina didn't appear every evening that he had a cup of tea in his red leather chair, and she never appeared when that particular teapot was not in the study. Nor would she visit Ian in any other room, even if he had tea with that teapot there. One evening Ian found out she could materialize in the study when he was not having tea, but had, nonetheless, brought the pot into the room.

Planning to have tea a little later, Ian was in the kitchen rinsing the teapot when the phone rang. Still drying the outside of the pot, he went to the study to pick up the cordless extension. As he talked, Ian sat down in the antique recliner and placed the teapot on the table to his right. When the conversation was over, Ian turned off the phone, and laid it on the arm of the chair.

For no particular reason, Ian continued to sit and stare at the teapot. Suddenly he felt Katerina's presence. Although it had not been that way in the initial visions, he had recently noticed that his awareness of Katerina was now instantaneous. No progression of sensations led to their connection. During the last few visits, she had consistently appeared someplace in his study, as if out of nowhere, without warning. Or, more likely, Ian had suddenly found himself in her world.

On this particular visit, Katerina was sitting on a bench near the very statue that had caused him trouble in a previous visit. She was playing a wooden flute. Of course he couldn't hear the music she was making, but she painted a serene picture and seemed to be enjoying herself.

Quite content that he could move only in proximity with Katerina, Ian got her attention and pointed at the statue, to make sure it was not too far away. She nodded to confirm his intention.

The countenance of the statue looked uncannily familiar. It was a woman who looked very similar to Katerina, but it was not she. The stature and dress were regal. Ian leaned forward and stared right into the eyes of this stone woman. Even in marble, those eyes implied a wisdom that could recognize a person by his or her spirit within.

An unbelievably loud, grating noise rose right up Ian's spinal chord. When it reached the base of his head, a shattering pain shot through the top of his skull. Ian jerked away from the statue, unable to believe that even in this place stone could generate such a sound.

"What *is* that?" he said.

The noise stopped. But he was back in his study as well. The noise had been the phone ringing and it stopped only after Ian's convulsion knocked it to the floor, breaking the connection.

In panic he looked at the table next to the chair, where he always set the teapot.

"Thank you, thank you," Ian said. He had flung out only his left arm to silence the phone. The teapot sat safely on the table to his right.

He got up, disconnected every phone in the house, and pulled the curtains closed. He made tea and had a cup, hoping to return to Katerina and relax. He was unsuccessful in both pursuits.

"Tomorrow I will disconnect the doorbell as well," he said, finally rising from the chair. "I'll never again be yanked back before my visit is complete!"

From then on, Ian went through an invariable process of closing the house up, sealing himself off, and switching off all the phones before each tea.

The day soon came when Ian was able to visit Katerina in her cottage. With all his precautions in place, he settled into the recliner one night, hot pot of tea prepared and on the table beside him. He had not poured himself a cup. Yet, an old room of large stone and timber-frame opened up before Ian. The interior reflected the same grand artistry and craftsmanship as that he had previously seen on the exterior.

It took him a moment to become aware of his new surroundings, but Katerina was already smiling and talking to him—as she worked with some herbs.

"Hello, dear one," he said. "Your home is even lovelier inside."

With her hands in a pot of a liquid mix, she motioned with her head for him to look around. Fearful of encountering the limit of his energetic tether, he turned slowly around where he stood, taking in every detail of the environment.

The room was reasonably large, perhaps twenty-five by thirty feet. Judging by what he had previously noticed about the exterior size of the cottage, the staircase to the left of the area, and the windows he had seen from outside, Ian knew there were several other rooms in the house. This room seemed to serve as the all-purpose area. It was kitchen, dining room, and study. Shelves of books and a couple of large, comfortable upholstered chairs sat at one end. He and Katerina were at the opposite end.

The primary entryway was through an arched door in the center of one wall. The floor beneath Ian's feet was of stone similar to slate, but more rustic. A few feet in front of the door was a sturdy, old rectory-style dining table, flanked by benches. Opposite the door was a very wide span of deep-set leaded transom windows, set over a kitchen counter made of large, handmade ceramic tiles. The cabinets under the counter were handmade, with wooden knobs. Shelves holding many kinds of ceramic jars covered the wall on either side of the windows behind the countertop. Between the windows and the back of the counter top, there was a window box filled with various flowers and herbs. Dried bunches of plants hung from the ceiling in several locations.

While Katerina worked with the flower essences, and another pot of dyes, Ian stayed near her. He could not assist her with her chores, for he still proved to be without substance in her world. Though unable to hear what she told him about her tasks, Ian could smell the aromas and was happy just to see the sights and pastimes of her life.

Obviously, Katerina had acquiesced to Ian's innate inability to lip-read, no longer seeming to expect further progress. Ian was convinced that they understood much more of the intention of their communication by speaking naturally. One thing he was certain of: the silence did not diminish their enthusiasm for communicating with each other.

"What is your vocation, Katerina? I still don't know if I visit only when you are away from work," he said. "That happens to be the case with me because I initiate the visits, and can only do so at home, after work."

Katerina watched him, considerately.

"At least I *imagine* that I instigate the visits—perhaps foolishly." Ian had to question just how much of this experience he could afford to make assumptions about. It was all so anomalous.

He looked back at Katerina. She warmly smiled, continuing her work and patiently waiting for him to go on.

Ian speculated that the image of his form must be clearer to Katerina than it was to him in her world. When he spoke, she was always attentive for the duration of his monologue. Ian considered that this conduct might have been due to a difference in their cultures, but the ardor of her attention sometimes made him uncomfortable. If not for the familiarity that she also expressed, Ian might have thought she believed him to be a visiting dignitary or luminary. Maybe such a visitor as himself was not so common in this reality either.

"Never mind talk about work. I'm finished for the day," he said.

Starting another look around the room, Ian changed his focus. "I think I like your world better than mine. With you being here, I am certain of it."

It appeared that Katerina was reasonably well-to-do, for even if the house was an old, inherited family home, it would have cost a fortune to maintain the structure and its ornamentation, not to mention the extensive gardens that surrounded it. Even though the gas oven and the lighting that was similar to electricity implied that Katerina lived in a time with some modern technology, the furniture, doors, and windows of her home followed the décor of an architectural "period display". It crossed Ian's mind that he had only seen a home furnished with such a disassociation to present time when it was a part of a cultural heritage display, or perhaps a church property used as the home of a vicar in a wealthy parish.

When Ian returned his attention to Katerina, she began a very lively, cheerful conversation. He watched closely and picked up what little he could. From her animation and facial expressions, he took in the joyfulness she was conveying. Ian caught his name a couple of times, and a few hand gestures certainly were referring to him. She seemed to be speaking of some interaction that she had had with others, concerning him.

Stopping mid-sentence, Katerina jerked her head toward the heavy, arched door. The top half of it was open. She rose quickly from the stool where she had been sitting, and wiped her hands dry on a towel that lay on the counter. Ian had no idea of the sound she was responding to, but it now had her full consideration.

She moved quickly across the room, and swung open the bottom of the door. After a momentary delay, Katerina stepped out onto the stoop, awaiting some arrival. Of course, Ian followed, as he knew he must if he expected to continue the visit.

A little boy charged up the pathway, crying. Katerina kneeled and scooped him into her lap. She rocked and stroked him, speaking all the while. Ian slipped out the door and came close to watch her perform this magic. His movement disturbed neither the child nor Katerina. Though Ian believed that no one but Katerina could see him in this place, he suspected that the little boy would not have noticed anyone else anyway. The boy was completely focused on the comfort he was receiving from Katerina.

Apparently the child had scraped his leg. Katerina was consoling him, his head on her shoulder next to her face. She had one arm wrapped around him, and the other hand pulled various salves and herbs from her pockets and applied them. It was quite a ballet of motion. No wonder the children came to her. Ian could see how the rhythm of her speech and the loving way she touched the little boy would soothe him. Watching it was enough to hypnotize Ian into a state of tranquility.

Katerina must be the village godmother, Ian thought. He didn't doubt that she was particularly adept at healing small injuries, whether to body or to spirit.

After a while, the boy was sufficiently soothed. His energetic predisposition returned, and he slid off Katerina's lap. She gave him a little advice and a peck on the cheek. Away he went as fast as he had come. Katerina's face was sublime radiance as she rose and returned her attention to Ian.

"Lovely," he said. "What a lucky child." What a lucky man, he thought of himself.

Fully returning from what almost seemed a meditative state, Katerina beamed a smile at Ian and continued with what he assumed was her previous conversation. They moved back into the cottage.

Thinking about Katerina's manner with the children, Ian wondered why she was the only other adult he had seen in this place. But that question was soon to be resolved.

Ian and Katerina had a particularly long visit that day. As they talked Katerina sketched some pictures. Then she painted for a while. Later, she wove fragile baskets from the stems of the flowers that she had used in the essences earlier that morning. Ian was so comfortable and involved in their visit that he did not even notice when he started to return home. There was no warning at all. Instantaneously, he was sitting in his chair, still wrapped in the warmth of Katerina's company. But he was alone now.

Without thinking about it, Ian looked at his watch and realized it showed he had eased into his chair only a few minutes before.

Enjoying his immediate memories, he thought about Katerina with the children during his various visits. It crossed Ian's mind that she was not only supremely attentive with *them*. She paid the same special consideration to him as well. She possessed a remarkable selflessness, a singular thoughtfulness that made one feel more significant with her than when outside her company.

Ian's visits with Katerina continued to be silent, but with every visit he felt a greater intimacy with her. He knew that much of what he felt was all in his mind. Ian became acutely aware, however, of the value of kind and loving gestures—of touch and conversation. He began to give greater value to the many other ways people can convey affection to each other, but so often take for granted.

Ian became certain that the teapot was the most crucial element in invoking the visits. During two lapses when he had no visits, however, it proved evident that removing anything else from the room also had a disruptive effect. He could only speculate why, since the combination of those items never caused the experience before the addition of the teapot.

The first period of Katerina's absence began when Ian removed a balloon-back chair in front of his desk in the study to have its seat re-caned. At the time, Ian had no idea why Katerina ceased to join him in the tea ritual during the two weeks that the chair was being repaired. As the days passed he became quite distressed by her absence. He only hoped that the remarkable circumstances that made her visits possible had not ceased to exist.

On the evening Ian picked up the repaired chair, he had a flat tire on the way home. There was a light mist of freezing rain, which made changing the tire all the more frustrating. He was chilled when he got home. He brought the chair in, placed it beside the desk, and immediately started to make some tea, for a little warmth and comfort.

Concentrating on his warming brew, he looked up to see Katerina sitting in the newly caned chair, smiling and talking to him while she worked on a book of handmade paper.

His body was suddenly filled with warmth, and his heart gladdened.

"It is so good to see you, dear, dear friend," he said. "Until this moment, I didn't realize just how much I had missed you." Ian was so overwhelmed with happiness that he was trembling slightly. He had to put the teacup down until he could recover.

Katerina smiled and nodded. Looking directly into Ian's eyes, she spoke for a few moments, her facial expressions seeming to reciprocate his feelings. As usual, the only words he heard were his own.

Picking up his teacup, Ian rose from the chair and moved toward her. "How do you like the new caning? Does it sit well?"

Katerina was looking down, tying the binding on her book. Ian saw that she did not know that he was speaking. It didn't matter. He was so content though, that as he neared her he continued talking.

"Do you think the absence of the chair could have interfered with our visit, Katerina? I don't understand how it could. We were never able to come to each other before the teapot. I am sure the teapot is the source of our connection."

Midway through his last sentence, as Ian was standing just in front of her, Katerina looked up at him. Raising her eyebrows, she questioned him for what he had said.

"I said that I wish I could do better at lip-reading. I am sure you can understand what I am saying, but it won't help much for me to ask you a question because I won't be able to understand your response."

Her fingers finishing the knot on the binding, Katerina raised her shoulders and then began talking to Ian about something, very casually. He was sure it was intended to provide some comfort. She reached out to "touch" him.

After a couple of minutes, she quickly turned her head to one side, as if she had heard something.

"What is it, Katerina?" he said.

She lifted a finger, retaining her focus outside his study.

"Is one of your children calling?"

Katerina tilted her head and started to rise. Instead of coming to her feet before him, she vanished.

There he was, teacup in hand, looking at his newly caned chair. Comforted by her return, he moved back to the recliner and admired the caning that Katerina had been sitting on only moments before.

"Welcome back, Katerina," he said as if she were still with him. "Come back to see me anytime."

It was rare that they visited in his world, and Ian could not discern what determined who would visit whom. Though Katerina's world was much more interesting to him, he would have preferred to always have her visit him in his study. When visiting in his home, Ian had independent mobility, the experience of moving about at will. He was also afforded the comfort of being fully corporeal. Katerina appeared to be solid flesh in either environment.

Much to Ian's pleasure, his and Katerina's teatime visits occurred regularly after that, and were uninterrupted for a couple of weeks. Then one night, he sat down with tea, and was surprised to find that he remained alone. He lingered, having several cups, thinking Katerina might return.

"What is keeping you away tonight, Katerina? Hope you are having fun. I miss you."

He was disappointed, but not overly distressed. After all, Katerina did not visit *every* night.

The next night, still alone, he was a little more anxious. Just drinking tea and letting his mind wander, for no particular reason the incident with the balloon-backed chair came to mind suddenly.

"Oh, no. Is it I that have been keeping you away?" he said.

Ian began to frantically go over the inventory of the room, searching for what he might have done to disturb the ambience of the room.

"Think, Ian. Something tells me you've done something that you shouldn't have."

Midway through the second cup of tea, he realized what it was. The day before he had moved a Fauvist-style painting of a male angel—painted by a local artist—to another room. Without thought of any consequence, he just decided to try the painting elsewhere.

"The painting; I moved that angel! What was I thinking?"

He rushed to the painting and brought it back to its previous location in the study. Confidently, Ian headed back to his chair. Before he could raise his cup from the table, Katerina had come and gone. He could not remember any of the activity of the visit, but he had the sense that she had been with him. It was as if she made the connection, imbued him and the room with her presence, without ever needing to materialize.

Never again did Ian allow any article to be moved from the study.

Dark Visits

For some time to come, Ian was content to understand nothing more about why and how he and Katerina were brought together. The fact that their time shared gave him great happiness was enough. The experiences had no perceptible impact on his day-to-day life. The joyful sensations that he had in trade for a few unaccountable seconds during his daily cup of tea were precious.

Ian knew he was growing increasingly attached to an experience that he could not explain to most people, but what was the harm? Just like many others, he had dinner or a few drinks with friends after a day of less than fulfilling employment. So what if he then came home and had tea with his mysterious friend Katerina? Though theirs was not the most orthodox relationship that he had ever known, it made him inexplicably content.

Unfortunately, Ian's time spent outside the domain of his conscious world did not remain confined to only a few seconds during each visit. He did not mind initially when the time span increased a little. But after a while, there was evidence that he actually was losing consciousness during the sessions and for unpredictable amounts of time during visits with his tea companion.

When the visits began, Ian felt as though his perception was briefly being expanded to include some part of reality not ordinarily seen by him, and he willfully chose to concentrate his full attention on that redefinition of his world for a period of time. What he was now beginning to experience was more like an unavoidable blackout. Sometimes for seconds, sometimes for hours.

Despite the implied danger, he continued to desire contact with Katerina. Common sense forced Ian to consider that he might be out of control. He could no longer avoid the blackout experience if he had the ritual cup of tea, and yet he could not deny himself visits with her. Of additional concern to him, the visions had begun to leave Ian with the sensation of a particularly noxious poison flowing into every cell of his body.

After a time, Ian began to notice disconcerting changes in Katerina's appearance. Since he believed that it was the traveling that was affecting his health, and he was generally the one doing the traveling, Ian had not imagined that their visits could have a corresponding ill effect on Katerina.

Tea was later than usual that night. He had stayed at work late to catch up on some things that had been delayed due to his developing health issues. Feeling like he had just dragged himself across the infinite space between their realities, Ian strained to focus on the likeness of Katerina that was available to him. No longer was her image fully formed and substantial. It was more phantasmal like he had seen of his own form when he first visited her world.

He didn't know if he would be able to remain this time any longer than the other visits of late. Why have I come back with no more answers than before? he wondered.

Ian had to ask himself why he was making so much effort to

bring Katerina's image into view. He knew it would only sadden him. Even if he could overcome the visual distortion, it was evident *much more* was going terribly wrong.

In the beginning, Katerina's face had been radiant. Now it was growing haggard and unhealthy looking. She moved like a completely different person, with a labored step rather than her former gracefully flowing movements.

The haziness of her present form kept Ian from being able to make out much of Katerina's countenance. He hoped all this unpleasantness was the result of the delusional consciousness that now seemed to take hold of him during recent visits. If Ian could trust what he saw, her bright eyes, with their bold spirit, had become dim—and perhaps angry.

Thinking the details of his facial expressions were probably no clearer to her than hers were to him, Ian raised his hand to say hello. She threw him a kiss in return. Though the action told him she was not angry with him, it actually made him more depressed about the situation. It was disheartening to see Katerina struggle through the visit as if she was also victim to a poisonous atmosphere, even though she tried to be congenial. If she was subject to any of the same physical effects that he was, Ian did not want to impose the situation on her.

In desperation to express his feelings for her, Ian tried to move toward Katerina, but he could not budge. He could sense that he had a fever, and that it was rising rapidly. He knew he would not be able to remain much longer. Maybe this is only a delusion from the fever, he thought. How he wanted to believe that was the case!

Transitions in and out of the visions had lost their unheralded nature. A flood of input to Ian's nervous system signaled the beginning to his return home: nausea, tension, and pain. It warned that he would pay for this transition. These days, he increasingly felt some of these symptoms while in the visit. However bad it was during the visit, it was much worse as the visit ended.

Ian reached out as to try to touch Katerina, just before the scenery reverted to his study. With his high fever, sweat was rolling down his face. The only way Ian kept the pain in his poisoned muscles from making him vomit was by clenching his teeth. With long, slow breaths, he started to calm his stomach. This, however, was not all good news. Recent experience told him that as soon as the physical distractions subsided, he would have to fight the onset of a round with depression. Though the vision seemed relatively short, his watch told him that he had been "out" for half the night.

His blackouts had become extended, and the nasty aftereffects lingered long after his return. Quite often, Ian "awoke" with his body fighting off this resulting fever. He also had the sensation of a sleeper who had not been fully released from a dream.

He made his way to the bathroom sink, to throw some cold water on his face. Ian hoped it would cool him off and shake him completely free from this nightmare. The face in the mirror was looking as strained as Katerina's had. After each visit, Ian swore that he would not attempt another one before coming to an understanding of what was happening and how to combat the deterioration of their experience together. Yet, as soon as his health recovered enough, he could not resist returning. He knew better, but each time he managed to convince himself that the two of them would not suffer ill effects in the next visit.

The breaking point for Ian came when he started to feel the same erratic waves of distorted perception when he was not with the teapot, or even when he was not at home. In these experiences, he never remembered Katerina appearing, but he would suddenly become conscious of the sensation of returning to awareness—an abrupt regaining of his consciousness—which almost always followed recent visits. This situation was proving to be particularly tricky at work.

One day, Ian was making his way to the office when his supervisor joined him in the hall.

"How are you feeling today, Ian?" she said.

Without slowing his pace, he responded, "Good morning, Mary. I'm doing pretty well. How are you doing?"

The look on her face said that she thought he looked terrible. He knew he had dark circles under his eyes and that his skin was ashen. Ian's recent visions were costing him much sleep, and his appetite was not good.

"Are you *really*, Ian?"

"Yes, I really am," he said.

"And how is the testing going with the doctor?" she asked. "Is he getting any closer to finding the source of the allergy?"

Ian felt he had everyone in his daily world convinced about the causes of his health issues.

"Food allergies can be very complicated to pin down, you know," Ian said. "There are just too many variables. But we're making headway, Mary."

"I hope so, Ian. I would be a lot more comfortable if I knew you were taking time off and focusing on your health. You have enough seniority and vacation to take as much time as you need.

"If the effects of this allergy are causing a lot of insomnia, like you say, you should be home, resting."

Ian stopped to make eye contact. Mary took a step past him, and then turned to face him.

"I know you've been concerned about my health, Mary. I very much appreciate the fact that you are letting me continue to come into the office. With the exception of time needed for doctor's appointments, and the infrequent time that I can catch a little extra sleep, the best thing for my health is to be here, focused on work instead of my health."

The last thing Ian wanted to do was remain around the house when he had no idea how to resolve the issue and did not dare to make additional visits.

"Okay, Ian. If you assure me that you will take any time you need," she said.

"Yes, I will, Mary. Thank you."

She momentarily put a hand on his shoulder, "Now, if your health allows you, I need for you to do me a favor. I was hoping to ask you for some assistance for an associate working on one of the projects that you are doing research for."

"Sure, whatever you need," he said, glad to have the conversation change.

"Do you remember Thomas Hutchins?" she asked. "He is a talented fellow, but his group is a little short of senior-skill-level help and he has been put into a position that might be demanding more than he has experience to handle in the timeframe we need. Can you give him a few pointers in some of the more problematic functions for their code section?"

Mary's concern was now fully shifted to schedules and performance. That motherly look had completely left her eyes; she was viewing Ian solely as programming talent. He was much relieved.

"No problem at all. I'll give him a call and set up a work session with him," Ian said.

Without further delay, she started to walk away, returning to her usual fast pace of making sure each of her current projects was bustling along productively. "Thanks, Ian. He'll be expecting your call."

Ian had always preferred to work alone, more now than ever. But if he was going to be under someone's scrutiny, he much preferred it to be a junior associate rather than his project manager.

A couple of hours later, Ian was sitting at his laptop, going over a code structure with Thomas Hutchins. All had been going well and they were just about to clean up most of the group's areas of confusion. Out of nowhere, Ian felt faint, as if his consciousness was being forcibly pulled elsewhere. This sensation was similar to the initiation of the recent visits, but he had never been threatened with such a strong experience outside of his study.

"If you move this value to temporary storage . . ."

Ian knew that he had stopped speaking in mid-sentence, but he could not force further words out.

"Are you all right, Ian?" Thomas asked.

Ian's eyesight was getting patchy and the sense of touch was fading from his fingers, as they became numb. Ian looked down at his right hand, at the fingers frozen in place on the keyboard. He tried to tap the keys, but no finger would move.

Though Ian did not see any vision of Katerina, and did not fully lose sight of the office around him, he experienced many of the unpleasant physical responses that had become common during his recent visions. He managed to avoid blacking out, but it took every effort he could muster. Ian didn't know for sure whether Thomas believed that he was conscious during the entire episode.

Thomas had placed a hand on Ian's shoulder. He was leaning forward to look into Ian's face. "Ian?"

Fortunately, the immobilizing spell snapped at just that moment. Instantly, Ian's vision recovered, and the cloud in his mind vaporized. He found his voice. "Sorry. What were you saying, Thomas?"

Thomas quickly pulled his hand away and shifted his weight back to the center of his seat. "Are you all right?" There was an obvious concern in his voice.

Ian tried to cover up. "Oh, yes. Sorry, I was completely absorbed, thinking about a possible solution to that database screening. I just might have a solution."

"Oh? Sure," Thomas said.

"I'll work on that later," Ian said. "Now concerning this module." He pushed ahead without hesitation, gave the junior programmer an important bit of code to work on, and sent him on his way.

Ian knew Thomas did not believe his explanation for his peculiar behavior, but Thomas was young and unsure of his status in the company. He would not cause any problem for Ian by bringing up the episode with anyone else. Ian knew he would have to spend a good bit of time instructing Thomas on how to work through that module, but the effort was well worth the trouble if it bought his silence. Thomas would benefit, in turn, from Ian's instruction and from the recognition he would receive once the code was completed. Still, Ian was sorry to have to use his seniority in such a way.

Ian had had other experiences when he was away from the study. Fortunately, the incident with Thomas was the worst. However, it had become evident that Ian could have the blackouts not only at unpredictable times, but in random places as well. He was afraid he might even black out while driving. He needed answers, right away, concerning the recurring visions of the alluring but silent Katerina. And he felt confident that a visit to the original home of the teapot would provide some resolution.

Liz

Ian had acquired the teapot from his friend Liz's bed and breakfast the year before, while on vacation in the mountains with his long-time girlfriend, Beverly. Ian thought he wanted her to have it as a reminder of the good times they seemed to have had on that trip. Sadly, a few weeks after returning from the mountains they found it necessary to accept that the relationship was not fully providing either person's needs. The only resolution they could agree on was to separate.

It was a sad time for Ian. Their relationship had been his most enduring since a short, failed marriage when he was much younger. It had seemed obvious that his relationship with Beverly had been falling apart even before the trip, but he had not wanted to see it.

When Beverly tried to pack the teapot with her things as she moved out, Ian was annoyed—and thus became aware of whom he had really bought it for. He was irritated, yet somewhat amused, that Beverly would now choose to claim a gift that she had all but rejected when Ian had given it to her. If anything, she had expressed almost contempt for the teapot and had repeatedly indicated an interest in giving it away.

Ian was also surprised, however, by the attachment he found himself expressing for the teapot. After all, it was wholly unremarkable in appearance, manufacture, and function. From the beginning, however, the teapot's impact on his life proved to be much the opposite.

Ian's fondness for that simple teapot had seemed to have a special ability to upset Beverly. He could not understand how they had such opposite reactions to a simple ceramic pot. As he looked back on those days now, Ian felt fortunate that Katerina had not visited the few times Beverly used the pot to make tea. He was sure that such an inopportune visit would have spelled doom for his beloved teapot.

Despite its association with the end of Ian's relationship with Beverly and the beginning of some strange activity in his life, it was good to see Elizabeth—Liz—Fontilineau's bed and breakfast again. It had been the centerpiece of his vacation with Beverly.

When seen while driving up the country road, Liz's bed and breakfast appeared to be a one or two-story flat-roofed building with some Victorian enhancements. But once past a green border of trees and bushes on the approaching side (or sooner when it was winter), you would become aware that the house was deeper than it was wide. It was built on a steep bank bordering the road. This fact hid the extra height of the building. If you were not stopping at the upper guest parking, on the approaching side of the B&B, you made a right turn on the opposite side of the house and drove down and around back to Liz's parking place and gardens. From there, the south side, the B&B looked like a townhouse, three stories over a basement.

Liz told him that the building had once been a general store and feed supply. Though it took a lot of work to fix up, she had bought it for the location and the space it provided for the price. Now Liz had multi-bed guest suites on the upper two floors. The common dining area and her private living space were on the bottom floor. The basement, exposed only on the east and south, was used for storage and gardening supplies. The two upper floors had balconies, and the first floor was wrapped on two sides with a wide deck.

Liz was a joy to be with. She and Ian had become good friends since they met on his trip with Beverly. Over seventy years old, she was a tall, remarkably elegant woman . . . elegant for any age. She spent much of her time in the bountiful gardens that spread around the house.

Ian would not have expected to find Liz inside, except that it was winter. She opened the door to greet him. Three weeks of abstinence from visiting Katerina had not brought about quite the health recovery that he had convinced himself it would. Though it would take far more to force Liz from her usual decorum, her eyes betrayed fleetingly her shock at Ian's haggard appearance.

Then she said, "Give me a hug, darlin'." She spoke in a charming deep-South accent—not heard very often in the mountains of the Northeast—and opened her arms to greet him.

Ian stepped through the door, glad to wrap his arms around her.

"Hello Liz. It's wonderful to see you again."

The year before, Beverly, Ian, and Liz had had many enjoyable conversations. Liz proved to be not only gracious, but a very wise, fascinating woman. During those leisurely conversations, Ian had never been able to extract from Liz just how she came to her knowledge. Her attention was focused on the "here and now," to caring for her gardens and being cordial to her guests, which she did so intently that it was almost a mystical art.

Now Liz led Ian through the door to the dining room and said, "The water for tea went on as soon as I saw you pull up."

"Thank you, Liz," Ian said. "You are such a wonderful hostess." He pulled back a chair from her large, double-pedestal dining table and sat down. She always had a way of making a person feel special.

"It is what I enjoy. It is what I do," she replied, and she disappeared for a moment through the double hideaway doors that led to the kitchen.

Every move Liz made, everything about her appearance, and all the choices she made were graceful and genteel, Ian thought. He realized that the music playing softly in the background was a recording of a Mozart concerto, performed on original period instruments.

He got up and looked through the windows toward the river west of the inn. Ian called, "How have you been, Liz? Did you have a nice Christmas?"

"I've been doing very well. Thank you for asking, Ian." Liz came through the door, carrying an exquisite silver tea service with a plate of the most fragrant scones. "It was a lovely Christmas. The weather was cold, with just enough snow for the mood of winter, without being troublesome. I spent time with many dear friends, of course . . . By the way, thank you for sending me that lovely Christmas card."

Just being around Liz brought out Ian's best manners. "My pleasure, Liz."

"How have you been, Ian?" The tone of Liz's voice held none of the alarm Ian had seen on her face when Liz had first greeted him.

"I'm alright, Liz."

Liz paused for only a moment before responding, "I'm glad to hear it."

Ian could not overcome feeling guilty about his obvious lie, so he added, "Though I've been working too much. It's been wearing on me lately. But I think that's about to turn a corner."

"That's good," Liz said. "One always needs to care for the spirit."

Ian looked around the room, seeking to diffuse the nervousness that was starting to build within him. Against the wall next to the kitchen, Liz had a pie safe with glass doors. If this had been her busy season, the cabinet would have displayed several cakes and pies. Now it was empty. The standard flower arrangement was absent from the center of the table, replaced with holly for the winter season.

Placing the tray on the table, Liz looked up at Ian, "I hope you like scones."

They sat and sipped green tea, spending the next hour relishing the maple-flavored scones and finding out what each had been doing since they had last been together.

"I was sorry to hear about you and Beverly," Liz said. "You two seemed so happy together when you first arrived."

"Thank you, Liz. Obviously something was not quite what it should have been. Anyway, the separation seems to be best for us both."

"Well, that's good. I know it had to be painful. But if you are both happy, I'm glad for you," she said sympathetically.

Liz's enjoyment of the simple pleasures of the moment and her unwavering attentiveness were, as always, so infectious that until she brought it up, Ian had completely forgotten about the teapot and the visions that he had been obsessed with for months.

"So, tell me, sweetie, what is it that you want to know about this teapot of yours?"

As comfortable as he felt with Liz, Ian realized that their conversations had never entered into esotericism. If Ian had to guess, he would have speculated that Liz had no such interest. He'd wondered whether she had never been drawn to such things or had just passed beyond the need of like expressions.

Ian answered carefully, not wanting to sound insane, "Oh, I don't know, Liz. I've just come to believe there is something very special about it."

Liz leaned back and gazed at Ian in a way that made him feel she was looking right inside of him. He was becoming uncomfortable. Always before, she had maintained a mix of Southern politeness and New England reserve. Never had he felt the slightest impulse in Liz to be openly curious. He would have assumed that she considered prying to be bad manners. But today, her quiet look felt almost intrusive.

Eventually, Liz shifted her gaze, smiled, and tilted her head to one side as she lifted her teacup. "It's a pretty teapot, darlin,' but there is nothing special about it. I was glad to give it to you when you asked to buy it. I'm not really sure why I kept it after that couple said they didn't want it back."

When Liz had given him the teapot, she had told Ian that a previous guest had left the teapot behind, but she had said nothing more. Its history had seemed unimportant at that time. He had been happy to have a token to remember a wonderful, peaceful time, and the teapot had served that purpose well. Beyond that, Ian had not thought much about it.

But all that had changed. Now he was curious. "A couple left it?"

Ian's question was not as telling as the quick way he spoke, the tone of his voice. He was embarrassed, and he hoped Liz failed to pick up on his expressed eagerness.

She smiled and put her teacup down. "Yes, it was a couple, a husband and wife." She paused. "Now it's your turn, dear."

Lost in his thoughts, Ian was slow to respond. He had hoped that the previous owner had been a single woman. It came as a surprise to see how much of a romantic fantasy he had built up. Ian imagined that he had been experiencing a connection with a proverbial "soul mate," through the mutual connection of the teapot. Ian had not been aware of it until now, but despite all the elaborate trappings of the visions, some part of him had adopted the notion that the person he was visiting had previously owned the teapot and was "of this world."

Liz waited patiently for his response, smiling and giving him all the time he needed. She took a bite of scone and gave him an encouraging look.

Initially, Ian was not ready to accept his disappointment. "Excuse me?"

Liz leaned forward and reached across the table. She touched his hand gently and said, "I will be glad to tell you everything I can about the teapot, Ian. You don't even have to tell me why you want to know. But I think you'll be surprised to learn that I know a little something about a lot of things you might never imagine."

Still unsure how to proceed without appearing unstable, Ian said, "Liz, have you ever had a possession, which seemed to have more to it than just its physical properties? It's hard to explain . . . well . . . when you're relaxed, quiet, and unguarded, it makes you feel as if you know something about its past? Or the people who owned it before?"

Liz's response almost scared him to death. "Oh, you mean an energetic imprint? Energy stored in an inanimate object, which can affect those in contact with it?"

"Um-m-m." He didn't know how to respond. Liz smiled kindly, and then Ian knew she had not asked with any judgment in mind. Still cautious, he replied, "Ye-e-es. You could call it that."

"I told you, I can be a surprise," Liz said. "Now, sweetie, maybe we can have the conversation you came here for."

Ian felt the tension drain from his shoulders. He could not say if it was because he finally felt relaxed about pursuing this topic with Liz, or if it was merely a result of exhaustion from trying to dance around the subject. One thing Ian was sure of, whether she thought he was crazy or not, he now felt much more at ease about asking his questions.

"Liz, when I asked to buy that teapot, it was only to remind me of the wonderful time that you, and your B&B, provided Beverly and me. I expected nothing more of it.

"But I soon began having a certain experience every time I used the pot in my study." Ian paused to summon his courage. He started to speak to Liz of "visits," but suddenly felt fearful, and restricted himself to calling them "visions" instead. His suspicion was that the concept of visions required much less indulgence on the part of the listener.

"I began to have visions of a woman, about my age, with long, auburn hair. She speaks, but I cannot hear her words. Crazy as it seems, I have to admit that I've come to an intense feeling of intimacy with her. I am certain, that in the deepest meaning of the word, I *know* her well."

"And you think the woman in your vision has some connection with the woman who left the teapot?" Liz asked.

With this question Ian went from being afraid of sounding delusional to feeling shame for being ridiculously naive. "Well . . . yes. It seems so. Do you think that is unlikely?"

Liz topped off his tea. "This will go more quickly if I tell you a little bit of what I know about the pot's previous owners.

"They were here about two months before your visit. It seemed they had some business in the area and used my place as a base. Though they stayed for three weeks, I did not see much of them. As I do with all my guests, I tried to make them comfortable and welcome. They did not want to be bothered. Even though they never expressed it in so many words, they made it clear they saw me as a servant, not as a friend or a social equal.

"After they left, I noticed that they had left behind a number of items, including the teapot. So I called to ask if they'd like me to ship the pieces home. The wife was indignant. 'Oh, no! We left them intentionally. We only bought them because—because they were more—familiar,' she told me.

"She stumbled over the words when she realized that she had been more truthful than she'd meant to be. It was quite clear that she liked those tea things better than the ones I had in the suite, but even they were not suitable for her home. I pitied her, despite the slight, and thanked her for her generosity.

"This lady looked nothing like the woman you're describing in your vision. She was a good bit younger than you, though she acted older than both of us. She was short and thickset, had short, dark hair, well cared for, but with a style weighted on convenience. Her clothes were also more practical than becoming. In fact, passionless pretense seemed to be her defining focus.

"I think I'm a pretty good judge of character. My years of serving people have given me time to observe and to learn. I feel safe in saying that this woman, bless her soul, is a person so afraid of living that, if you were to tell her your story, even if she *were* single, she would do everything she could to have you put away—for presenting possibilities that terrify her."

With the insight that Liz provided, Ian decided that it might be helpful to have some outside input on his experience. "Liz, what is your opinion of what I've told you?"

"Ian, I do not question your experience. I'm only telling you what you already know. Be careful to whom you speak of this experience. There are a lot of people who are more interested in maintaining the illusion of knowing than coming to any real understanding of reality. They will make every effort to stop anyone who upsets their self-deluding beliefs."

Ian felt suddenly downcast. "That is true."

Liz leaned forward quickly and said eagerly, "But all is not lost! I cannot help you much with your exploration. I've always preferred to spend my time with my flowers and my guests, rather than in explicit consideration of such things. But, I have a friend who *can* help you. This old fellow is a little unconventional, but he can give you just the kind of assistance you need for something like this."

"That would be great, Liz! Thank you. Can we invite him over today?" Ian asked excitedly. No matter how peculiar this fellow might be, Ian felt like he was getting nowhere alone and he knew of no one who might be able to explain the kinds of experiences he'd been having.

"It's not so easy as that," Liz said. "But we are in luck. Normally, we'd have to traipse all over the woods trying to find my friend. He doesn't have a phone, but I happen to know he is house-sitting this weekend for a neighbor, who does have a phone."

Liz got up and went into the kitchen to make the call. Ian could see her through the double doors.

"Hello, Djalma. This is Liz. How's the house sitting going, sweetie?

"Oh? Nice . . .

"I need a favor, darlin'. I have a friend here who could use your special help. He's been having some unusual visits. Do you think you could see him sometime soon?"

Ian noticed Liz's choice of the word "visits". Was it merely coincidental? He had not used that word while talking with her.

Liz got a pad and pencil from a kitchen drawer. As she listened, she took notes.

"In two weeks? On Saturday?"

Liz looked at Ian for confirmation. He nodded.

"He says that's good, Djalma. Do you need to go to his place? I can drive you. Ian lives several hours away . . ."

"No? Okay, I will tell him how to get to your cabin."

Liz listened a minute and then said, "Okay, on the stone by the bridge . . ."

"At seven in the morning? That's a little early, sweetie. Are you sure?"

"Oh? Well, okay then."

Again Liz looked to Ian. Feeling he was in no position to bargain when asking a favor, Ian nodded while shrugging his shoulders.

"That will work," she confirmed.

Ian could tell by listening to Liz's side of the conversation that his meeting would be a challenging one.

"Ian says these visits started when he acquired a certain teapot. Should he bring it with him?" She paused. "No teapot."

Liz returned her attention to Ian and gave him a questioning look. He knew of nothing else to ask, so he just nodded.

"Thanks, sweetie. He'll be there. Again, his name is Ian. Stop by if you have questions later . . ."

"You too." Liz smiled widely. "What do you think about that cat of theirs? A real Buddha personality wouldn't you say?"

She listened for a bit longer and then said, "Yes, amazing. Enjoy. Bye now, see you soon."

Liz returned the phone to the cradle and brought her pad to the table.

"There you go, Ian. You're in good hands now."

Looking at his instructions, it crossed Ian's mind to ask, "What if it is raining or snowing that day? It does that a lot in the winter here."

"Djalma said there is no need to worry about that."

The sheer certainty of her voice didn't completely alleviate Ian's concerns, but he could tell that was all the comfort he was going to get from Liz. She brewed another pot of tea, and they spent the rest of the afternoon chatting about other things.

During the next couple of days, Ian was too busy at work to even think much about his visit with Liz or the upcoming meeting with her friend. In fact, for some days Ian didn't even have time for a cup of tea. It was just as well. He did not want to risk inadvertently doing additional harm to Katerina.

Djalma

Ian was sitting by the riverbank, about a mile from Liz's house, atop a massive stone, under an old hemlock, within view of the bridge on the state road. It was seven o'clock in the morning, just when he'd been asked to arrive, which had required that he start down the road for this meeting in the middle of the night.

It was cold on the top of a rock by the river, a little after sunrise in January. Ian looked out over the water. If Liz's psychic friend is worth all her claims, perhaps he's brought me here for a frigid dip in the river, to bring me to my senses, Ian thought bemusedly.

"Not at all," someone responded out loud, seemingly from nowhere.

Ian's legs jerked and he had to grab the rock to avoid falling into the river. Fortunately, the top of the rock was mostly flat and Ian had been careful not to sit too close to the edge. He had seen no path except the one coming from the bridge. Being surrounded by thick rhododendron, Ian felt justified in watching only the bridge for signs of another person's arrival.

Ian jumped to his feet and looked down in the direction of the voice. At the base of the stone, on the edge of the river was a muscular young man. His hair was long and pulled back into a French braid. His face had a peculiar combination of both male and female characteristics, strength and softness.

The young man's voice did not give any indication that he had noticed Ian's embarrassment. "Good morning, Ian. Thank you for meeting me here. Sorry for the inconvenience. I needed to gather some things along the river this morning."

This was Djalma, Liz's psychic? Now Ian was aggravated. He had driven half the night and sat on a freezing rock to meet an eccentric, longhaired, blond Anglo kid? Ian had wanted a legitimate mystic.

Ian's mind exploded in doubt. Where did this guy get such a name? The exotic choice was probably with the idea that it added some credibility in his chosen vocation. If he truly had any talent for the preternatural, what difference would it make if his name were something ordinary like Joseph?

As an imagined defense, considering that a psychic might be capable of reading minds, Ian forced his thoughts into silently quoting the first thing that came to mind from *Hamlet*. "Whether 'tis nobler in the mind to suffer the slings and arrows—"

Unfortunately, Ian found that his frustration was stronger than his fear of Djalma's possible talent. His mind went on the offensive again. He distinctly remembered Liz referring to Djalma as "this old fellow." Didn't she know that psychics and mystics should be of a more mature age? How else would they be able to project the bearing of wisdom? Here I am in the mountains with an eccentric kid half my age, a junior psychic sorcerer!

Ian went back to focusing on lines from *Hamlet* to mask his real thoughts.

If Djalma was reading Ian's mind, the calm of his face showed no evidence of taking the hysterical mental chatter personally.

Finally, Ian slowed his mind down enough to say, "Good morning, Djalma. I didn't hear you come up." From wherever you came, he thought. Ian looked about to see from just where that could have been. "Nice morning for a hike."

"A little cold for my liking, Ian. We'd better get on with our business. It's going to start raining in an hour."

Oh, great, Ian thought. Now I am going to get caught in the mountains in a blizzard or an ice storm. No way was it going to be just rain at this temperature.

Forcing himself from his true thoughts, still neurotic about Djalma's possible talents, Ian returned to *Hamlet*. What a piece of work is man! How noble in reason! Noble in reason, indeed, he thought ironically.

Amazed at how much of *Hamlet* he actually remembered, Ian struggled for self-possession. Okay, how would he and Djalma go about the real subject at hand?

Djalma climbed around the side of the rock and started toward the bridge. As he passed by, he touched Ian on the shoulder and spoke with a gentleness that Ian normally associated with someone much older. "I'm sorry I've disturbed you. This wasn't my idea. Let's move over there in the sun, where it's a bit warmer."

That brief touch, even through a bulky jacket, gave Ian a remarkable sense of reassurance. He no longer felt any hard feelings toward Djalma for having brought him out at such an odd time. In fact, he was suddenly content to be where he was. He replied in all honesty, "We don't have to have this talk today, if it's inconvenient for you." Ian truly felt freed from his own need and full of concern for Djalma.

"Oh, I wasn't referring to our meeting. I really *am* glad to meet you. What I meant was that I didn't ask to be useful in such matters. It's sometimes as uncomfortable for me to be consulted about these things as it is for the people who come to me."

Never breaking stride, Djalma looked over his shoulder and smiled. "By the way, you'd have to ask my parents what they had in mind with the name. I've considered changing it."

I knew he could read my mind, thought Ian.

Djalma led them to a warmer spot, out from under the trees, and a little removed from the river, but there wasn't much more warmth. The sun had barely crested the mountaintops and the clouds were rolling in.

Djalma started the conversation, "How did you come to learn this talent of visitation?"

"I might be learning now, but it began more as something stumbled onto, I think," Ian said.

"Oh, I doubt it was purely by chance, friend," Djalma said. "It requires something much more than luck."

Djalma asked Ian a few more questions. Ian was surprised at how comfortable he became in sharing information with this stranger. Every question Djalma asked unleashed a flood of response from Ian. It was a relief to share his full experiences with someone who fully accepted what he said. Ian felt immensely closer to a solution.

As wrapped up in warm clothing as Ian was, the cold damp weather was beginning to get to him. Djalma was periodically brushing his hands up and down his own sleeves, too.

"Are you up for a little walk?" Djalma asked. "No need to move your car. It will be all right. My house is just through the woods, and I have a fire going there."

They wandered away from the road, through the trees and rhododendron, on a worn path through the thick evergreen forest. Suddenly, a tiny house appeared. It was the size of a small storage building. Made of rough-sawn lumber, it had a high-pitched tin roof. A covered porch, which was mostly storage for firewood with a narrow path left to the door, extended about eight feet from the front of the building.

Djalma grabbed a couple sticks of wood from the pile as he made his way to the door. Inside was a tiny woodstove whose fire had all but gone out. Putting the new pieces in, Djalma stirred the coals. Even though the temperature in the cabin was much colder than what Ian was used to at home, just to be in a place that was dry and warmed by the dying fire was a welcome luxury.

The interior of the cabin could not have been much more than 250 square feet. The space was divided into two rooms. The back room, more the size of a closet, appeared to be Djalma's sleeping quarters. Through the drawn cloth that served as a door, Ian could see a thin pad and covers on a raised platform.

Benches sat against the opposing walls, just inside the door, and were the only seating. A very small table and an old, cast-iron sink, with large water bottles stored under it, were against one wall, farther into the house. Over the sink were a window and several shelves, sporting only a few pans and dishes. The woodstove faced the door, against the wall between the living and sleeping spaces.

Ian suspected that the massive number of books, which covered every inch of wall space not otherwise occupied, provided most of Djalma's insulation. The weight of books seemed to exceed the sturdiness of the shelves perched over the bench where Ian sat. He hoped, however, that they would not collapse this morning.

Djalma made some hot tea and brought Ian's over to him. Ian held the cup for warmth and Djalma put his own cup on the table next to the opposite bench. In a single step Djalma was back in the kitchen, pulling a large pot from the wall over the stove and taking a small knife from the sink. He sat down on the bench across from Ian and placed the pot on the floor in front of him.

With one hand, Djalma grabbed the bottom of the bag he had carried from the river and dumped it onto the floor. Roots, bark, twigs, and an occasional green sprig, along with a lot of dirt fell out. Paying no attention to Ian, Djalma picked up a handful of items and started to scrape, cut, and shred portions of his collected treasures, tossing parts in the large pot, parts in a bucket nearby. If Djalma had swapped receptacles for this work, Ian was certain that he would have never known which was to be compost and which was to become stew (or whatever it was that Djalma was creating).

In time, the reawakened fire required that they shed some of their outer garments. Ian forgot about the growing heap of ingredients in Djalma's pot and the books perched just above his head. He talked easily about more of what had been going on while Djalma worked and listened. Ian told Djalma about his experimentation of moving items in and out of the room, as well as why he felt the teapot to be the central key to the event. Changing expressions on the young man's face assured Ian that Djalma was absorbed in every word. Djalma rarely gave any response other than a grunt of acceptance now and then, until finally Ian was silent. For a few minutes, the only sounds were the fire crackling and the rain that had begun to fall on the tin roof.

When Djalma finally spoke, it was with a tone of concern. "What you have believed to be thoughtful furnishing of your home has actually been a bit of energetic alchemy. From what you tell me, you have been stirring this brew for a long time, and with some purposeful intent, though subconsciously."

Djalma was proving to be most of what Ian expected of a generally proclaimed "wise" person, unerringly peaceful, possessing an occasionally disconcerting insight, and impossible to predict. After this brief statement, the young man seemed content to sit silently, as if waiting for Ian to process his diagnosis.

Ian wondered, is that it? Is that all he has to say, after all I have told him?

After fruitlessly waiting for Djalma to expound on his statement, Ian said, "Please explain what you mean."

"First of all, you are comfortable, are you not, with the idea that everything is made up of energy, and the physical world is an illusion?" Djalma asked.

"Sure," Ian responded. "In theory, anyway."

Djalma spoke quietly, his eyes intently focused on Ian's face. "Though not often experienced as you have recently, it is more than theory. It is so. How are you with the concept of infinite realities?"

Ian defaulted to an attempt at humor. "I like it, but no more than a couple nights a week."

Djalma's smile still conveyed seriousness.

"Sorry," Ian said. "Just what do you mean?"

"There is a single, all-encompassing energy field, call it the Whole or the Absolute. Within this infinitude are a limitless number of overlapping subsets, let's say segmented fields, that vibrate at unique ranges of frequencies. Each field is a separate reality, which more often than not remains unseen by any of the inhabitants of the other fields because of the frequency differences between them."

"Everything that appears to be physical within a subset of a specific reality adds a unique energetic signature onto the base resonance of that field, while remaining within the defined range of that field." Djalma waited to make sure Ian was following.

Ian could see that his confusion was not going to dissipate in the near future. So he nodded once, to suggest that Djalma go on.

"We may have to come back to this wider scope, but for now let's focus specifically on a single reality—our illusory, 'physical' reality. At the very least, those things we perceive as material will resonate according to their molecular makeup," Djalma continued. "From there, every entity gives off emanations based on what it has experienced, no matter if it is physical or not, sentient or not. In addition to this vibration, those entities, which we recognize as living, stir in their own personality or nature, which can be, for example, predatory, genteel, or whatever. Additionally, the resonance one picks up from self-aware entities is very affected by their individual assessments of their own experience and by their sense of self."

Ian was glad to drop the implications of those other fields, subsets, or whatever Djalma wanted to call them. Even with limiting his focus to his own reality, what Djalma was presenting was giving Ian a bit of psychological discomfort. Sure, Ian accepted such things as scientific fact, but he had not expected to deal with them in his personal life.

Djalma kept working with the roots and herbs. "Some people are completely unresponsive to these psychic emanations. Almost always, their total imperceptivity indicates a psychology of disassociation, dangerous to the individual and those that share their world, known and unknown. Such a lack of responsiveness should be corrected. Most people have some degree of sensitivity, which varies, depending on the situation and the range of vibrations they are naturally attuned to.

"These vibrations provoke the feeling of otherwise unwarranted pleasure you might experience when you meet certain people, or the sudden weakness that may come over you in a particular environment. When acquiring possessions, we're sometimes attracted by the resonance of the item, rather than by its more commonly perceptible characteristics. These emanations continue to affect us, and their surrounding environment, after we acquire the piece."

The implications of what Djalma was saying began to overwhelm Ian. "That would suggest we take on an enormous liability every time we choose a prospective possession!" he burst out.

Djalma looked around the room, and then said casually, "Rarely is there any need to be apprehensive. Most people are engaged in some degree of the same type of choosing based on the emanations that people and things give off. Russian roulette alchemy, if you will. Fortunately, the cylinder of this theoretical revolver has an infinite number of chambers, providing minimal odds for any perceivable alteration within the so-called normal reality, much less any threat to an individual."

"If that is the case, how do you explain what I have been experiencing?" Ian demanded.

With the equanimity one would expect of a person with his apparent achievements despite his youth, Djalma picked up the distress in Ian's tone. He smiled as if he knew that Ian was asking to quiet his own fear. "Perhaps it's just the luck of the draw. Lightning has to hit somewhere every time it strikes."

Ian stared hard at Djalma. He wanted answers, not just to have Djalma offer vague speculations.

Djalma responded to Ian's unspoken plea, "Theoretically, if one was able to attune one's personal resonance to another range, another channel, say, such a person could slip from one reality to another.

"In your case, I'm inclined to believe that some part of your deeper self has been pursuing this kind of access for many years. Perhaps up until now your quest has been exclusively subconscious. It's possible that the process has taken all the previous energetic mixes in order for these visits to happen. In addition, your conscious mind may have been going through preparation, so to speak, so that it could perceive what has happened.

"Perhaps your subconscious was always experimenting, armed with no more than a desired result."

"Considering the dark turn these visits have taken," Ian said, "I can find no reason for believing some portion of me intends this bit of self-destructive experience."

"It's your conscious perception that calls your experience self-destructive," Djalma said. "How do you know that what is happening is not creative in a positive way, rather than destructive?"

Ian sometimes found Djalma's insight to be infuriating. It was easy enough for Djalma to speculate, Ian thought. He was not living with the situation or its after-effects. Ian knew that the experience had taken an unhealthy turn. He could now admit that he was scared. He needed more *real* assistance from Djalma.

Looking into Ian's eyes, patiently, peacefully, Djalma waited for Ian to decide where he wanted to go with the conversation.

Ian mulled over the information he understood Djalma to have presented. Then he reverted to his speculations about what had been happening. "What I would really like to know is: If this is an energetic imprint, does that or does that not mean that a particular woman created the impression I'm receiving? The teapot is not that old, so the imprint could not have occurred that long ago. Liz says the couple who owned it bought it new, locally. Not many people could have come in contact with it since it was made."

Ian was getting more excited as he went on. "It can't be that hard to find out who she is. If Katerina and I have some connection, or she has something to tell me, I should find her and solve this!"

Djalma leaned back and slowly raised both palms, as if to ward off Ian's agitation. "I don't think this is an imprint, but if it is, I am certain it's not *that kind* of imprint," he said.

Djalma rose and took the pot of root mix over to the stove. Pouring water into it from a large jug, he continued. "Not all imprint manifestations are the result of a playback or representation of a specific person or event to which the item has been exposed to. It's likely your teapot was never in physical contact with . . . Katerina, as you call her. I would say this is not even a secondary imprint, which occurs when an item comes into contact with someone or someplace that has been in direct contact with a person exuding a strong psychic signature.

"Your visits are very specific to the one room. Also, as you told me, if you remove a single item from the room, Katerina ceases to appear."

"This doesn't make sense," Ian replied. "If she is *not* imprinted on the teapot, why does the teapot set off the vision?"

"It's not just the teapot that is causing the experience, Ian. You have come to this conclusion because the visits started after the teapot was brought into the room for the first time. Apparently, the teapot is the final ingredient in a *combination* of psychic emanations that have been developing for a while. Hence Katerina's absence if *any item*, and not just the teapot, is removed."

Ian's exasperation was heightened when Djalma said, "I am certain none of the items in your study have ever come into contact with Katerina."

If no item had come into contact with her, Ian thought, why was this particular woman appearing? He panicked. How can I locate her if I cannot associate her with some item or event in the physical world?

Djalma spoke quietly, as if in direct response to Ian's thoughts. "How would a woman from such an exotic culture, perhaps unearthly, come in contact with an ordinary teapot?"

Maybe it was just a simple mind-reading trick, but it brought Ian to his senses. Wrongly or rightly, each such inexplicable display of this telepathic talent increased Ian's trust in Djalma's ability to help him solve his problem. Ian suspected that the only reason Djalma performed these "tricks" was to calm him.

Feeling less tightly coiled, Ian took a slow breath and looked Djalma in the eyes. "That thought has crossed my mind, but I suppose I never completely dropped the idea of an energetic imprint because, for whatever reason, my logical mind found it the most comfortable—or familiar—of all the fantastical possibilities I have considered as an answer . . .

"What, then, does cause Katerina to appear? And why this woman, in particular?"

"Why her—that is something only a deeper part of yourself will know, Ian. What causes her to appear is the part I can help you with."

With his pot of herbs simmering, Djalma came back to sit across from Ian.

"Remember back when we were talking about a base range of resonance within a reality or field? Just as everything has its unique energy signature, a grouping of items within a certain space near each other will combine to produce a collective signature. To varying degrees, almost always unintelligibly, these collective signatures affect the reality experienced by anyone within the scope of their influence.

"Most people aren't sensitive enough to perceive even a fairly wide range of fluctuation from the base emanation of their own field of reality. Those who do sometimes perceive such fluctuations rarely interpret their resulting experience as anything more than a gut feeling, maybe the hair standing up on the back of their neck for no apparent reason. Sometimes a particular area has such a strong collective signature that even the general populace will acknowledge the location as possessing some preternatural influence. The usual extreme end of the spectrum would be widely experienced apparitions in the area."

"Are you saying Katerina is a ghost?" Ian cut in.

"Not at all," Djalma responded.

Without really hearing the response, Ian continued. "Wouldn't that operate much the same as an imprint?"

Djalma slowly shook his head, and waited for Ian to relax enough to take in what he was about to say.

"Whether by the unlikely accident or subconscious intention," Djalma said, "I'm content that you have constructed a collective signature within your study that is affecting your perceived reality—or rather, periodically expanding your perception of reality.

"Now remember I said the different fields or realities are almost always invisible to each other because of differing base frequency ranges." This time Djalma waited as if for a response from Ian, giving him a questioning look.

Concluding that they would not go forward otherwise, Ian offered a cautious "Yes."

Satisfied, Djalma smiled and continued, "More than just unveiling something from the sensory fringes of our shared reality field, the collective signature of your study seems to have created a vibrational doorway, making it possible for you to move into another reality, an alternate or parallel life.

"There are an inestimable number of realities, overlapping the very space of this room and even our very bodies. We never become aware of them, though these worlds appear just as substantial to their occupants as we believe ours to be. Only the most achieved Masters and Adepts expand their consciousness sufficiently to achieve a glimpse across these boundaries. It requires a very precise balance of vibrational signatures, external and/or internal, to perform such a pass-through.

"It's almost impossible to stumble across exactly the right combination to produce such an access. Even though you were not consciously aware of it, you did not stumble across this doorway. I believe your visitor is not a result of chance."

"Expanded perception," Ian said, "would explain my ability to see her world, to see her there, but how does that explain my own experience of traveling to her world or reality?"

"It's not traveling, really," Djalma replied. "That's a concept of the illusory physical realm—moving your form from one place to another—that your analyzing conscious mind has imposed on the experience, to make what is happening more comfortable, more familiar."

"Travel seems an apt description," Ian said. "I am here, and then I perceive myself, although not really solidly, in her reality. She has also *traveled* to my study.

"I can comprehend that what I see of Katerina could be just a visual projection into my room, a holograph, but my experience in her world is that I have something like a bodily presence there, just as I do right here."

Djalma smiled. "Well . . . actually you are neither here *nor* there."

Semantics are not helping, Ian thought.

Undisturbed by Ian's stern expression, Djalma smiled and continued, "Technically, we are not here. We are not physical. But we are an illusion of physicality, a manifestation of our consciousness, from energy.

"The energetic doorway in your study is doing more than just expanding your ability to *see* into this parallel reality. The experience could have been limited there. But your doorway appears to have allowed you at least a partial transfer, or fluctuation, between two separate reality fields . . . what you are referring to as traveling. Your ability to perceive this other reality makes it as real and accessible as the one you and I interact in right now. After all, what is reality except the 'perception of choice' at any given time?

You are manifesting a reference point for your consciousness, a body—even if not conventionally physical—in that place. You *are* in both places."

Ian agreed that this was how the visits felt. Now he saw this explanation could help him get his situation under control. The dark path the visits were taking demanded some remedy very soon.

"Why do you think her appearance and some aspects of her personality seem so strained at times, Djalma?"

"This is only my speculation," he said, "but I think that some development has not been achieved within a necessary period of time. This would also explain the unpleasant physical effects you are experiencing."

Troubled by that thought, Ian asked, "Are you saying that she's unhappy because I'm not performing some task I am unaware of, and therefore she is exhibiting some ill will toward me?"

"Ian, I don't think that is the case. You may be feeling an impact on your health just because you've spent too much time in the transitional range between the two fields, never fully achieving presence in her parallel world.

"As far as the nature of your visitor goes, I cannot be certain yet, but I believe she is a dear and trustworthy intimate to you."

Ian could not have anticipated the effect of those words. When he heard Djalma speak of Katerina and her affection just as if she were any other beloved. As irrational as it sounded, Ian felt some validation. His longing to truly experience her company in his world caused him to lose any calm focus he may have managed to exercise up until that point.

"Am *I* the cause of the changes I have seen take place in her?" This possibility had already been worrying Ian. "If so, what can I do to help her?"

Djalma sat down in front of Ian again. "The full extent of what you see may not actually be happening to her. The image may be distorted because the psychic connection between the two of you has been damaged."

Ian found this analysis dubious. "Well, what has been happening to my health is definitely not an illusion!"

"True, but we don't know if the interaction is capable of having the same impact on her."

"Will you help me then?" Ian asked, emphatically.

Djalma was silent.

Ian pressed him. "Can you, or do you know anyone who can, help me achieve the full connection? It sounds as if I need to do something immediately . . . And why do you think Katerina and I have been able to make this connection?" Ian started to speak again and then stopped short, releasing his breath. He realized there must be a reason for Djalma's silence.

"What you have been experiencing is defying time and space," Djalma said. "You and she could be making contact to exchange some information, to strengthen a bond, or to fulfill some preexisting promise. I cannot say just what with any confidence. You're asking me for information only you possess. Your experiences so far, however, especially the inability to touch or hear each other, imply you and she are currently incompatible in each other's reality."

Ian suddenly felt sure that Djalma's extreme calm, the most he had exhibited so far, was something the young sage was intentionally projecting with the intent of helping him calm down. Yet he was becoming more anxious that he would not be able to continue to visit Katerina.

"That's not something I can just sit back and accept," Ian said. "Look at what is happening to us."

Djalma nodded. "I said you are not currently able to fully exist in the same reality. I did not say that things should, or could, remain that way. Assuming this darker path that the visits have taken is not natural or intentional, the first thing we have to do is to figure out when they started to change. Then, maybe, we can figure out why."

They sat silently for a while. Ian thought back over the last few months. He hadn't really considered when the journeys had started to take the darker turn. "The situation has been developing all along. Even before things became unpleasant, the experience was ever-changing."

Djalma forced him to try again. "So, tell me the first time you had an unpleasant reaction to anything within the visits. Was it when you started to black out for longer periods? And do you remember when Katerina's appearance started to change?"

"I remember that I started to remain disconnected from my conscious world for longer periods of time as the experience got progressively more pleasant. At that time, I was glad to extend the visits. And, as far as the change in her image, I have been so infatuated with Katerina that I don't know if I would have noticed any initial progression of small negative changes in her appearance."

Ian struggled to recall the time before things "got bad," his first unpleasant reaction to one of their teas. Then he remembered one day when everything about the tea had seemed as beautiful as usual. Katerina had radiated a captivating sense of joy. Savoring the experience as he returned to conscious awareness, Ian unexpectedly felt a rush of distress that he could describe only as a panic attack.

"I just remembered! One day, instead of feeling comforted and joyous after my visit with Katerina, I was fiercely shaken. Something set off panic in me. I was consumed with dread. I forced myself up from the chair, as if to escape a threat, and stumbled toward the door. In just a moment, I got a grip on myself and felt rather foolish about my reaction. Still, the whole afternoon remained clouded by the experience of my return.

"The next few times I brought the teapot out, I was a little cautious, but all went well, and I soon forgot about that incident. It was months later that the visits became progressively more difficult."

Djalma's eyes were fixed on him, as if demanding more than Ian had given. "I'm sure I already know the answer, but had you recently brought something new into the room before that experience?"

Ian responded to the suggestion as if Djalma had accused him of sacrilege. "Not one thing since I realized the impact it could have!"

"Has anyone besides you been in the room?"

"No." Ian had to smile, thinking of it. "My friends think I'm a bit demented because of the way I protect the sanctity of my study, but I've managed to keep the room private. They tease me, but I've continued to entertain as usual. The study is somewhat secluded in the floor plan. Privacy wasn't the problem it would have been if I had been trying to secure certain other rooms in the house."

"What about the teapot? Has anyone come into contact with the teapot when you have people over?"

"Again, no, Djalma. I've been a little crazy about it, but I'm unwilling to take a chance. None of my friends even know I have the teapot. Except to rinse it and fill it with hot water for tea, the teapot has remained in the study since the early days of my experience.

"The first time I had someone over, after the first visit, I had already realized that changing things in the room could affect the experience, so I hid the teapot away in the study. From that day to this, I've kept it there."

"That's fortunate for our purpose," Djalma said. "It limits the range of possibilities we have to consider, but it's unlikely any casual contact would have affected the teapot. Most people would not leave an imprint that lasted much longer than their immediate contact with the pot. Those whose emanation lasted longer would have caused only a temporary change in the vibration of the teapot and, therefore, the collective resonance of the room. You might have noticed a minor modification in your entry into a visit, or the reality shift might not have occurred with the very next tea, but any effect would have dissipated in a few days."

Djalma leaned back, relaxing a little, obviously considering the options. "No one was in the room? Is it possible that someone doing some service in the house, or even one of your friends, could have come into the room without your knowing it?"

Looking away a little embarrassed, Ian had to say, "Not possible, unless someone broke in without leaving any trace. I invariably lock the door to my study, and that's the biggest source of banter on the nights I have the guys over for cards or to watch a game."

"Still, good for our purpose." Djalma smiled. "The room was not changed. The teapot was not changed. So that only leaves you."

"What do you mean? How could *I* have been changed?"

"Just as everything else in the room can be affected, so could you. Again, the same rules of impermanence would apply, *unless*—" Djalma emphasized the last word to make sure Ian was listening, "—the effect has been expanded by your continued thoughts or response to a person, thing, or experience.

"Let's concentrate on the time just before this unpleasant return to consciousness you mentioned. Can you remember anything or any person you came in contact with, which seemed to have a lasting effect on you, good or bad?"

It had been several months since the experience of the tense return from the visit with Katerina. Ian didn't recall right away what had been going on at the time. As best he could remember, it was just like the months that had preceded it. He spent his days with computers at work, went out with friends, came home, and then did this all over again. Ian's initial memories of those uneventful times were faint. He had been a little preoccupied with more recent concerns.

Trying to think what may have had a terrible effect on his paranormal teas, he tried to summon unpleasant memories. Actually, Ian had to admit that things had been going particularly well through that period of life. Work, his friends, all seemed to be going through a positive phase. His time working and socializing had been carefree and happy.

Just as Ian was about to throw up his hands in defeat, he remembered a project member at work whom he'd found particularly irksome. It was not that the person ever did anything that truly warranted such feelings. This fellow was just one of those people whom Ian always felt conflict with, even when they agreed.

"I've got it. Dixon Peerit! For the whole time I worked with him, I felt a strange tension."

"There is a way, Ian, to get a little better idea if your contact with this person had the type of consequence we're looking for. It sounds like you've probably had a previous experience similar to what I'm suggesting. This is something like a guided meditation. It's not hypnosis, just a method of relaxation to help you focus on a subject. It will allow me to get a feeling for your subconscious mind's assessment of Dixon. So, if you're willing, get comfortable and close your eyes."

Certain they were on the verge of a solution, Ian closed his eyes without hesitation. "Ready."

"Just relax," Djalma said. "The first thing you have to do is to let go of all your conscious beliefs about what has caused a change in the visits."

Djalma was silent, and Ian made every effort to let go of his hope that they were about to find the reason his visits had become distorted.

"Now, slowly, breathe deeply into your diaphragm, not your lungs. Hold that breath. Slowly, breathe out."

After a few minutes of this, Djalma asked him to remember Dixon. Despite instructions, Ian had already been revving up this memory. In his mind, Dixon was inextricably guilty as the source of Ian's misfortune.

Djalma peacefully coached Ian: "Bring up the memory of Dixon. Release any thought of him, but hold the image.

"Hold it. No thought, just hold the image."

As soothing as Djalma's voice and instructions were, Ian was ready to jump into action when Djalma said, "Okay, now let the image go, and we are going to come back to full awareness . . .

"Breathe deeply, and open your eyes when you are comfortable."

Ian stared at Djalma, anxious to hear his conclusion.

"It's not him," Djalma said when he opened his eyes.

"Are you certain? That guy used to give me the worst feelings—"

Djalma cut him off. "And there might have been a good reason, but it seems as soon as he left your project, you were no longer concerned with him."

True, Dixon had not crossed Ian's mind since he was moved to another project area.

"You're certain?" Ian was having a hard time letting go of his hope that the only unpleasantness he could recall during that time was the answer to the problem.

"I'm certain. Dixon did not have a lasting effect on your consciousness, and that would have been the only way another person could affect the journey through you. We'll have to try again."

Shaking his head, Ian said, "There's nothing. It was a particularly good time in my life."

"That does not preclude the type of effect we are looking for, Ian. You should also be trying to remember anything you found uncommonly pleasant or enjoyable during that time. It could be an impressive or exceptionally agreeable person whom you had just met, or a wonderfully satisfying experience that happened shortly before that time. It could even be new music you had just discovered, something that had an unusual impact."

It seemed like an odd request. Look for the good as the root of the bad? Ian just sat there in disbelief.

After a few minutes he began searching for the best, not the worst, of his memories of that time a few months earlier.

"Of course, there are always new songs on the radio," Ian offered.

"Any that you continued to listen to once they were not played on the radio or that changed your musical tastes?"

"No . . . there were movies that I saw and enjoyed, but none I've given much thought to since."

They went through everything Ian had done for several months leading up to the first unpleasant experience. Ian was almost regretting that he had such a precise memory and that he had so many good things to remember. By the time Djalma was finished, Ian was beginning to grow weary of that stretch of time, which he had just remembered as so satisfying.

Djalma latched onto Ian's mention of a fellow who was the team leader of the same project that he'd worked on with Dixon, Peter (pronounced Pay-ter) Rostich. Ian assured Djalma that was a dead end, but Djalma was having none of it. The more tribute Ian paid to Peter, the more adamant Djalma became.

Peter was one of those people everyone liked, a natural

leader. He could get any member of his team to do just what he needed done. It seemed to be a talent that he had always had. No matter how much he asked of a person, that person felt it was no more than was reasonable, and Peter always showed his appreciation of his or her cooperation.

Even outside work, Peter was an exceptionally interesting individual. It seemed he must have begun to pursue his many interests when he was very young. He was musically talented, proficient in violin, piano, and several other instruments. Hanging from his office wall was evidence of considerable talent in acrylic painting, pen and ink, and digital art. He had used his very keen mind to become proficient in each media—and it seemed, many other accomplishments—one by one.

Peter loved his wife, adored his kids, and was dedicated to his community. Ian admired Peter's way of looking at life; he believed Peter "had his heart in the right place."

So Ian had to admit the positive experience of meeting Peter had stayed with him longer than his negative feelings about Dixon. One doesn't meet such admirable people that often, he thought. But he could not imagine how that positive experience could have brought on such unpleasantness.

"Djalma, to be honest," Ian finally said, "I don't like the idea that something satisfying might set off dreadful experiences."

Djalma's look was disarmingly kind. "Peter didn't cause the change. Bad results are not inherent in good things. Your experience is just the product of an accident. The energetic signature of your tea environment was perfect for the outcome you achieved and desired. *Any* significant alteration was going to make a change. It so happened that this time the resulting change was undesirable.

"Remember, few people, not even you in most cases, are likely to encounter such a doorway and generally have no need for concern. It was not meeting Peter that made the difference but rather his continued effect on you, your perceptions, and therefore your energetic signature. But this is assuming that Peter is the element we are looking for. If you'll close your eyes and relax again, we'll know soon enough."

They went through the guided meditation process again. Several times Djalma asked Ian to hold onto the vision of Peter. Ian could not excite much faith in this pursuit, and the image faded. He was glad to have met such a person, glad there were people like Peter in the world, but Ian had no desire, then or before, to spend time visualizing Peter.

Finally, Djalma told Ian to release the image and come back to an alert state.

Ian sat silently this time, looking into Djalma's eyes. Djalma had somewhat of a dazed look. For several minutes he just sat without speaking or blinking, barely breathing. When the trance broke, a smile spread over Djalma's face, and he pulled from his pocket an ornate metal disk, about the size of a fifty-cent piece. He handed it to Ian, saying, "Take this into the room with you for your next tea."

Ian turned the token over and over, enjoying the artwork of it, without making any comment or asking any questions. There was something innately reassuring about having the item in his palm. He could hear Djalma taking in one long, slow breath after another.

"Your response to Peter *is* what we were looking for. It had a positive impact on your spirit, but it also changed your vibration, and therefore it changed the portal for your reality shifts. I'm expecting the token to counterbalance that change."

Ecstatic at the prospect, Ian rose immediately to his feet, almost knocking his head on the ledge of books above him. Clutching the token, which felt like his salvation, Ian hurriedly expressed his appreciation. "Thank you, Djalma. This is wonderful! Thank you, so much!"

Ian reached down, shook Djalma's hand longer than he needed to, and pulled Djalma to his feet. Mixing goodbyes with more gratitude, he hardly let Djalma speak again. He was too eager to try Djalma's solution. Besides, those herbs cooking on the stove had become a little too intense for his comfort.

As Ian made his way quickly through the woods toward his car, Djalma called from the porch, "Find out why you and she are in contact."

Later, during his drive, Ian felt bad about the hurried, even discourteous, way he had fled from the meeting with Djalma. He had been able to tell from Djalma's several attempts to speak that there was more to tell about this solution than Ian gave Djalma time to do so.

The truth was that Ian did not care to hear about any possible side effects or be given any precautions. He felt like he had a reprieve from a terminal disease. Anything that might happen had to be better than what he had been experiencing.

The Journey

Parallels

On his drive back home Ian gave a lot of thought to Djalma's description of the "doorway" to Katerina, and how it was opened. He was excited about the implications that he had subconsciously been constructing the proper combination for a long time. Ian wondered what other information might be harbored within his mind but just outside his present understanding? Had some part of him known all along about Katerina and the ties they had?

How little we know, he now thought, about our true motivations and the effects of even our simplest choices.

The items in Ian's study now took on almost a sacred importance for him. Just to think that only that combination of items would allow him—and only him (since he was part of the required collective signature)—to experience Katerina's world and allow her to experience his world made him extremely aware of everything in that room. Djalma's speculation had validated something Ian had realized about himself for quite awhile; he sometimes felt compelled to acquire certain items for his home, and he was never quite sure why. If that compulsion had been leading him to create a collective signature, then that was very comforting.

Since childhood, Ian had been accused of giving inordinate importance to the selection of his personal belongings. Somehow he always knew that those who taunted him simply did not understand its importance, though he could not explain what "it" was. Secure in his perception of a calling to possess specific items, or to be involved with certain people, situations, or places, Ian had moved through life responding to his internal guide. Invariably, this was his path, despite his own conscious mind's frequent discomfort due to its lack of understanding.

Ian could discern neither rhyme nor reason in the motivations to choose things—by now he had come to accept the urgings of his intuition. Most of the time he went about his business making choices in as whimsical a manner as anyone else—except those times when he felt a choice rise *from his depths*. Once he verified that the urge was genuinely intuitive, Ian did not question the choice further.

Those "must-have" possessions came from greatly varied sources: yard sales, antique stores, discount chains, exclusive art galleries, trash discarded on the curb, or just about anywhere else. Ian didn't go looking for these "significant" pieces, but could not ignore his response to such an item once it was discovered. Much less often, there were items that elicited an equal demand of avoidance.

Over the years, Ian had frequently sought a logical rationale or discernable pattern for his choices, only to acquiesce eventually. Intuition alone seemed to make an item "wrong" or "right" for him. There were even times when Ian truly did not like the look of an acquired item, but early on realized he could not pass it up or get rid of it once it was identified.

The most challenging expression of this instinctual demand was the house that he had lived in for many years now. Prior to encountering it, Ian had never had any desire to live in a town on the coastline. One year, he was on vacation and saw that old gray saltbox. Abandoning what most would have considered good sense, complying with a vehement call from his inner guide, the next thing Ian knew, he had bought the house, carted all his worldly possessions there, and begun a new job nearby.

True, once Ian did acquire something, he had developed an inescapable ritual of moving the item from room to room, and place to place within a room. Ian would bring the article in and place it in the first possible location, usually closest to the door. Sometimes the new piece would stay in that initial spot for weeks, even if he found the placing to be very inconvenient. He was simply awaiting inspiration by the inevitable process that he knew would eventually take place.

Other times Ian had barely set the piece down before he felt compelled to move it again. Sometimes again and again. He bought a beautiful green vase of blown glass on a base of smooth, gray river stone, which he eventually had a strong urge to destroy just so he could be released from its obsessive, but indecisive, drive to find its proper "home." For weeks Ian was obliged to move that vase to a new location just about every time he laid eyes on it—and he was grateful when it accepted a final location!

Usually, Ian would allow a piece to remain in its first location until he inadvertently picked it up as he walked by and deposited it elsewhere. There it would remain until the item "magically" found some place better suited for itself. After a time, Ian would realize that a particular possession had been in the same location for an extended period. A feeling of relief would come over him: knowing the item's proper place had been found, and he was free from further obligation to it.

Once back in his driveway after his visit with Djalma, Ian sat in the car in his driveway and stared at his saltbox home, which he had once believed unexplainably atypical of his tastes.

"Thank you," he said aloud, releasing a charge of gratitude

for all those unexplainable intuitions that had attracted so much playful—and sometimes harsher—ridicule over the years.

 Ian was sure that Djalma was right about what had caused the unpleasantness in the recent visits. The first tea after receiving the token was glorious—the completely flawless experience of joy that is the delirium of new love. When their visit began, Ian watched Katerina as she read a large book in her home. This was like being given back his early experience, except now he knew more of who she was and what he felt about their time together. Ian did not have the uneasy feelings that he had experienced with the first few trips. Djalma had given him back the beginning, but this time the journeys had—Katerina and he had—a history.
 Katerina's face had the same radiant beauty of months ago. Her smile was back, and her eyes were bright and clear.
 Ian remembered what Djalma had asked him to do. But what had he meant when he said, "Find out why you and she are in contact"? This may not speak well of my mental health, Ian thought, but Djalma's question makes as much sense as it would to tell young lovers to figure out why they are enamored.
 Ian was thoroughly enjoying his life again, and especially time in his study. His friends made a point of expressing their relief that he was regaining a healthful appearance. To them, Ian credited the change to an herbal concoction, cooked up for him by a curious new friend in the mountains.
 No longer was Ian drawn into another reality when outside his study. He regained the clarity of mind that he had been used to before the visits had become dark. He went back to enjoying his previous routines, going out with friends, and even enjoying his programming work. Now that he had Katerina back, Ian no longer felt a need to know how or why the visits were happening. Though it may have seemed insane to some to say so, he liked his life, as unorthodox as it was.
 Ian's only concern was he hadn't been able to put to rest

Djalma's parting words. Ian wanted to forget them—he tried to forget them—but they persisted in his thoughts. Despite that, Ian gave most of his attention to the additional time he had been given with Katerina.

They were again seeing each other regularly. Their visits were as varied, yet as routine, as they had been early on. All their exchanges remained extrasensory and pantomimed. Ian continued to feel closer to Katerina after each visit. With each interaction, he felt even more satisfied within his own spirit. Then one day something a little strange happened.

Ian had always experience a momentary loss of awareness of the present when he visited Katerina. He would be looking at something, and then he would be seeing her. When the reality shift finished, he would find himself staring at an item within his room again, quite often the same thing as before the visit began. The shifts had always been instantaneous, except when things had gone dark, before the use of Djalma's token. At that time, the returns to consciousness had been less distinct, leaving his mind cloudy and his emotions distressed.

Usually, Ian would start a pot of water. He would not wait for the kettle to whistle, but instead keep an eye on the heating water, while he put leaves in the strainer and generally tinkered around the kitchen. Once the hot water was in the teapot, he would set the timer for brewing time.

For some unknown reason, one night Ian took the teapot into the kitchen and before putting any water on the stove, he returned to the study, looking for something, but he could not remember what. Perhaps losing his sense of purpose, he sat down in his old recliner, per his normal ritual, but without that all-important teapot.

The next thing he knew, Ian was slowly returning to awareness from something he had to describe as a meditation. It was not abrupt like the returns from his usual tea visits, and yet he was much too conscious to have been asleep. He had a feeling of glorious warmth rising from his inner depths. As he became more alert, Ian realized he had been with Katerina. In all the months past, he had never been graced with a visit while the teapot was not in the room.

A feeling of joy flooded his spirit, as if he had just had the grandest good fortune. He was used to the good visits mostly passing in seconds. Tonight his watch said he had been *elsewhere* for almost two hours.

Sitting there, both confused and delighted, the memory of what had happened during the meditation pleasantly broke into Ian's conscious mind. Once he saw the first pictures of recollection, the rest of the memory began to flow freely. The experience felt like a lived memory, something recalled from his own life, not a dream, a vision, or other indirect experience.

His elation became mixed with fear. Everything about this visit was very different from any other journey he had experienced. Katerina was different. She looked years younger. Her surroundings were not the house that he'd become used to seeing her in. Despite the changes, Ian had no doubt it was Katerina. It did not matter how her appearance might have changed. A visceral part of him recognized her spirit.

Katerina moved about, attending to her interests and concerns, in a parallel life, previously unknown to him. She cooked a meal, read a book for a while, and played a stringed instrument Ian was unfamiliar with. This all seemed to go on and on. And he heard her speak! He could hear everything going on in that world.

Ian thought the memory of her voice would make him pass out as he recalled it. He fought to stay conscious, because consciousness was his means for savoring this experience and he was not willing to lose one instant of that memory. From an objective perspective, Ian could not say that her voice was anything special. Except to him, who had so longed to hear that voice, her voice was like an angel's song. He now sat with eyes closed, watching those images passing and listening to her voice. His entire body resonated to her vocal tones.

Ian did not move from his chair for the better part of the night. Never having been much on remembering more than morsels of the occasional dream, Ian was stunned at how much he remembered of this meditative reverie. He would have been glad to go over and over the same small sequence of memory that evening, but there was no need to. This one journey seemed to cover days of time spent in *this* Katerina's life.

Another very definite difference was that this Katerina, without question, was speaking to someone other than himself, who stood exactly where Ian perceived himself to be. She called the person of her attention by another name. Though the name did not give Ian any indication of gender, it was obvious she was interacting with a male partner.

It was as if he was looking through the eyes of the male in her presence, as a spectator only. Ian remained a distinctly separate consciousness from this individual, but he was anchored to this world within the body of Katerina's partner. Ian could not experience this man's sense of touch, but could smell the aromas of this world. He was not privy to this man's thoughts, but he felt a mysterious sense of *unity* with this individual, even more than that of merely sharing a body.

One benefit of being hosted in this unfamiliar place seemed to explain why he understood the words spoken by the couple—though he knew it was not a language he should understand. Unfortunately, he could not always comprehend the intention of the conversation. The couple referred to events and situations in their life and relationship that Ian did not have knowledge of.

Ian's awareness seemed to expand long enough to allow him to watch several days of that life: those several days took place in only two hours that passed in his world, despite the implied temporal conflicts. This made it clearly apparent to Ian that he was experiencing a parallel life with Katerina, an alternate reality—

Parallels

one always before him, but not usually available to his primary world's perception.

Katerina's home was now situated in a lovely, open countryside. The surrounding flora and fauna were unfamiliar. Only the attire and the odd customs separated the occasional neighbor whom Katerina and her partner met from the people Ian had met in the countryside near Liz's B&B. In both cases, they were all courteous and giving of themselves.

Ian did not know if it was because he was exhausted of because he had simply came to the end of his trance, but finally, there seemed nothing more to see. Whether he had eyes closed or eyes open, the scenes no longer flowed into his consciousness. The most Ian could do was to bring up repeat portions of his experience to savor as memories.

That meditative trance had had the intensity of the earlier visits. This experience was as real as the best of Ian's experience in his everyday, waking world. He could have sworn he had experienced these few days firsthand.

One Who Knows

When he got back from work the next day, Ian was still charged from the previous night's experience, even though he had lost several hours of sleep to it. Without brewing tea, he tried sitting in another meditation, hoping for an additional visitation. He tried sitting in the study with the teapot, but with no tea. Then he tried sitting without the teapot in the study. Unfortunately, Ian was too energized to relax. Nothing happened.

Even knowing that it would further delay his getting any much-needed sleep, Ian brewed a pot of tea and had a cup. He wanted to see Katerina right away. If a few seconds with her, here in his study, were all he could have, Ian would be glad for it.

What he really hoped for was to visit the Katerina of his *tea visions*. Since he was able to hear Katerina in this other life perhaps that was an indication that he would now be able to hear the Katerina he had been visiting for months, if he could only get back there. Ian longed to share with her what he had discovered.

From the moment he had initially seen her, walking through the forest path in their very first visit, Ian had been left with the unsettling conviction that she and he shared more than just the ongoing exchanges that he was experiencing. He had not been able, however, to find any rational justification for such strong feelings. But after the vivid memories of the night before, Ian felt he had seen pictures of a life that Katerina and he had lived together, or *were* living together now, in some parallel existence.

With the night before, he had experienced some additional portion of their story together. He had known her voice, her laugh, and her direct interaction with him in that life. And he wondered how this previously unrealized parallel life had subconsciously affected his experiences in his *primary* world.

Ian drank the tea, but he was disappointed. After taking his time enjoying two more cups, he was even more awake and yet had no additional experience of Katerina. Lingering in his recliner, he did not immediately notice when he started to go through the memories of the evening before. Soon Ian questioned why he was determined to have a new visit, since he was so blessed with a rich memory that he could relive with such vivid detail and sensations. His recollections of that experience were unlike any memories he had ever known before. They were just as authentic as the original experience.

After a while, Ian got out a notebook and began writing down every detail he could recall. The location of that new visualization was definitely not the world of his consciousness, or in his time. He wanted to firm up all the details in his mind. Perhaps he could find some answers to his recent experiences within the memories of those few days. He wanted to be able to share what he had experienced with *his* Katerina.

Again, he was late getting to sleep.

For the next several evenings, no visit occurred. Though short on sleep, Ian continued to feel fully energized and happy. Night after night, until he had gone carefully through the entire experience of that simultaneous life with Katerina, he recalled an unbelievable amount of detail from that single visit. He concluded that something had changed. He was no longer merely visiting another reality, but actually living a portion of a parallel life. This had obviously resulted in a change in him, right down to his definition of self. Then it hit him.

"A change in me?"

From what Djalma told him, Ian realized that such a change could alter the vibrational rate at which he resonated, change the signature of the study! He had been so busy recounting his extended visitation with Katerina that he had not worried himself about whether there was any significance in her recent absence. Ian tried to reassure himself by recalling that in the early days she had been gone for extended absences and there had been no reason for concern. Maybe sleep deprivation had caught up with him, but he felt overwhelmed by apprehension.

His first instinct was to immediately call Djalma and beg for help. But Ian felt guilty for departing their meeting so hastily and not keeping Djalma informed. Besides, Ian couldn't just call him. He would have to call Liz and ask her to hike up to Djalma's forest home. Although she tramped through the woods quite regularly, Ian was not willing to ask her to do so at his request.

The next thing Ian knew, he was drowsily responding to the alarm clock. He'd finally slept, but apparently not for very long. He woke, exhausted.

Later that day at work, Ian's anxiety about losing contact with Katerina overcame his reservations. He made the call to Liz. It was comforting just to talk with her for a while. He asked her to ask Djalma to call him collect any evening, whenever she next saw him. She agreed not to go looking for Djalma, but would wait until he came for one of his frequent visits to her B&B.

Djalma called that night. Ian hoped the prompt response was due merely to his good fortune, not to any extraordinary efforts on Liz's part.

"I'm surprised to hear from you again so soon," Djalma said with a pointed but friendly irony.

Ian apologized and groveled appropriately. "Oh, I know, Djalma. I've been meaning to call. The charm you gave me worked so beautifully that I did not want to trouble you. I really have to thank you. You knew what you were doing with that."

"Thank you," Djalma said.

Ian paused for a moment. "I believe I have a related question."

Then he told Djalma about the reality-transfer during meditation. He did not go into details, just mentioned the fact the teapot had not been in the room, how it had felt, and the impact the experience had had on him. Then Ian told how since then he had achieved neither a new meditative transfer experience nor a *tea visit*.

While he was relating his story, Djalma made no real response. He just made the kind of slight diversionary sounds one might make when distractedly turning a strange or unexpected idea over in his mind: "Uh-huh." "Hm-m-m." "Really?"

Ian assumed the limited responses meant Djalma was surprised. Ian had thought the new kind of experience might have been caused by the token. This made Ian wonder why he had assumed that all that happened was part of Djalma's plan.

Ian concluded his story and said, "Maybe the token you gave me needs a new charge."

"I'm afraid it could never have been more than a temporary solution, Ian," Djalma replied. "It performed its only intended function. Your visits ceased to pose any immediate threat to your health.

"You need to realize that the visits, in their previous form, may not be meant to continue forever. It sounds as if you have moved into another phase."

"Yes, the dearth stage. That's what troubles me, Djalma."

"I don't think you realize the extent of what you've achieved, Ian. You removed a distinct part of the portal, and yet it continues to function. Not only that, you now have a degree of access beyond what the collective resonance of the study gave you. You can hear the sounds of that place and seem to be somewhat embodied within a physical form.

"This new development is almost unbelievable! I wish I could manage such an experience."

Initially, Ian swelled with pride. Seconds later, he deflated back to humility—realizing he had no idea how his experience had been induced. Then he sank to sheer terror. If he had no idea, and it had not been the specific result of Djalma's assistance, how would they know *how* or even *if* the portal would function again?

"It's only been a few days since your last visit," Djalma continued. "It's possible that your nervous system can only take so much of such high-intensity experiences. It's quite probable this kind of a connection would be very demanding on your spiritual energies. This was no ordinary visitation. I wouldn't push for the next journey too soon, Ian. You found your way there, and it is likely you will do so again when you're ready to handle it."

Ian felt too anxious to adopt a wait-and-see approach. "Is it possible that my reaction to the extended trip has changed me in such a way that Katerina and I can no longer contact each other?"

"That *is* possible, Ian, but I think it unlikely. It's too early to tell. We can only wait and have faith that your inner intelligence knows what it's doing, and knows when you'll be ready for more."

"What about making the kind of counterbalance adjustment within me that you made with the token? Wouldn't that be a more direct solution?"

"Oh, no. Even if I were capable of such a thing, Ian, I wouldn't do it. Attempting to sculpt another's energetic resonance would be a very dangerous undertaking. Not only would such a reckless venture endanger *your* body, mind and spirit, it could also harm me."

"What about giving a new charge to the token?" Ian asked.

Gently but firmly, Djalma said, "You don't understand the

delicacy and potential danger of what you're suggesting. When we used the token, we weren't in full control of the result. It was a calculated gamble at best. I tried because you were caught in a situation that was damaging you. The alteration seemed to be the best of a number of possible choices, all of them questionable.

"This is an entirely different situation, despite what you may believe. Your subconscious is in a recuperative phase. Whenever that recovery is complete, you will probably return to Katerina. But this visit may have yet other new aspects."

Ian was frustrated by Djalma's rational path. Djalma, however, had never given Ian reason to doubt him or his wisdom. Until given reason to do otherwise, Ian would trust him.

"Ian," Djalma said. "I need to point out something that I know you know, but seem to have momentarily lost track of. I have the terms to describe what is going on. I have studied the relative theories, and even have the odd talent that suggests possession of some superlative information. But you are the 'one who knows' in this situation.

"I cannot do what you have done, nor have I ever done anything similar. You lack the conscious understanding of what is going on and why. But your spirit knows. Within you is all the information you will ever need.

"If you allow me, I can be a support to you. I can point you back to yourself when you stray. But that's all I can do."

Djalma went silent.

For the first time since he had given Djalma the position of acting as his personal source of wisdom, Ian was forced to return to the place of his own insight. It was both powerful and painful to retake control of his direction. He too became quiet, trying to reclaim the energy, the will, to take charge. Ian accepted that what had begun as his respite from this responsibility had gotten out of hand.

After a few moments, Ian remembered Djalma's offer of assistance. He was not alone, and for that Ian was genuinely grateful.

"Is there anything I can do to repay your kindness, Djalma?"

"Call Liz and leave me a message—better yet, come by—after you see Katerina next. I would really like to see you again."

Ian was both surprised and comforted.

Djalma finished their conversation by saying, "Ian, I'm not trying to intrude, but if I were you, when you see Katerina, I would not assume this new access will remain open forever. You two are too intertwined to take these opportunities casually. There *is* a purpose for this connection, and I would say a very important purpose considering the energy it takes to overcome the obstacles that generally disallow such cross-reality reunions."

Sacred Vow

Soon after his call with Djalma, Ian achieved his passionately sought goal of meeting Katerina many more times, but he could not have imagined what the feat would demand of him in return. Ian knew that in pursuing love, one never intentionally asks to be made defenseless, gullible, and imprudent, but many a love, as well as countless other great treasures, would not have come to pass without first coming to possess some degree of those more dubious gifts.

For some people, but not for him, it might have been debatable whether Ian's next visit was a gift of benevolence to lure him onward or a cruelty. For him it was, unquestionably, kindness.

All that was necessary was for Ian to cease to pursue the next visit so fervently, and to rest comfortably with the confidence that he was connected with Katerina. After a month of ignoring numerous invitations, Katerina visited Ian during his meditation one evening. Perhaps it was coincidence—or had it become necessity?—but the teapot was not is the study this second time as well.

As had become his habit while meditating, Ian sat cross-legged on his woolen couch. Sitting there, Ian began to perceive the Katerina of his original tea visions, the very same woman in appearance and manner. She sat, with her back to Ian, on a tall stool at a fine old-time writing desk of a dark wood. She was reading an ornate, thick, old book with a leather cover. Contentment spread through Ian, along with caution. He was afraid to breathe; afraid he might disturb the connection.

His view of the scene started to arc to the right, moving nearer to Katerina. At first, Ian was alarmed, as he had not willed this movement or even desired it. By then he was used to being out of control of his location in her environment. Today, Ian could determine that his view was not through the eyes of another person in the room with Katerina.

He expected Katerina to become aware of his presence. She always had been when he had visited in her home before.

This was indeed the very Katerina with whom he had become so familiar during the tea visits, unless his memory was playing another cruel trick. And, this was the room in her home that he had visited many times. Just as Ian remembered, her desk was in front of the window to the right of the exterior door. On either side of the desk were bookcases. He had watched her laugh, read, and write here many times before.

Katerina slid to the back edge of her stool, looked upward, and was silent for a time, perhaps in some prayer or meditation of her own. Ian felt close enough to lay a hand on her shoulder. With all the power of focus he possessed, he tried to reach forward and touch her shoulder. No hand obeyed. No touch occurred. Clearly, Ian had no body for this visit to her home.

Lost in the midst of this frustrating perception, Ian heard Katerina speak. After a moment of pleasant surprise, he noticed that her voice had a sad tone.

"Are you listening to me? Can you hear me, dear one?" she said.

"Yes!" he said. But his response made no sound. Katerina evidently did not hear him either. She did not reply.

Was that truly Katerina's voice? he wondered. Her sadness troubled him. Though he had not been able to hear what she said during his previous visits into this life, Ian had never observed anything before to indicate that she was leading less than the most fulfilled of lives. His belief that she was happy had made the separation between their existences acceptable, at least until he could find a way to be with her. The melancholy rhythm of her words caused him sorrow.

After a moment of silence, she lowered her attention to the tome on her desk. "Where have you gone to, my friend?" she asked in that same sorrowful voice.

"I am here, Katerina," Ian replied.

Katerina continued to talk to herself as she flipped slowly through the pages of the book. She appeared to be searching for something in particular.

Ian was looking over her shoulder. The pages of her book had detailed scrollwork painted around the edges. The paper was thick enough to be vellum. The book seemed handmade. The text was not written in English, and the formatting of the lines in most places implied that it was more like poetry than prose. Most pages had a variety of images in the text area, more like hand-drawn or painted artwork than printed pictures.

This particular book was not something that he remembered from any previous visit to her house, but it was not unlike other books Ian had seen Katerina use, or that were spread about her home. Based on what he had seen before, this could be a rare collection of ancient volumes of poetry. Or it could be something more along the lines of the esoteric writings, with which she was also so familiar. There were many such tomes on the shelves on either side of her desk and spread about the house, extraordinary in their appearance and their content.

In his previous visits, Katerina had impressed Ian as being both an artist and a mystic. He did not need to see her work with such manuscripts to come to this conclusion. The way she responded to children, flowers, or any other living things provided evidence enough for this speculation. She always exhibited the wonder of a child, the wisdom of an ancient, and a unity with nature rarely embodied by any member of humanity.

This day, Katerina periodically stopped to consider a particular page and traced her finger over a design or picture. Sometimes she sang lowly, barely loud enough for him to hear. One song reminded him of a children's lullaby. Another was more of a hypnotic chant.

After the chant, she quickly flipped through several pages, as if remembering something, or returning momentarily to a section she had already viewed.

"What are you looking for?" Ian asked, needing to speak though he knew his effort would be silent.

"I am looking for you, dear one," she said precisely at the right moment. "Are you looking for me?"

Ian was shaken.

He hoped Katerina would turn to look at him. Had she finally realized that he was there?

Without turning, she spoke again, "When will you return to me?"

"Oh, Katerina," he responded, "I *have* returned. Why can't I make myself known to you?"

She flipped through a few more pages, silent now.

"Look at me, Katerina," he said. "Please turn around and see me!"

Abruptly, she stopped turning pages. It gave Ian hope. But she did not turn around.

She read aloud from the page she had found. At first her words seemed to be in a language unknown to him, but she spoke too softly for Ian to be certain. At a later point in the verse, Katerina suddenly began to speak clearly, and in English.

Twice known.
Eternal waters of unlimited life.
Three times shown,

Mysterious ways of freeform flight.
I have seen,
Been forgotten, but revived.
I have died,
But never been denied.
Somewhere near,
The immortal dance begins.
Swirling sphere,
From which all life extends.

Was this a favorite poem of hers? Ian wondered. Or was she reciting a potent spell for some specific purpose?

Sitting back in her stool, Katerina closed the book with a heavy thump. "I do not believe you have chosen to forget about us and our commitment to one another," she said.

"Don't believe it, Katerina! I haven't forgotten!" he promised.

Katerina pushed her stool back from the desk. She rose, walked away from him and disappeared into another room. Ian stared at a piece of paper now lying on top of the book she had been reading from. The script was beautiful. He was certain it was Katerina's own handwriting.

The paper was well worn—obviously a favorite keepsake. If for no other reason than its value to Katerina, Ian wanted to be familiar with this verse. There was only a single paragraph. Unlike the book, the words on the page were in English. Ian started to recognize them as something he was already acquainted with.

Katerina returned and stood between his vantage point and the desk. She had brought a candle and lit it, releasing a fragrance of an exotic smelling spice that Ian did not recognize.

With her back to him, she pushed the stool under the desk and stood with her hands on its back for a moment. Then she dropped her attention to the paper that he had been trying to read.

"Why are those words familiar, Katerina?" he said. "What is it?"

That piece of paper had to be significant, and Ian was certain he was familiar with those words—but, he could not remember how or why. He felt a rising sense of urgency, a need to know that verse. He wondered why—was it because he would soon be leaving there or that he might need the verse for some future purpose? He felt completely helpless. His view of the page was blocked now, and in this reality he had possessed no ability to direct his point of view...

Katerina turned as if to look straight into Ian's face. She took a couple of slow steps toward him. They stood nose to nose; a couple of inches separated them. He could feel her breath and smell the mingled aroma of her old books and the candle that was burning.

Could she tell that he was there?

If so, Katerina gave no indication. She stood entranced, with a faraway look on her face. Ian wanted to believe that she could at least imagine his presence. If she was unaware of him, he had no idea what she was doing.

Ian wanted to keep taking in the whole sight of her, but his attention was drawn into Katerina's bright, intense eyes. Time after time, he felt overcome as if he were falling into her eyes. Surprisingly, he felt inclined to resist the experience. He instinctively knew the visit was about to end. How he wanted to continue to remain with her, to be this close to her!

Her soft lips slowly formed a first, intentionally precise word. And then she spoke:

I offer this Sacred Vow to you alone. If ever you are in need, expect me to reach beyond possibility and take your hand. As you feel the warmth of our bond, know that you will never be forgotten, never be alone, and never be without this one enduring love.

Katerina was reciting the verse from the paper on top of her book. Ian struggled to justify the deep familiarity he had with those words.

After drawing a long, slow breath, Katerina began the same

rhythmic recital again. As she did so, he was again drawn into her eyes. This time he let himself go. He could feel some part of himself blending into a single existence with her. Physically he was becoming part of her. When the verse was complete, he settled again into his sense of separateness.

A third time Katerina began to recite the same words. This time Ian gladly let go of any perception apart from hers. And this time, losing himself resulted in losing her as well.

As serene as his transition into Katerina's parallel world had been, Ian came back into his awareness of his world with a charge. His heart was racing the moment he became conscious. He forced himself from the couch so quickly that he tripped over his feet and almost fell over on his face. He knew now why that verse was familiar!

There was a chance that the same *Sacred Vow* was in his house, somewhere. He had written it down after a stirring dream he had had some time ago. And he was going to move every item in his possession, one by one, until he found that scrap of paper—if he had not thrown it away.

Ian had a bad habit of disregarding musings and inspirations that he scribbled down as time passed. This particular bit of writing had sparked such uncomfortable emotion within him that he had almost destroyed it immediately. In fact, he remembered that the only reason he had not done so was he couldn't believe a few words from a dream could force such an uncontrolled emotional response within him.

Now he knew why he had reacted so strongly to the passage. Ian resolved to find it.

It proved unbelievable how much a single person could store into every hidden space of an entire house. This became especially evident to Ian when he decided to inventory everything he owned. Half of what he sifted through over the next two days had certainly long lost its value or purpose in his life.

The task he was performing was almost a perfect situation for a thorough spring cleaning. Or, it would have been, if not for the fact that Ian was completely intimidated by the idea that he might accidentally overlook and discard just the item he was searching for. He unearthed everything, examined each thing, and put it right back in its original place—just in case he didn't find what he was looking for and had to do it all again.

It was a good thing no one happened to come by the house during that little obsession. Ian was sure they would have had him carted away. He rarely moved away from his place of excavation, except very briefly to attend to life's necessities. Several times he woke after having fallen asleep right in the middle of his work.

Ian was beginning to worry about what would happen if he didn't find the paper. Months later Liz or Djalma might come looking for him and discover that he had expired during his fixated searching; unsatisfied but unwilling or unable to give up.

Eventually, Ian was successful. The crumpled bit of paper was one of several unrelated scraps in a box of old pictures. Ian had not imagined the impact holding that paper in his hand would have on him. Here, finally, was a concrete link between his reality and Katerina's.

He was almost giddy in his exultation. He felt like a foolish child in his needing something tangible to reassure him of his connection with Katerina. But he didn't care. Holding onto that bit of paper, he leaned back against a stack of boxes in the attic, too tired to move. Letting his guard down, he went peacefully to sleep.

Birthday

After finding the paper on which he had written the Sacred Vow shared between Katerina and himself, Ian was enraptured for the rest of the week. Later in the week, Liz called, asking him to come to a party for Djalma's twenty-seventh birthday. Ian was honored by the invitation and quite interested in meeting some of Djalma's other friends. Liz was a normal enough sort of person, but Ian was certain that friends from Djalma's inner circle would prove to be some entertainingly unusual characters.

When Ian arrived a bit early for the party that weekend, Liz's car was the only one in the drive. Perhaps the rest of Djalma's friends all live in the woods nearby, Ian speculated.

Liz was opening the door as Ian reached it.

"It's so good to see you again, Liz." He handed her a vase of bright purple Japanese lilies. "These are for you."

"Thank you, sweetie. Come in." She kissed his cheek as they embraced. "Let me take your jacket."

Ian followed as she headed for the dining room. "I hope my being early isn't inconvenient for you. Is there anything I can do to help you get ready for the party?"

"No inconvenience, and I'm all prepared for our gathering. Djalma is here."

As they stepped through the dining room door, Djalma rose from his seat at the table. Ian's two friends had already been having tea. The table was dressed beautifully, in just Liz's style, with a number of tea snacks, though Ian thought the amount of food was rather modest for a party.

"Happy birthday, Djalma." Ian stepped forward and offered his hand.

"Thank you, Ian. It's good to see you again. I hope you had a good trip."

Ian hadn't fully realized it before, but Djalma had very kind eyes, the eyes of a wise, old man, clear and bright but gentle, and with an undeniable expression of loving concern. Concentrating on those eyes, Ian didn't notice at first that Djalma was not releasing his hand.

"It was a good drive," Ian said. The next thing he said came without thought. As Ian stood looking into Djalma's eyes, he said, "And it's very good to see you again."

Djalma smiled and let go of Ian's hand.

Ian stepped back and began to scan the room. There was only one more teacup on the table, so it appeared this would be a small party. Djalma's other interesting friends would remain a mystery to Ian.

Ian gave Liz a questioning look. He suspected now that the invitation was to provide Liz and Djalma a chance to check up on him since the use of the token.

"It's an intimate party, honey." She smiled shyly. "You know there aren't a lot of people who live around here during the off-season."

Ian just nodded his head. "Yes, I know."

Turning to Djalma, Ian handed him the present that he'd

brought. "Well, I'm sorry. It looks like you won't be getting many gifts." Then he hesitated. "This is your birthday, isn't it?" he said.

Djalma grinned and nodded. So Ian handed him a package.

Liz resumed her role as hostess. "Now you just sit over here. We've been having some Oolong tea." She put her hand on Ian's shoulder and directed him to the seat in front of the remaining teacup. "Is that good for you? Or would you like some green, black, or rooibos tea? Or perhaps something altogether different to drink?"

"Oolong will be wonderful, Liz."

They took their seats, and Liz poured a cup of the tea. The hot, earthy smell of the steam rising from the cup relaxed him.

"Open your present, Djalma," Liz said, as she passed Ian a tray or two of snacks for his choices.

The gift was a good paring knife to replace the warn knife that Ian had seen Djalma use in the cabin. The handle of the one he had was about to fall off and only a sliver of a blade remained.

"Not to deprive you of an old friend," Ian said. "But you'll have a replacement whenever you decide your current knife is due for retirement."

Liz had a good laugh when she saw the contents of the box. She must have seen Djalma whittling at his herbs at some time.

Djalma laughed along with Liz, but his face was red. "Or," he said, "one for someone else to use in helping me prepare the herbs while we talk."

Ian felt lucky to share company with two such remarkable people. He sat back in the chair, sipped his tea and laughed with them. They had a party of three. Like little children, they laughed and joked, ate Liz's treats, and gaily passed away several hours in good company.

They talked about what they had each been doing, books they had been reading, music they had been listening to lately. Ian had many good friends with whom he enjoyed sharing and laughing, but Liz and Djalma knew about a part of his life that he had not shared or felt he could share with anyone else. For that reason, even though these were not his oldest friends, they felt like his dearest.

The subject of Ian's travels did not come up until Liz suddenly asked, "Have you seen Katerina lately?"

Ian looked at Djalma, who did not appear surprised. Liz and Djalma often seemed deeply in tune with each other.

Ian looked back at Liz, "Yes, I saw her again last weekend."

Ian stepped into his sharing of the latest journey slowly. But soon the three were talking about Katerina and his visits with her as if she were a mutual friend in their physical world.

Djalma and Liz paid rapt attention to the story Ian told them of the *Sacred Vow*. He asked their opinions about what it all meant, but they offered few responses.

"It sounds as if you two have a very old connection," Liz said, and Djalma agreed.

As Ian reached the end of his story, he knew it was getting late and he had to leave for home.

"Is anyone interested in a real meal?" Liz said.

"Not me, Liz. I have to start back. Tomorrow is Monday," Ian said.

"You could take a vacation day. I have plenty of rooms, sweetie—all made up for company."

"I wish I could, Liz. This has been wonderful." Ian looked over at Djalma, meaning to include him as well. Djalma gave him a very focused look of seriousness, which Ian had hoped not to see this day. He knew Djalma now wanted to comment about Ian's relationship as the paranormal thing that it was.

Ian decided to take the lead. "What is it, Djalma?"

"If you don't mind, Ian, I need to ask: Do you feel any different than you did the last time I saw you?"

The question was easy to evade. "Well, yes. The last time I was here, I was still involved in the dark journeys. I feel better since they have ended. Remember how hard they were on my health?"

"My mistake," Djalma said. Then after a pause, he went on.

"Accounting for the recovery from the dark experiences, do you recognize any impact on yourself after these new visits?"

"After seeing Katerina this last time, I feel great. I'm telling you the truth."

With each exchange, Djalma's eyes became more focused, more serious. "Yes, you may feel great in your body. But what I mean is, when you're in that relaxed place, just after the meditation ends, have you noticed even the slightest feeling of weakness or evanescence?"

"I've only had the meditative transfer experience twice." Ian looked at Liz, hoping she'd interrupt. She did not. She had the same concerned look Djalma had.

"Everything is fine, Liz," Ian said to her. He looked back at Djalma and addressed the heart of his concern, "Just what are you troubled about?"

"Though your health has improved, your energetic signature has much weakened since the last time I saw you," he said.

Ian reacted with a defensive remark aimed at Liz. She'd been the one who had set up this meeting for a reality check that he did not want and could not now escape. "Do you think so, too?"

He immediately repented this childish response. "I am sorry, Liz," he said.

She smiled sadly and empathetically. "You can trust Djalma," she said.

Ian reached out to squeeze Liz's hand and looked back to Djalma. Like it or not, Ian knew that he'd better consider what Djalma was worried about. "Tell me what you're seeing, my friend."

"It's not visibly affecting your health yet," Djalma said, "but I think it will, if the pattern continues. The materialization into other realities seems to take energy from you here. Perhaps this is because we don't know how to guard against or restore the energy displaced in the process ... What concerns me most is that I know of no one who can even speculate on what impact such visits would have on body or spirit, or the precautions that should be considered."

Ian cut in. "Djalma, if there has been any negative impact, why doesn't it impair my ability to visit Katerina? I don't even need to use the teapot anymore."

"I find that absolutely incredible. I wish you could tell me how you do it. Apparently, you are now able to adjust your personal resonance to create this portal, which used to take a whole roomful of energetic signatures to achieve. I'm speculating that when the collective signature of the study failed your purpose, your subconscious automatically simulated what it remembered about the experience, allowing you to continue to achieve the transfer during meditation.

"What's most remarkable to me is that, so far as I understand it, with every reality shift, your signature should be greatly changed, requiring your subconscious to recalculate the proper resonance to achieve the desired end for each additional attempt. I hope you'll someday be able to teach me how you do that."

"I'll be glad to," Ian responded, "as soon as I have some idea of what I'm doing! Do you have any suggestions on how to overcome the displacement of energy?"

"I wish I did, Ian. As I said before, you're doing something outside my scope of understanding. The only thing I know that would help is to stop materializing in her reality—"

Ian looked sharply across the table, and Djalma continued, "—which I'm sure you're not going to consider. I can't honestly say I would do so if I was in your position."

Ian smiled, glad for the understanding.

"I can only imagine the connection with Katerina that you're feeling inside," Djalma went on. "It doesn't surprise me that such an experience would lead you to risk your health and the stability of your mind. If I may, I'd like to offer a few things you might wish to consider further."

"Anything that you think will help."

"You're not making these trips by your own spirit's efforts alone," Djalma began. "I am as convinced as you are about the connection you and Katerina have. This being so, if you continue to go down a path that eventually causes you harm, you certainly risk harming your link to Katerina and possibly also Katerina herself.

"It's not only this one manifestation of Katerina with which you share the connection. Remember, you have now had a visit that seems to be the two of you as a couple simultaneously occurring in another reality. There could be many, many more expressions of your bond out there. Before I met you, I would have said that what you are doing is no more than a theoretical possibility. After seeing what you experience, my concern is that we cannot tell what impact this journeying might have on other lives, not only you and Katerina. Through the interconnected ties that bind us all, if you recklessly bring yourself to harm, who knows how many others of us may feel the effects?"

Ian sank back into his chair to consider the options. "You know that I cannot stop visiting her, Djalma. What other choices do I have?"

Liz had come around behind Ian's chair and laid her hands on his shoulders. Feeling her supportive touch, he took a deep breath.

Djalma continued, "I can only suggest you don't try to rush the period of recovery between each trip. You will definitely need to do some healing, and although your recuperative talent seems exceptional at this time, you must give yourself the full measure of rest that you might need.

"Your spirit may need considerable time for recalibrating the necessary energetic emanation after each journey. Should you force the next transfer before that calibration is ready or your energy is properly restored, you could end up lost somewhere in the transition. We would not be able to help you from this side and Katerina might not be able to find you."

Ian silently considered the implications of Djalma's words. From the look in his eyes, Ian could tell what he was about to impart next was very important.

"Now, this is purely intuition on my part. I have no other justification, but please remember it. If you run into any trouble, hold onto that piece of paper with the vow you expressed in the writing, which you and Katerina both possess. That could be most important."

Djalma got up from his chair and gave Ian a big smile. "Just like any friend about to make a journey," he said, "we wish you a safe trip and send you off with our support and love."

They said their good-byes, exchanged hugs, and Ian started back home. As dominant as his experiences with Katerina were in his consciousness those days, on this long trip home, all Ian could think about was how fortunate he was to have two such dear friends in his life.

Eyes of Another

On Monday Ian called Liz to let her know he'd gotten home safely. After thanking her for inviting him to such a lovely party, he asked that she pass his thanks to Djalma.

"I love you, dear friend," he said.

"And I, you, sweetie," she replied.

"I'll let you know when I've made another visit," he assured her.

A couple of days later, Ian realized he had not taken the teapot into the study since the evening of his last visit with Katerina. Remembering Djalma's speculation that *he*, not the items in the room, was the portal now, Ian removed a few more items from the study. In an act of daring, he moved the Fauvist painting into the guest room, and the cane-bottomed chair to the living room. He had really wanted them in those rooms for some time but had not dared take the chance. He also made a note of what he had moved and where, just in case he still needed their psychic assistance.

Just so his friends would not worry, Ian called Liz a little later that week. They had a good talk. She had not seen Djalma for a few days. Ian told her he was not considering attempting a visit until the following week.

As eager as he was to see Katerina again, Ian's inner wisdom seemed to provide a contented patience. He could not say why he felt he needed to wait. But as long as the respite felt right, he would wait.

In time that same judicious part of him gave Ian the go-ahead for more time with Katerina. The next few visits, however, made him question whether that supposedly wise self really knew what it was doing. He did not know what made the difference between the visit that had introduced the *Sacred Vow* and the next few that followed, but it turned out not to be an easy time for him.

With no more rational understanding than Ian had when he knew not to attempt a visit, one day after work, Ian's intuition led him to go into the study and sit on the couch. For a little while, he leaned back thinking of nothing, shaking off the workday. Without particular forethought, he pulled his legs up and crossed them.

Katerina and he (or the person whose eyes Ian saw her through) lived in a city. They were in a windowed apartment of a multistory building. Their large living space was not without considerable evidence of affluence. There were expensively framed, original paintings on the walls. Much of the furniture was ornate, solid wood. Several of the articles had the uniqueness of handmade work, and Ian felt certain a number of the pieces were antiques. The floor had an exotic pattern of inlaid wood, covered with finely crafted rugs. The technology of appliances and the buildings he could see through the windows suggested this life took place in the present, the very near past, or in the near future.

Only intuitively did Ian recognize the woman in the room as Katerina. Maybe Djalma would have said it was honing in on her energetic signature. Her behavior and appearance was different, but Ian had no question this was she.

"Where have you been?" Katerina asked, sounding mildly annoyed.

"Visiting friends. What difference does it make?" The tone of the voice Ian felt resonate within his host body, her partner's voice, showed he was unconcerned.

"More likely, visiting *a* friend," she said.

Now Ian understood the environment and was having a hard time imagining the purpose of this visit. It took too much effort to make a journey just to watch this annoying alternate life where Katerina and her partner so thoroughly disregard each other.

They have no idea who they are or what we all share, Ian thought to himself.

The words between the couple made it obvious the husband was having an affair. His responses sometimes implied that they were both frequently unfaithful. With that kind of wounding behavior, Ian expected some strong emotion to be flowing with their words. Ian, though not his host, seemed to be the only one in the room feeling any such passion about what was happening to their relationship. Katerina and her mate stepped through the conversation with a choreographed precision, without any real emotional effect.

What the hell are you people doing? Ian thought. He felt no lack of excitement: he could assure them that the field of play was not completely without passion on this day.

Strike. Parry. Step and speak again. This "argument for display" that they were carrying on was unnatural to Ian. They must have been practicing that pattern for years in order to achieve such threatening accuracy without actually imposing any evident damage on each other. As their dance flowed, Ian was being drawn in ever deeper. Unable to resist, he responded, though silently, to the pernicious nature of their actions.

Then suddenly the couple appeared to throw in a new step. The cadence of their argument staggered at just that moment, and the man took the lead, seemingly out of sequence. Ian had to wonder if the performance was going as expected, because even his host seemed surprised by what he did next. Some evidence of true feeling started to filter into his voice. Ian had a strong sense that this direction was something neither of the couple expected.

"You're being ridiculous," he said as he—or he and Ian—stood completely immobile for just a moment, seeming not quite sure what to do for the first time. Then Katerina's partner walked toward the door, as if to leave the room.

She followed closely behind him, "Don't you walk away from me!" Her voice was full of an emotion that was more appropriate to the words she spoke. "I may be a fool for staying here, but I am not stupid. What do you think you are doing?"

Her partner turned and stared at Katerina, but did not say anything at all. She may have known what he was doing, but he did not seem to.

There Ian was, gambling with his health and risking his spiritual well-being for any possible hope of interaction with the woman with whom he shared a multitude of lives. What he was seeing instead was a time where Katerina and he—assuming that his host was some version of himself—had utter disrespect for the relationship they were then sharing.

What was the purpose of that particular visit? Ian knew there are always two sides to a coin. Undoubtedly, Katerina and he shared many happy lives and some Ian would rather not know about. But he did not enjoy paying the price required for an experience such as this.

Ian speculated that the couple had never dealt with the real issues that were causing their callousness toward each other. It was not each other they were dissatisfied with, but themselves.

"If you want to leave me," Katerina continued, "have the courage to tell me so, but do not treat me with disrespect." There was no question she was feeling truly angry now. She was crying.

After a little more delay, her partner snapped back. "Yes! It's over. It was always a miserable mistake. We never had anything. I don't know why we ever got together!"

No! I hate this reality! Ian screamed inside his own head.

Then Ian found himself back on his couch. In his own world, his heart was as broken as had been the heart of Katerina when he'd left their most recent parallel life. He did not want to accept that there would be unhappy lives, even if they were part of his great bond with Katerina. It seemed that they simultaneously lived in many alternate lives, and he could not control which Katerina he would visit at any given time. If what he experienced in this last visit was going to dominate the visits to come, Ian did not know if he could continue.

The next few visits Ian had with Katerina were not any more satisfying, nor did he ever visit the same place twice. He continued to be little more than a spectator, pulled along for some unknown reason. If he'd had any sort of control on over his destinations, he would have chosen to return to visiting the Katerina of the *tea visits*. He would have loved to meet her in that French country house again.

The new experiences were not completely without interest for him, however. He came to know many manifestations of his dearest Katerina, and he was blessed with the knowledge of many of their parallel lives.

At first, Ian tried to meet with Katerina every evening after work. But after a time, he began instinctively to accept a limit to the frequency of the visits. He allowed himself a period of recuperation after each visit. In due time, he would be moved to sit for meditation again.

Ian decided that the purpose of the recent visits was only to expand his definition of his relationship with the woman he first visited. The most frustrating parts of the experiences were his lack of control during a journey, and his inability to return to a particular manifestation of their lives together.

During a given visit, even if Ian was certain that his point of view was through his eyes in a parallel life, his consciousness from his primary reality could do nothing but follow along. He wanted to communicate with the Katerina of the other lives, and with the manifestation of himself as her partner in those places. What a benefit it could have been to us all, he thought. The couples he visited stumbled about, sometimes not fully appreciating each other, never understanding the scope of their relationship as Ian understood it.

Every so often, Ian called Liz and reported to her—and through her, to Djalma—what was going on with the journeys, assuring her that all was fine. Djalma would periodically ask Liz to remind Ian that he might not be able to continue the trips forever. Ian had no doubt Djalma was correct. Transitions between his normal consciousness and his destinations were getting more complicated, a little tricky at times. Now and again, Ian was aware of being in a place that was merely a void, neither in his original world nor in one of the alternate realities to which he visited.

Liz frequently invited Ian to come and stay for the weekend, but he made excuses why he could not visit the mountains during that time. He could definitely feel the growing weakness within himself as he continued the visits. Ian knew that if Liz and Djalma laid an eye on him, they would be worried about what he was doing to himself.

More than likely, Ian thought, Djalma already knows, even without seeing me face to face. Djalma had merely acquiesced to Ian's choice.

After a few more visits, still never returning to the same place twice, Ian had a visit in which he started to experience what he believed were the emotions of his parallel selves, during the visit. Up until that time, Ian had felt only his own responses to what he saw and heard. This new aspect of the experience was a little complicated, but it helped him come to some understanding of why Katerina and her partner made such foolish choices and failed to understand how precious their times together were. Gifted with his recently acquired perspective, Ian had the larger comprehension of the great web of his and Katerina's many lives together. At the same time, the emotions of his host in the visited reality seemed to dominate Ian's feelings during the visit—making it hard for him not to get lost in the same pettiness that hindered his host's understanding.

The same thing happened several more times. And then it evolved into something more: Ian started to share the physical experiences of Katerina's partner within the host environment. He would have liked to put an end to this added involvement. Once the bodily connection developed, he was subject to any physical ailments his parallel self was experiencing in the visited world. Further, after returning to his primary reality from such a journey, it would take Ian anywhere from hours to weeks to separate his actual, physical self from the parallel self's sensations. This, along with Ian's increasing weakness in his primary body, forced him to spend longer periods of recovery between visits.

Once, a host in the visited reality was sick with a fever. Ian's body exhibited that fever after he returned home. Three days afterward, Ian still had the fever and was almost delusional from high temperature. In desperation, he went to the doctor. She ran test after test but found no organic cause for his symptoms. Ian had hoped she could give him something to combat the discomfort, since he had the symptoms.

Just as no tests explained the fever, nothing was effective against it. Luckily, the fever broke as mysteriously—to the doctor—as it had developed. Ian could only hope that his host had become well in the recently visited parallel life, since Ian knew there was no chance he would be able to return to that particular life and check on his parallel self.

One other possibility that dawned on Ian was his symptoms had subsided because his parallel self had died from the fever. The union Ian had experienced with his host only a short time before caused Ian a unique sense of remorse over that idea. Even more unsettling was the implication that the experiences of Ian's parallel selves could have a direct consequence on his physical body in this world. What would happen if he landed in a reality in which that self was dying? What if the parallel self died while Ian was still in the host world, bonded to that consciousness?

Through all the changes in the visits, Ian hadn't been able to forget the visit when Katerina and his parallel self were ending their relationship. It seemed like somehow they were comfortable with a well-traveled, though unhappy pattern. Then Ian began to wonder if the influence of the parallel lives went only one way. Might he have disturbed the emotional balance of that couple's life together? Were they truly surprised when the repetitious path of their quarrel took a new turn that day? What had he done? Ian knew any impact he'd had on them would influence his life here in this world as well, even if the impact was immediately unrecognizable.

No matter the threat to himself, Ian knew he would not be able to stop going into the parallel lives. His life had been redefined: it was something more than he had ever imagined before the visits began. But, Ian didn't know exactly what his life *was* now. The idea that he had been directly affecting the visited lives, without realizing just how or to what extent, was disturbing to him. His "visiting" was sometimes more frustrating than it seemed worth. But as little sense as it made occasionally, he was still certain there was a purpose to it and a need for him to continue on.

Dangerous Choice

Ian did not like what he saw and felt when he arrived in the next parallel life. If it had been an option, he would have gone right back to his couch; better an ordinary day after work than where he found himself. It was hard to imagine that this place had anything to do with Katerina, or with any time they had spent together.

He was moving through filthy, stinking streets filled with huge numbers of poor, destitute people without resource or hope. He could hear many sounds in this world, mostly a cacophony of voices—too many voices—sorrowful, angry, and suffering. The voices drowned out even the sounds of machines and big-city racket.

Ian's point of view seemed to move too fast, and he was too high to be seeing from the eyes of a person. He watched from significantly above the heads of the people below, as if through the lens of a camera guided by some intention unknown to him. Why was he here? Was Katerina in this reality at all?

Then his point of view began to lower. He turned a corner and slowed as a tattered woman carrying a baby came out of a dilapidated building just in front of him. Ian resisted admitting it, but an all too reliable intuition assured him that this was Katerina. Oddly, he had no feelings of curiosity whatsoever as to the identity of the child. If the child was his and Katerina's, this would be the first alternate life in which they were parents. But what a place to raise a child!

Ian drifted behind and somewhat above Katerina. She was hurrying along as if she were being pursued. Since Ian seemed to be disembodied, he did not believe it could be he, whatever he was, who troubled her.

She spoke to the child. Her language was foreign, but Ian was not surprised that he understood her. He had become accustomed to this. Despite all the overwhelming babble of the people on the street, he was tuned into her alone.

"Don't worry, Eestu. Momma will find a place where he cannot hurt us," she said.

Perhaps because the baby was being jostled as Katerina rushed away, perhaps because it could feel its mother's distress, the child began to whimper.

"Sh-ssshh, baby. It's going to be all right. I'll get you food soon."

The mother and child also had to contend with hunger? Ian definitely did not want to see this. But once he knew this was Katerina, he could not wish to leave. Even if he tried, it never appeared that Ian had a choice about when to leave or what do to once he entered into these parallel lives.

The baby continued to be bumped about, as the mother tried to force her way through the crowds. All the people were as dirty and ragged as she was. Some cursed her as she pushed by them. Once, someone struck out at Katerina as she moved past. Ian tried to lunge to her defense, but his bodiless self left him unable to pursue the desire.

Why am I here? he demanded of himself. I cannot interact with Katerina. I cannot help her.

Just below Ian, entering his field of vision, two men were walking up behind Katerina very quickly. Ian was terrified that they intended to harm her.

Katerina had obviously expected someone to follow her. As

the men forced their way through the crowds, people responded angrily. When the men got closer, Katerina saw them and tried to run, but the wandering crowds held her back. All she did was bounce off the back of the man in front of her.

She abruptly turned down an alley. It was less congested and allowed her to run.

Of course, as soon as her pursuers got to the same alley, they were also able to speed up. Still Ian followed, now behind the men chasing her. A hungry woman carrying a baby could not have outrun them for long, even if a huge pile of trash had not blocked the entire alley a little further down.

The baby was screaming now, as loud as it could. Katerina tried running up the pile but slipped back down. She backed up against the wall and tried to use it for support to climb. Still she slid down on the loose rubble as the men approached confidently. They were no longer in a hurry, knowing she could not escape.

Ian's own movement was slowed in response, but his emotions were rampant. He felt her panic as if it were his own. He thrashed about within the uncontrollable restrictions of his invisible confinement as desperately as Katerina did below.

Forced to accept that she could not overcome the pile, Katerina turned and dashed toward her pursuers. As she ran she added her own tormented wail to that of the baby's. Her pursuers laughed, delighted at her suffering.

The larger of the men stepped to one side, as if he would let Katerina go by. Just as she saw the opening and moved toward it, he grabbed the arm that held the baby and jerked her toward him. It was amazing she did not drop her little bundle, given the force he used.

"And just where d'ya think ya're going? Thought ya would slip away without paying Mr. Chen-ye what he's owed?"

"Leave her alone!" Ian yelled, heard by no one but himself. The dim light that filtered into the alley began to flicker.

Katerina was looking only at her baby, trying anxiously to soothe its fears, speaking first softly to the child. "Shh, Eestu, Sh-h-h." Then she raised her face to respond to her attacker. "I'm going to get food for my baby. You can see that she is hungry."

The smaller man responded, "You got no money to pay. Where ya gonna get food? Maybe you were shopping at the alley mission here?" He laughed nastily, looking at the larger man for approval.

Defiant and trying to maintain her dignity, Katerina jerked her arm to free it from the big man's grip.

"Let go of me!"

He raised the back of his other hand, to slap her. Ian fought to intervene, but could not overcome his limitations.

The large hand froze in the air. Then he slowly lowered it and said, "There's no hurry for this. First, ya tell how ya're going to pay what is owed."

Katerina looked with horror, at one man then at the other. She clutched the baby all the tighter. "My husband, he took Mr. Chen-ye his due this morning. He left out just before I did."

"Husband? What husband?" said the big man.

"The baby's Da—" she shot out. "—My husband has what's due."

Ian suspected the mid-morning skies were as clear as they probably ever got, considering the air was dense with smog and stench, but even that limited light was wavering in the alley.

The smaller man snorted. "How about that, Ammon? She's got a husband." Showing his contempt for her hope, he spat on the street near Katerina's ragged semblance of a shoe. "There ain't no marriage on the streets."

Stroking the baby, she said stubbornly, "I have a husband! Just because you didn't see him—"

The larger man jerked Katerina's arm again, demanding her attention to their business. "Forget that craziness! Something is owed and no husband has paid it."

Katerina was crying silently. Tears left tracks down her dirty cheeks.

Ian lunged for the larger man, hoping against hope that the tension building within him would translate into effect. But he was denied once again.

Katerina was stroking the child and mumbling to herself.

"He won't forget. He's always with us." Over and over, she repeated this. The chant was starting to annoy her captor.

"Shut up, you! Listen to me!" To get her attention, he jerked her arm again, harder, shaking her whole body side to side, but she seemed scarcely aware of what was happening. Then everything went black and silent.

"What the . . . ?" Ian screamed.

He fought to see, but with no physical eyes, there was no place to direct his focus. Then, just as suddenly, the vicious nightmare in the alley was back.

"Ya only got one thing worth somethin'," the larger man continued. He applied his free hand to the baby daughter that Katerina held. "You're too feeble to work, in the alleys or 'Under,' but the baby—"

His companion took the cue and grabbed Katerina by her shoulders. The two men began to separate her from her only interest in life. The small man pulled her arms back while Ammon, slowly, but effectively, pried the baby from her hands. Now her cooing chant rose into a piercing scream. Her lungs were strong enough. The sound she made quickly irritated her attackers. Ammon yanked the baby from her grasp and shoved her to the ground.

The two men turned to leave with their payment.

Ian managed a quick movement toward the men. Finally, he could help her! But all went black again. Katerina's cursing screams went dead. And Ian could hear nothing.

Then the screams shot through his nervous system once again and Ian saw Katerina kicking the huge man in the back of his knees.

"Give me my baby, you bastard!" There followed a jumble of words spewing out too emotionally to be completely formed. Most of what came from her mouth was nothing but the unintelligible sounds of a suffering soul.

Ian managed another convulsive move, but he could not sufficiently direct it.

Katerina's feet did little but make the man hunch his shoulders in anger. He slowly handed the howling baby to his companion, who grinned excitedly. Then the larger man turned and drew back a foot to kick her.

Before the kick was released, Ian experienced complete darkness and then a blast of light. But, the light was the light of his own home. He was sitting on the couch. A roar forced its way out of his mouth. The cry was not merely due to his frustration, but in response to the physical pain that shot through his nervous system.

Coming back from the trip so abruptly, Ian felt like he had been slammed at high speed into something solid. His body felt broken in many places; and his spirit was still bleeding for Katerina's defeat. He tried to rise from the couch. But before he got all the way to his feet, he fell back again, about to lose consciousness from the pain that still surged through him.

Ian had to fight hard not to lose the light again. This was his primary reality, and he had some control here. He would not allow himself simply to black out! Waves of faintness battered him. The throbbing in his body was working against him.

"Katerina," he shouted, "I am coming back!" Ian could not accept that there was nothing he could do for her. He had to try again to help her. Despite Djalma's warnings, Ian was determined to force himself back into the transfer immediately. There was no time to wait. Maybe his inability to return to the same location was a matter of temporal proximity. Ian feared that if he waited for his spirit to recoup and recalibrate, the next shift would take him someplace else.

He had a fleeting sensation of being connected to her again, and he grabbed it. Instantly he felt a shift in his consciousness. Either he passed out or he was successful in projecting himself into back-to-back visits. He could only wait to see what sight unfolded in front of him.

The Void

Nothing unfolded. The densest black veil swallowed Ian, smothering every sensation.

He waited patiently for images to appear, hoping he was in time to help Katerina retrieve her baby. Transition between consciousness in Ian's physical world and his parallel lives had been taking longer recently. But after a few minutes of nothing, he could not remain patient.

"Come on," Ian tried to scream, "before he hurts her!"

He heard no scream, felt no sensation in his vocal cords. Instead, he felt a physical—or at least neural—sensation of something being drained from him—whatever he was in that dark place.

The sensory deprivation under this shroud of absolute black was both internal and external. His mind twisted about, trying to cope with no sensations at all. It soon became uncomfortably obvious to Ian that his mind had never before been without some form of sensory input. Even when one is asleep there is a steady flow of messages, if only from the body's involuntary functions.

Ian wondered what his body was doing. He had never been aware of any bodily sensations from his primary reality when visiting before, but this was not one of the ordinary reality shifts. In a usual shift, it was possible, Ian imagined, that he continued to receive messages from his body back home but was always distracted because of what was happening in the visit. He seemed now to be lost somewhere between his primary reality and the place he hoped he would visit soon.

Or, he thought, maybe this place is just a different reality, one that I'm having a harder time than usual comprehending. Maybe I just have to let go of my preconceived expectations.

It dawned on Ian that this place might not have been where he originally intended to go, but Katerina might well be here anyway.

What he was sure of was that Katerina in that last world needed him. He *had* to go back there. No matter how he tried to ignore it, Ian knew he was going to have to accept that even a reduced time frame between trips would not help him return to a previous life.

He wanted to flail about and curse, but the void he was in had sucked all anger out of him. Instantly, he had a sensation of collapse where anger should have been, and he felt all the more exhausted for it. More than exhausted. Diminished. As if his existence was less certain than it had been a moment before. The threat of losing not only his life but his entire existence to this void was filling Ian with a unique sense of fear.

No matter how much Ian wanted to help that unfortunate manifestation of Katerina, he had to accept the possibility that he might not even be able to help himself. Every emotion or thought he experienced seemed to take away more of his life energy.

The loss of energy from his feelings was worse than that of thought. Ian decided to clamp down on any emotion. Each time he got upset, he experienced an excruciating void in its place. Thus he knew he could not afford to allow himself to feel anything. So, he used the process of releasing emotion that he learned in his mediation practice. Just let it go, he told himself, breathe in

. . . It was easier when he'd had the sensation of breathing to focus on.

Suddenly from nowhere, Ian was blindsided by a new rush of fear. What if I am dead? His emotions took off running. And the backlash of the emptiness that followed was unbearable.

"O-o-oh hell-ll," he wailed.

Just then, Ian realized something positive. If he was hurting, he was not dead! For the first time ever, he was thankful he could feel pain. It allowed him to release the fear and drift in the void.

Thought did not have as negative an effect, Ian had noticed. He had only a slight twinge of pain after a thought. Still, he had to ration his activity. He decided that he had better focus any thought on getting himself out of whatever he had gotten into.

Ian was sure he had to be lost *in-between*. Djalma had warned him it could happen. "You could get lost in the transition," Djalma had said. So, here he was, no good to Katerina or to himself.

Ian searched for an answer. Was there something else Djalma had said that might be helpful? He is a smart one, that Djalma, Ian thought. If he thought something would be useful, he would probably have repeated the phrase or idea more than a time or two.

His mind was proving particularly intolerant of limited sensory input. Ian's thoughts alone were not providing enough stimuli. This had to be what it felt like to die, awareness collapsing in on itself.

But there had to be *something* Djalma had repeated most. He would have done that. He would have tried to prepare me without being pushy, Ian thought.

Then Ian remembered: the *Vow*! Djalma had said to remember the *Vow*!

"Think on the *Vow*," he told himself. "It doesn't matter if it makes sense."

Who could know about the *Vow*, except Katerina? Thinking of not being able to help her and her child caused Ian to feel pain again. For feeling that flash of sympathy, he suffered another ripping sensation of the void.

As loud as he could muster, he recited the Vow:

> *I offer this Sacred Vow to you alone. If ever you are in need, expect me to reach beyond possibility and take your hand. As you feel the warmth of our bond, know that you will never be forgotten, never be alone, and never be without this one enduring love.*

Over and over, Ian repeated the *Vow* to himself. The rhythm of the verse was hypnotizing. Ian noticed that the darkness seemed slightly less oppressive.

Blurry light broke through to his eyes. A shadow appeared in front of him—a figure leaning over as to touch his head. It was the Katerina of the *tea visions*. Ian yearned to touch her . . . and he did not feel the pain of losing a part of himself!

"Oh, Ian, what have you done to yourself?" she said. "Go home and be healed. This is very dangerous for us. Come back to me when your spirit has recovered, dear one." She fanned some herbal smoke across him, and Ian lost consciousness.

When he woke up, Ian saw that he was in his study, and that it was sometime during the day. Judging from the light in the windows, it was around midday. It had been early evening, right after work, when Ian had first entered into the meditation. He could not see a clock or even manage to raise his watch arm, so he did not know if it was the next day, or some day following. What he did know was that he was miserable.

Lying flat on the couch in his study, he tried to move. He knew he needed food, but the pain from the first attempt to stir almost made him sick. He gritted his teeth and tried to hold on to his awareness, but he could not. He blacked out again.

Woodland Soup

The next thing Ian knew, he was propped against the arm of the couch with pillows behind him. He was covered with a sheet and blanket, and there was an aroma of lentil soup in the room. He was so weak he had to struggle just to open his eyes. Once he had them open, he couldn't focus well enough to see. The most he could make out was the shadowy shape of a person in front of him.

"Welcome back, Ian." It was Djalma's voice. "Yes, you're still in your house. I apologize for intruding."

To Ian's knowledge, Djalma didn't have a car. How could he have managed the four-hour trip? Even more confusing, how did he get into the house?

"Not to worry. I didn't break anything getting in."

This was Djalma all right. Ian didn't really care if anything had been broken. However he had entered, Ian was grateful for it. He wanted to thank Djalma but didn't have the strength to speak. Right now, remaining conscious was all he could manage.

"I've been able to get you to drink some juice and water, but you haven't been eating," Djalma said.

Ian had no memory of drinking.

"It's been a couple of days since your return. Maybe you could eat something now," Djalma said. "I brought you some of my special woodland soup, gathered on one of my hikes just before I left home—Remember? I was making some on your first visit." He laughed. "Just kidding. It's regular soup."

Ian could smell the spoon of soup below his nose.

Djalma coached him. "Try to open your mouth, buddy. You can't heal without nutrition."

A very little soup was all Ian could manage to eat. It seemed like only a few minutes passed, and yet he must have slept, as he was waking up again.

Djalma had pulled the desk chair beside the couch and was sitting there reading poetry out loud. The poem was referring to the mist and the mountains. It sounded like Taoist poetry.

When he saw that Ian was awake again, Djalma stopped reading and said, "Welcome home again."

Ian could focus a little better than before. It was good to see Djalma's smile. He tried to thank his friend once more, but abandoned it for a mere, "hello." Even that sounded feeble.

"Is there anything I can get you, Ian?"

Ian's reply of "woodland soup" was almost unintelligible, but Djalma laughed and patted his arm. He was back in just a minute. Ian suspected the soup was already on the stove, as he heard no sound from the microwave.

Ian sat up and fed himself a little. The effort of doing so hurt immensely, and he quickly lost the ability to use his arm. He did not mention this, but Djalma must have realized what was going on and began to help Ian with the soup.

Needing the assistance of a young man to feed him was humbling. It was not quite so humbling, however, as the affliction that had brought Ian to need the assistance.

For the next few days, Djalma made sure Ian had food and water. He did the laundry, kept him company, and helped him hobble back and forth to the bathroom. Ian was grateful for the company and the help.

Knowing that Djalma had to help him out of a mess only because he had ignored his advice shamed Ian considerably. Whenever he tried to apologize, though, Djalma cut him off and asked to be repaid with a promise of full recovery.

Until Ian was able to maintain consciousness long enough to carry on conversation, Djalma entertained them with reading poetry and philosophy aloud. Some of the books, he had brought. While waking to some of Djalma's readings, Ian was reminded of items from his own shelves that had not been read in some time.

Several days later, Ian finally became cognizant enough to realize he had been out of work without explanation. When he tried to get up for the phone, Djalma explained that he had already told Ian's manager that Ian had a severe virus and might need a couple of weeks to recuperate.

For some reason, Ian found that bit of magic a little harder to believe than most. Work was something he had never spoken to Djalma about. It was hard to accept that Djalma's little inexplicable feats could have made their way into the stiflingly rational world of software. The doubt must have been apparent in Ian's face. Djalma smiled and nodded.

"No big deal. You are very organized. The personal phone book under the phone has your manager's name and numbers."

Even so, Ian knew his manager's name wasn't listed under "I" or "M," for "Ian's Manager." Who cares? he thought. By the time he considered the possible ways Djalma could have found the information, his interest in the subject was exhausted.

In another day or so, Ian was still too sluggish to function well at work, but he could have managed well enough at home. Ian was certain that Djalma stayed partially to make sure there wasn't another rushed journey back to Katerina—and partially just as a good friend, visiting. Ian thought of telling Djalma he could go back to the mountains—but he didn't know how his friend would get there—and besides, he was enjoying the company.

Card games passed the time. Some of the games Djalma knew; some of them Ian knew. Djalma's poetry readings revived Ian's interests and he in turn shared some of his own favorites, such as Emily Dickinson's "Much madness makes divinest sense," and pieces from a locally published collection called, *Strike a Chord of Silence*. Ian came to enjoy the Taoist poetry that Djalma introduced him to. The poets' uncomplicated attention to nature, along with the accompanying ink drawings in one of the books, made Ian think of Katerina.

When Ian felt up to it, he told Djalma the story of his last visit—which had put him in the state in which his friend had found him. It was a way of thanking Djalma for his care.

"Thank you for making sure I knew to look for the reason Katerina and I were in contact with each other," Ian started.

Djalma looked up from his book and smiled. "So, you know what that is now?"

"I think I have a starting point. And that bit of information probably saved my life. How did you know it would be so important?"

"I didn't know," Djalma replied. "The suggestion was based on pure intuition. I knew how remarkable what you were experiencing was, the reality expansions. It's barely possible that one might encounter a sequence of random contacts over a very achieved lifetime, but this has been a repeating communication with a specific person. And if the contact isn't random, I speculated there would have to be some powerful initiator to make such a thing come to pass."

Djalma paused for a moment and then laughed to himself. "Most of all, I was making my suggestion out of a blind emotion. You could say I was being a mother hen."

"Whatever your reason, Djalma, I don't think I would be here if not for your insistence to repeat the *Vow* if I got lost. I am sure it allowed Katerina to help me out of a terrible situation."

Sitting forward on the edge of his chair, Djalma laid the

book on the table to his side. "Really, now? How did she help? I imagined that the only threat you might run into was the physical drain from visiting too frequently."

Ian tried to get off the couch alone. His body forced him to reconsider just what was involved in jumping from one reality to another. Ever since he ceased to be bonded to someone else's body when in a parallel life, most of the impact on Ian seemed to be mental or emotional. His experience in the void showed that if he mishandled the gift of reality shifting it could cost him his life.

Djalma was up and offering assistance. "No need to rush yourself."

"I was just going to get a piece of paper." Ian settled back onto the couch but remained upright. He pointed over to a stack of books to one side of the room. "Could you please? There is a piece of paper inside the flap of that top book. Have a look at it."

Opening the book, Djalma stared down at the inside flap for a while.

"Read it, please," Ian said.

As Djalma read aloud, Ian recited along.

Both fell silent before finishing the *Vow*—as if simultaneously realizing that it was something not to be recited without specific intention.

Djalma asked, "This is the *Sacred Vow*?"

"Yes. And I think it has something to do with the immediate reason that Katerina and I are in communication. It seems we have made a very strong commitment to each other. I am certain that quoting this verse allowed Katerina to pull me out of a disaster during my last journey."

"Would you like some tea, Ian?" Djalma started to walk to the kitchen.

Ian was surprised at Djalma's subdued response. Ian thought the story he was about to tell was something remarkable.

Djalma called back from the doorway, "I assume you'll need some food and drink while you fill me in on the gaping holes in your story."

While Djalma made tea, Ian managed to get up and move

about. It was an odd pain that he had, mostly internal, like that poison he'd felt in the dark days before Djalma had given him the token. Every part of Ian's body hurt, but he was much improved from when he first returned from that last visit—Ian suddenly thought about Katerina and her baby. Why couldn't he have helped her?

Ian stood motionless, lost in his memory until Djalma returned with tea and food, and broke into his thoughts.

"So your recent visit was something troublesome?" Djalma asked.

Ian moved slowly toward the couch. "Yes I had a visit with a manifestation of Katerina with a baby. It was really painful. Someone was taking the baby away from her."

Just recalling it drew Ian's consciousness back to that place. "I couldn't help her, and I was getting angry and panicked. I think my strong emotions about the situation eventually forced me out of that alternate life."

Djalma seemed to have some idea why Ian was stumbling over his words. "You're not completely disengaged from that place yet, are you?"

The question didn't make much sense to Ian. He took the residual emotions that he felt to be no more than anyone else would feel after a traumatic experience. Of course he would never be the same afterwards! He had been utterly useless in saving someone he cared about from harm. More than someone he cared about! Someone he was deeply connected to.

"Please tell me how the visit ended, Ian."

"I could do nothing but watch as they took the baby from her. Katerina was suffering greatly."

Djalma was very patient. He seemed to have some idea of his friend's need to take time going through his recounting of the event.

"My rage became so intense," Ian said, "that I found myself back on this couch just when Katerina was about to be harmed. I got bounced out of that reality. One moment I was struggling to help her and the next, I could only see the light of my study coming through my eyes.

"The return was painful, as though I physically collided with this location, and sort of rebounded, feeling not quite in this world, not fully out of it."

Ian became silent periodically. At each delay, Djalma would wait for a time and then call on Ian to continue. It was a good thing, because otherwise, Ian would become completely mired in the memory of that moment.

"I don't remember exactly how it happened, but I had an unfamiliar sensory experience. Instinct told me that this particular sensation was the doorway back to the place I had just left. I felt like I was still in the recoil of the returning bounce, and so I directed all my attention and emotion at the doorway."

Djalma cringed and ducked his head.

"Yes. You know what happened then," Ian continued. "You told me not to rush the time between trips, but I wasn't thinking straight. I was certain that if I could make the instant return, I would be able to handle the result."

"Did you make it back?" Djalma asked.

Remembering the place where he landed made Ian flinch. "I didn't see the woman again." Before continuing, he took a moment to mourn her misery silently.

Ian was realizing how entangled he remained with the alternate existence he actually visited—Djalma was absolutely right—he now saw that he had still not disengaged from the world of the suffering Katerina and child. There was something cathartic about exposing the experience to his conscious mind, and speaking about it. But separating from her was saddening. Now, he felt he was leaving her truly alone and abandoned.

"I feel certain that you're only a spectator in their worlds, Ian. You cannot affect what is already the reality there."

Recalling some of his own speculations he was left with over the last few visits, Ian stopped Djalma. "I'm not so sure of that any more, my friend, but let's talk about that later.

Djalma handed Ian a bowl of hot soup and placed a cup of tea on the table by the couch. They ate quietly.

After he finished his soup, Ian tried to continue with the

story. "When I tried to return to Katerina and the child, I got into some kind of in-between realm. There was no light, and it drained any energy out of me that I called up. I had to hold my emotions in check. Every time I allowed myself any emotion, it felt like part of my physical body was being literally torn away."

As he spoke, Ian reflexively raised his voice and said, "Damn, that hurt!"

Djalma recoiled at the loudness of Ian's voice.

Ian didn't say anything more for a while.

After some time passed, Djalma asked, "Are you all right?"

"Oh. Yes. Sorry, I was just remembering," Ian said. "Not good. I felt like I was dying in that dark place, being drained of my life energy. I was stuck in some kind of void. Then I decided to gamble that you were right about focusing on the *Sacred Vow* if I got into trouble. I directed all the energy I had left at it."

Djalma smiled. "That was a pretty big chance to take."

"Not really," Ian replied. "I didn't have any other option."

"Do you think repeating the verse was what got you free from the void?" Djalma asked.

"I think it made the Katerina of my tea visions hear me. Before I found myself back here and passed out, I was in her house. She fanned some smoky concoction over me. Then she told me to go home and come back when I was rested.

"The next thing I knew, I was on the couch, in great pain, and losing consciousness. After that, you were here."

Sitting back and drawing a big breath like a kid at the end of a grand adventure story, Djalma said, "It sounds as if Katerina is the one you should thank. Not me."

"Oh, I thank you as well," Ian assured him. "But I am grateful to her. I thank her for so much more than just getting me back home. I wish I could get back to her, to tell her so. But I have no control over my destinations."

Djalma made a funny little sideways motion with his head as if he were about to do something that he was trying to resist. "I may regret this," he said. "But I know it means too much to you not to mention it, if I think this is a possibility."

He had Ian's attention. "What have you got, old man?"

Realizing what he'd said, Ian wondered what was it about Djalma that made him seem like an aged familiar despite his youth?

"You may not have navigational control—"

Djalma paused as a tease, and it worked. Ian became fully alert, certain that Djalma was about to offer the treasure that he had been fruitlessly searching for.

"But it seems Katerina is able to help you." Djalma grinned and sat back in his chair.

"Come on now," Ian pleaded. "How is she going to help? If there is a choice, I will gladly return to the Katerina of the tea visits each time!"

"The verse," Djalma said. "That verse must be something that you and she can use to contact each other. You repeated the verse over and over when in the void, and she brought you out of it, directly to her. Maybe, just maybe, if you enter a meditation while repeating the verse, like a mantra, she can hone in on you and guide you to her location."

"All right!" Ian attempted to spring up from the couch. "Ooooh!" As pain hit him, he collapsed into a hobble. Eventually his movement smoothed into something of a walk.

"I think that might be it, Djalma. I won't have to fall into those random lives, suffering along with unhappy, unknowing versions of our existences together."

"Don't be careless and make me regret telling you," Djalma said. "It's only speculation. It's also possible your return to Katerina is not something that can be repeated."

Still walking somewhat clumsily around the room, Ian shook his head. "No, what you said about the verse rings true with me. I might have needed you to bring it to my attention, but now that I've heard the words, I feel its truth, deep within myself.

"I have to tell you, a few more visits as unhappy as the last handful, and I don't know that I could keep taking those trips. I'm certain Katerina and I need to be in touch with each other, but I don't believe the random locations are beneficial. In fact those interactions may be causing some harm.

"If Katerina and I can work to help each other, I'm sure we will be able to achieve our purpose—whatever it is."

Djalma picked up his book and went back to reading. Ian was concentrating on exercising his weak muscles. "One thing you'll need to consider," Djalma added. "Even if Katerina can consistently bring you back to her location, there's some reason she did not attempt to heal you after you were retrieved from the void."

Ian slowed down and stared at Djalma skeptically. He was about to take offense at Djalma's speculation.

"Don't you think she would have mended your damage if it was possible?" Djalma said. "Even though you two can communicate, you still exist in completely separate primary realities. Katerina may have sent you home because it was impossible to make you well in her home world."

Ian started to drop some of his defensiveness. "So, what are you suggesting, Djalma?"

"Keep exercising. Eat well, friend. I'm sure Katerina will share what she can, but you're going to have to attend to your own well-being."

Ian picked up a pillow from a chair close by and threw it at Djalma. The effort was feeble, posing only a comic threat to Djalma. It fell to the floor well before his feet.

"You need more practice, Ian. Get to work." Djalma laughed and returned his attention to his book.

Moving around the furniture, Ian said, "You're a good friend, Djalma."

Over the next week or so, Ian told Djalma about all his other journeys. The two friends speculated on what the experiences meant, and spent some time discussing unrelated philosophies and sharing their individual poetry favorites. Before long, Ian was able to move more naturally, and felt well enough to make some meals in gratitude for all the help he had been given.

As soon as he could, Ian drove Djalma back to the mountains. It turned out that Djalma didn't have a vehicle—but did not say how he had traveled to Ian's house. On the way home, Djalma asked Ian to stop at Liz's place. She had a fine meal prepared for the three of them, and they spent a few contented hours together.

At Liz's insistence, Ian spent the next few days with her. She didn't really seem to care to hear about his adventures. Mostly, she and he spent leisure time enjoying each other's company. The added stay was very beneficial to Ian. Exercise in the mountains, good food, and good company were returning Ian to prime health. The loving support of another dear friend did him more good than anything else could have.

Djalma didn't come back around Liz's house before Ian left. Ian wondered if all Djalma's nursing efforts had worn him out. He pictured his friend roaming in the woods for a month before Liz would hear any more from him.

Thanking Liz and expressing his love for her as he left, Ian asked that she pass his affections to Djalma as well.

"I'll be back in touch soon," he said.

Liz smiled and went straight to the issue that had not been mentioned since he got to her house. "You have some visiting to get back to, don't you, sweetie?"

"Yes, Liz. I'll be smarter this time."

"Katerina will be counting on that as well," Liz said, as she waved and went back into the inn.

It was true. His friends had completely revitalized him, and Ian was eager to put their results to good use as soon as he got home. He didn't mention it to Liz or Djalma, but he had taken additional leave from work, certain that he had more important business to finish.

Return

With his legs folded in a semi-lotus position, Ian sat on his couch, apprehensive after the result of his last meditation. Even though his friends' care had helped him heal, his body had a strong memory of the pain that had resulted after his last sitting in this position. Lingering fear was making it very hard for him to relax.

"Okay, Djalma, old boy. I hope you're right about this."

Ian closed his eyes but fidgeted, unable to get comfortable.

Nothing to do but to do it, he thought.

Taking in a long, slow breath, he tried to shore up his nerves. "Please don't let me bounce back on a convulsive reaction," he whispered

Finally Ian let the *Sacred Vow* occupy his mind. He repeated the verse several times before any calm came to him.

"I offer this *Sacred Vow* to you alone—"

A clear voice spoke in return, "Welcome back, dear one."

The last time Ian had heard that voice, he was in great pain and being guided home. His eyes shot open.

There he stood, in that glorious old cottage of Katerina's, facing her. She stood to the side of the lounge chairs, left of the exterior door.

"Katerina!"

"Yes, Ian?"

Ian could hear her voice! Djalma was right. He thought, I owe you one, my friend!

Ian brought a hand up in front of his face—and there it was, as clearly tangible as if he were standing in his own study. He lowered his focus to his body.

"I can see myself," he exclaimed.

"So can I. And it's wonderful to see you again!" Katerina seemed as excited about his improved physical condition as he felt. "Especially to see you looking so well. You had me very worried when you were here last time."

The next thing Ian hoped for was complete independent mobility. Timidly, he turned away from Katerina, stepped a foot out and propelled himself slowly forward. His face felt flush with excitement. Then, almost unable to believe his good fortune, Ian took several more steps, each time a little faster, each time confirming a direct correlation between his will and his movement.

He turned and smiled mischievously at Katerina. She returned a quizzical expression, obviously uncertain of his intention.

Ian spread his arms and moved quickly toward Katerina, bound on wrapping his arms around her. He didn't respond to her upheld hands, unaware it was a signal to stop.

At the moment Ian thought he would finally feel her touch, his vision momentarily blurred and he felt a nasty little electrical jolt. Then he was propelled to one side—literally through one of the couches and into the middle of the table beside it.

Ian jerked his eyes downward and saw that his legs had become embedded in the top of the table. His mind was objecting to what his eyes were reporting, and his body was objecting to what it felt. At just about the place where Ian's legs vanished into the table, his flesh was feeling like a pincushion, with every pinhead charged by an increasing voltage.

"Bloody hell!" he bellowed.

Katerina laughed aloud, "Oh, dear fellow."

The pain in his legs was getting worse. He twisted to one side and drew his left leg upward. It was like withdrawing it from some opaque liquid.

Determined to escape, Ian jerked to one side and high-stepped in that direction until he stood safely in front of the table. Then he turned and looked disbelievingly at what appeared to be a perfectly normal, solid, hardwood table.

When the pain subsided, embarrassment set in. Ian wasn't on quite the roll of good fortune he had imagined. Apparently, he couldn't come into contact with Katerina or anything else in this place. Worse yet, there was definitely some price to be paid for touching anything. Whatever object he waded into, like the furniture, repulsed him with some kind of electrical charge, bouncing his molecular energy about until he and it were fully disconnected.

Slowly, Ian returned his attention to Katerina. Her expression was sympathetic.

"I could have dodged out of the way," she offered, "but you'd have thought I was playing some silly game with you, Ian, or just being aloof.

"If what you felt from encroaching on the space of other forms is anything like what I have encountered previously, you're unlikely to forget that lesson soon."

He envisioned what he must have looked like, trying to get free from the table. There was nothing for him to do but take the situation as he found it and enjoy being with Katerina. Besides, what he imagined was rather amusing, if it had only happened to someone else. He couldn't help but shake his head and laugh a little.

"Did you feel hundreds of needles bringing charges into every muscle?" he asked.

"It was just that same way for me," she said, nodding.

He rapidly brushed his legs, to stop the post-surge tingling. "It's nice to know that I'm not the only one to make this mistake."

"The first time I made such a trip," Katerina said. "I tried to push open a door and went through it instead. It would have been a very undignified entrance as I was an official emissary, except no one was in the room to receive me. I had arrived at the wrong place."

Katerina's words indicated that Ian's home wasn't the only place that she had visited. Ian wondered if she had also visited their parallel lives.

"Were you visiting anyone I might know?"

Katerina sat with her back to the desk. "That was a long time ago, part of my early training."

Deciding to be more direct, he asked, "Did you ever visit parallel manifestations of you and me?"

"Yes, since I began to look for you, I have visited numerous other manifestations of us. You were the only one who ever fully acknowledged my presence."

"Were you able to control your movement and contact in those realities, Katerina?"

"Of course," she said. "My years of training with the Sisterhood provided me with that ability."

"Sisterhood? Training? Wait," he said. Obviously, their conversation was dependent on too much unknown information for him to keep up. In addition, his mind was flooded with thousands of belated questions, declarations, and full conversations that he had been silently practicing. He took a slow, deep breath and settled for an introduction.

"You know, Katerina, the very first thing I'd like to do is to say that it is wonderful to finally meet you—formally that is—when I can hear your words and we can exchange audible conversation between us." Then it crossed Ian's mind that he had a problem with the physical contact that usually accompanies an introduction. Since he couldn't shake Katerina's hand, or kiss or hug her, he bowed deeply and held the pose, waiting for her to respond.

Rising from her chair, Katerina said, "An excellent start." Her clothes were a combination he had seen her wear a couple of times—very loose, long pants, a top and the ornate, light green tunic. She followed his lead and curtsied. "Very much my pleasure as well."

In her presence, Ian always felt foreign to himself and, at the very same time, more natural than he ever had. From his initial encounter with Katerina, the mere sight of her consistently elicited uncharacteristic behavior from him—which he found forever surprising. This time was no different.

The next words out of his mouth were probably those he most wanted to hear himself say and wanted Katerina to hear. He didn't plan to say them at just this moment, and he certainly did not expect them at such an early point in their initial conversation . . . but the words just escaped from his mouth: "Katerina, I love you more than I have ever loved anyone. And I suspect I always have, even before I knew love."

Astonished at what he had said, Ian felt an instantaneous anxiety about how she would respond. Yes, Ian thought, they had wordlessly expressed love for each other in their actions, gazes, and mouthed commitments, but this was somehow different, blatant and undeniable. And what, he had to ask himself, did he mean by "before I knew love"?

With a funny little smile, the rise of one eyebrow, and the tilt of her head, Katerina reassured him.

"But of course you do. And I have always had just the same devotion to you, Ian."

Blind love is the perfect sedative for a phobic mind. Ian heard his rational self complain. What does she mean, "of course you do"? But Ian ignored the neurotic speculations of his conscious mind. He simply stood there, unable to release his gaze from her eyes.

After a moment of looking silently, Ian came to his senses. "Oh, yes. Thank you, Katerina, for helping me when I last saw you. I'm sure you saved my life."

Her face was joyous. "Thank you for calling to me, Ian. We should always be open to call on each other. Remember, we are seen as consummately bonded by the Collective."

He certainly felt bonded to Katerina, and was pleased that she felt the same. Ian was still considering what "consummately bonded by the Collective" might mean when she asked, "How did you get into the void?"

"I got repelled from a horrible journey and then tried to force my way back into it. Instead, I went to a place that drained the life-force from me with my every effort to get free. I started reciting the *Sacred Vow*. The next thing I knew, you were redirecting me home."

"That's a very dangerous thing you did. Please don't take such chances again."

"Not to worry," he said.

"Ian, I hope you won't be offended, but before that visit, I thought your people couldn't fully manifest when traveling."

Now, it was his turn to be amused with her words. "I won't be offended," he said, "if you won't be when I say I have no idea what you're talking about. I don't think many of *my people* visit this way very often. And what do you mean by *fully manifest*?"

"Oh, they don't visit parallel selves?" she said. Her expression was definitely one of surprise. "Your projection is fully manifested today—as you said 'you can see yourself'." When you have been here before, our connection wasn't fully manifested. I wondered why the *Sacred Vow* didn't function properly."

"This was only the second time I have used the vow. The first time was when you redirected me from the void," he said. "Were you always using it?"

"Of course."

"How did you know to use it, and how you should use it?"

Katerina seemed a little perplexed by his question. "By my training with the Sisterhood."

Under no circumstance did Ian want to take any chance of offending Katerina, but he couldn't avoid such a sense of familiarity as to say what came to mind. "Oh, I forgot, the Sisterhood," and laughed easily. He felt wonderfully joyous and playful being with her.

"Yes, the Sisterhood." She didn't seem offended at all.

"Unfortunately, I am at a disadvantage. There is no brotherhood back home, no one to teach me such things as recognizing magical verses to be used to identify the partner you are bonded with in another reality."

Katerina pulled an apron on over her head and took the stool from her desk to the front of the kitchen sink. Once seated, she took a large pot into her lap and began cleaning some kind of herbs and vegetables.

Looking at Ian as though she was quite concerned, Katerina said, "Why do you say you don't belong to an order?"

"Because it's true. If by 'order' you mean a religious or mystical society or fraternity, then my answer is because I never have seen any purpose for such an association."

"You're teasing me, aren't you, Ian?"

"I assure you I am not. To my knowledge, you are one of a *very* few devout people I have ever interacted with."

Katerina lowered her eyebrows and pursed her mouth. She was silent, occasionally looking from the pot to him, and back. Ian had the distinct impression she was having a hard time believing him, but accepted that he would tell her nothing but the truth.

"Katerina, are there no people in your world who do not belong to an order, hold to an established faith or practice a defined belief?"

"Of course there are."

"Are there many of these people?"

"No, not many."

"Where I come from, it is closer to being just the opposite. And of the people claiming any faith, those who are not fearfully religious or falsely professing—but truly learned in such mysteries and connected to the spirit—are few in number indeed. I don't know if I have ever met one, or even met anyone else who has met such a person . . . though I know such people do exist."

Katerina considered his claim for quite a while. Judging by her shifting expressions, she appeared to Ian so lost in her contemplation that he made a point not to interrupt her thoughts.

Eventually Katerina broke her trance and spoke. "You

might not be aware of such people yet, but I am sure the wise ones can be found in every realm.

"Besides, it seems to me that you know more than you imagine. You found your way to me on your own, and that was not a simple task."

Watching Katerina prepare the roots and vegetables with a small knife, Ian was reminded of Djalma with his herbs. "You might be right on both counts," he said.

They fell silent for a while. Completely content, Ian stood, fascinated with her presence, and watched Katerina as she worked. She looked up and smiled a couple of times, but it did not embarrass him into self-consciousness.

"Katerina?"

"Yes?"

"After so much time spent in fantasy of doing such, it is a crying shame that you and I cannot sit for a cup of tea together."

"I can teach you," she replied, still working with her fare, "to be able to sit on forms and use cups here, but actually ingesting drink could be a problem.

"When it comes to sitting or picking something up, you just have to sensitize yourself enough to recognize the electrical border field of the other entity."

Ian remembered what had happened when he tried to hug Katerina. "Will I be able to learn how not to bounce off the force field that surrounds you?"

Katerina stopped working and looked up. "I don't think we'll ever be able to experience physical contact between us. It seems the disparity between our worlds is too great. Unfortunately, we haven't come from sufficiently attuned realities.

"Higher life forms have the greatest potential for conflict. What you experienced when you tried to embrace me was sort of a protective mechanism between our worlds. Regulating contact seems to be a means of ensuring there is no intermixing of the atomic material that makes up the elements of irreconcilable realities."

"If that's the way it must be," Ian said, "it would have been nice if the Powers That Be had put up sufficient barriers to make sure that my elements couldn't mix with the furniture of this reality as well."

Katerina couldn't suppress a little chuckle.

"Wait," he said. "Did you get that same kind of jolt trying to kiss me when we first met? I remember you had a funny expression on your face, just before I returned home that day, but if you felt what I felt a moment ago, I don't think you would have been as calm."

"Actually, I had only intended to bring my lips as close as I could until I felt your barrier, but I never felt it, even after bringing my lips to what should have been contact with your face. I was confused. That was what made me certain we weren't fully manifested. That's probably why we didn't hear each other either."

"Well, if we had been fully manifested," Ian said, "that would have certainly been the most stimulating kiss that I had ever experienced."

A little silence of shyness passed between them. Katerina focused on her paring, and Ian just stood in the middle of the room, watching. After a time, he was amused at how two grown people in the midst of an extraordinary, paranormal relationship were acting like timid school children at their first dance together.

"You might get tired, standing all the time," she spoke up. "Would you like to be able to sit?"

Really, Ian had no interest in taking any chance of experiencing that electrical charge again. He was sufficiently inspired to be able to stand for days. He was even less inclined, however, to admit his fear to Katerina and so he replied, "That would be nice."

"Let's use the stool to your right. We'll start with a single surface of a seat only." Katerina's tone implied she was pleased with the opportunity to teach him something about functioning in her world. "Put the palm of your hand about two inches over the seat."

Ian turned his back to her and walked over to the rough-crafted, wooden stool. After taking a deep breath, he lowered his hand cautiously.

"Now close your eyes, Ian. It will help you concentrate."

He did so, warily. A moment later, he chuckled.

"Did it tickle you?" she asked.

"My silliness did," he said. "I'm standing here, with my eyes closed, sweating over the idea that an inanimate object might reach up and bite me."

"That's only silly within the confines of common assumptions of *your* reality."

Ian's eyes flew open and he jerked his hand from the stool. Katerina was calmly working with her herbs, but Ian's movement caught her attention. She looked up and burst into laughter.

"Oh, I'm sorry. I wasn't thinking about how that might sound. Inanimate objects don't bite here either—unless you wade into them as you did earlier." It was evident Katerina was having a hard time controlling her mirth.

"Oh, you are the playful one," he said, nodding. Ian began to wonder just how innocent her choice of words was.

"No, *really*," she insisted. "There can be places where a form we consider lifeless is able to bite."

"Maybe so." He turned back to the stool and lowered his hand, still carefully. "Let's save the speculation until I'm no longer in danger of being attacked by your furniture again." He closed his eyes.

Suppressing her last chuckle, Katerina said, "With practice, you'll be able to feel the electrical field of an object as you approach it. Very slowly, lower your hand until you start to feel the charge of the stool."

Ian was in no hurry to become a pincushion again. Slowly indeed, he lowered his hand. A couple of times, he stopped and opened his eyes, to see just how close he was. When he saw that his hand was still about an inch from the stool top, he closed his eyes again and moved closer. Suddenly, his hand felt like it was set on fire.

Shaking his hand wildly, Ian jumped away from the stool, cursing it for its deviousness. Katerina had to hold on to her pot of herbs to keep from dropping them as she cackled. Ian laughed playfully as well. They were like two kids playing together. He loved feeling this comfortable with a woman who also stirred such feelings of passion within him.

Once their laughter started to die down, Ian made his way to the stool again. This time he kept his eyes open. Katerina did not say anything as he moved his hand up and down, feeling for the first indication of the electrical field.

He worked at this for quite a while. They had several more good laughs as Ian got shocked a few more times. Katerina spread the herbs out to dry as he got better and better at finding the edge of the field without getting electrified. Finally, he felt he had conquered her challenge. He could consistently touch the stool top without pain. Katerina cheered as he boldly picked up the stool, grasping it on the top and underside of the seat, lifting it from the floor.

"Thank you for your instruction and patience, dear lady." Ian said in a playful spirit and bowed his head.

"As a reward, please take a seat, sir," Katerina responded in kind.

Suddenly Ian wasn't feeling so confident. His backside was a little more sensitive than his hand, and he doubted he had the same control with it. Still, he made the effort.

Sure enough, his first effort at sitting resulted in a resounding jolt that ran up his spine. His pride was hurt. Looking sharply around to see what Katerina's response was to his suffering, Ian was comforted to see she was cringing in sympathy. That was all the motivation he needed to get the trick right.

During the second pass, Ian started getting a little charge. Rather than putting himself in a position of having to start over, he resisted pulling fully away. Instead, he lifted slightly until the pain ceased and then he held still.

"The problem is," he said, "now I'm not really sitting, but I'm exerting more energy than I would be if I were standing, just in order to hold my behind a little above this minefield of a stool."

"Can you feel the edge of the electrical charge?" Katerina asked.

"Yes, I believe so."

"Then you can relax your muscles, Ian."

"Are you kidding me? I have seen what happens when I casually interact with this stool."

"Not at all," she assured. "It's just like touching the stool with your hand. You don't have to support yourself above the seat, but you have to approach the seat at a speed that gives your mind time to acknowledge the boundaries of the form."

"Katerina, you know, that would imply it is our mind's perception that dictates whether a thing is solid or not."

"This *is* the case," she spoke with enthusiasm. "In a familiar reality—like one's primary life—there's an autonomous interaction between the inhabitants that make this negotiation subconscious. In an unfamiliar reality, the language of negotiation may be initially unrecognized and, therefore, the negotiation must be learned consciously."

With his buttocks hovering over the stool seat, Ian drew a deep breath and let the tension leave his thighs. As easy as that, the stool supported him. Despite the apparent simplicity of the move, he was still a little anxious. If he shifted slightly, would he suddenly sink into the seat and feel the charge of his mistake?

"Congratulations!" Katerina said. She sounded like a child who just taught her best buddy a new game. Ian couldn't help but enjoy her delight at their achievement. He rested on the stool comfortably, proudly.

When Katerina started with a slow, happy laugh, he initially resisted joining in, afraid laughing might break his balancing act. As she clasped her hands and became fully engaged in her laughter, he could not help but join in. Laughing did not cause him any pain on his backside. At one point, he slipped off the stool, and promptly retook the seat before he had time to consciously consider his peril. As he sat without a hitch, he and Katerina were jubilant.

Ian thought it was almost ridiculous how much joy could be had from merely learning to sit, or any other simple activity, when one was experiencing it with the right person.

"You know, Katerina, it wouldn't seem to matter if I stood all the time I visit you. In fact, my body is resting on my couch all the while."

"You will find it does matter, Ian. You're undoubtedly aware that your body exists as much here as it does in your study."

Ian merely smiled in agreement. But he thought, that sounds like something Djalma would say.

"It's all energy." Katerina continued, "Energy that we perceive as a physical form. At this moment, your conscious mind is engaged with—and accepting the reality of—two simultaneous expressions of itself as physical forms. Energy you use and what happens to your perceived form here will affect your consciousness, thereby making a difference in your body in both places, just like the void did.

"Besides, who knows what benefit there will be at home from learning to function within another reality?"

Sitting was getting to be commonplace, so Ian got up and walked about, enjoying his return to this magically beautiful living space. He carefully slid his hand across the dining table, crafted of heavy boards that were smooth from many, many years of use. A hammered copper plate was at one corner of the table. Light from the kitchen windows made its surface glow.

"Ian, how is it you don't have a wife in your world?"

"I did have, one time." Ian hated being reminded of that fact, mostly because he was too much of a romantic.

"Did she pass away?"

"No. I made her a commitment I couldn't keep. And, I was too afraid of being alone to accept the fact that she wasn't the one. She knew I wasn't the right person for her as well. Neither of us wanted to accept the truth until we finally forced the brutal realization on each other.

"Mind you, once two people have improperly made such a commitment, I do believe it shows more love for each other to admit that mistake and end the relationship rather than continuing the suffering of the error. The trouble is understanding the difference between a true error and a challenge for growth."

For a while, there was only the sound of the birds outside and the couple's individual movements about the room.

As usual, once this subject was brought up, Ian could not be finished with it until he had made his full confession. "I am ashamed of that bit of personal history, Katerina, not so much for the promise I broke to her, for she is a thinking, intelligent woman and knew as well as I that our relationship was a folly. I'm ashamed for the impertinence with which I treated love and my true self, for willfully trying to validate such a false devotion though I knew it wasn't mine to claim."

Ian didn't know if Katerina's timing was just terrible, or if he should take it as a warning from her gods. This confession was something he would not have unveiled until much later in their relationship. It took the bold air of romance out of his sails. Ian wondered what she would make of his recent profession of love to her now that he had given her reason to doubt his credibility in romance.

"Do you feel such a promise is yours to make now, Ian?"

When Ian heard her question, he felt such a lift in his spirits that he was almost surprised he did not clear the floor with a yelp. Evidently Katerina was not concerned about his breach during his past. He tried not to respond like a fumbling schoolboy.

"What? Yes, without a doubt!" It was one of those times when more words poured out of him than were helpful. All of a sudden, Ian seemed to be trying to proclaim love every way he was capable of, and further failing with each effort. "I am certain that I made that promise to you long before I could even imagine you."

There you go with the "before I knew you" abstracts again, he scolded himself.

Ian tried once more to say what he felt, "In fact, I think the reason I have not been successful in lasting romantic relationships"— realizing that he was not helping his case, Ian continued in a slightly more subdued voice—"was because I was already in love with you . . . but had no way of recognizing it."

Okay, he was thinking to himself, one more attempt, and don't try so hard this time. Take a deep breath and speak slowly.

"Without question, Katerina. That is, of course, assuming you don't have a partner. Do you . . . have a partner or a husband?"

Trying to focus on something else to help him bring his spasmodic behavior under control, Ian stopped to test out the electrical field of a pottery vase on Katerina's dining table. Its resonance was noticeably different from the wooden stool and table.

Katerina had finished with her chore and was looking through the large book at her desk. "I do not. My obligations to the Sisterhood make it impossible for me to have a partner."

Ian was stunned. Her words were something he *did not* want to hear. Their meeting today seemed full of complications.

"You're a nun?" he blurted as he lowered the vase rather quickly to the table. He felt mild electrical charges, but nothing that became too uncomfortable.

"The members of the Sisterhood are not nuns, as the word is defined here," she started to explain. "What does 'nun' mean to you?"

Ian thought for a minute, trying to control his disappointment of what he had just heard. Then he said, "I believe I am right in saying this: a nun is a female member of a religious order, bound by vows of poverty, chastity, and obedience." The idea that Katerina was unavailable for his affection, by his full definition of a relationship, didn't please him.

"Please tell me how the Sisterhood is different from nuns," he said. "Also, is 'the Sisterhood' the full name of your order?"

Waiting for her response, Ian stretched his fingers out to the brightly colored, exotic flowers that were in the vase he had just been holding. He wondered if his finger would be diverted to one side, or if he would feel a shock from the flowers.

"The Sisterhood is a description, not a name. More accurately, the order is often called the Sisterhood of Crones. The exact name is something that cannot be spoken but is a symbol only."

"I find it hard to think of someone as lovely as you as a crone," he said without looking up.

"Please do," Katerina said. "The wisdom of Crones gives us all radiance beyond beauty."

Pushing his index finger toward the little orange flower, Ian never felt any sensation of its electrical field, but he noticed that the flower suddenly withdrew from him, as if dying in fast motion. "Dear thing," he said, sorrowfully.

"I'm sorry I didn't think to warn you," Katerina consoled him. "Some less complex life-forces cannot accept imposition into their energy field. They don't have force enough to fend off any intruding energy, so they're instantly destroyed."

Ian wanted to lift up the wilted little flower, but resisted the urge. This was the first time he had ever seen a plant go from living to dead instantaneously. The animation of the change made him feel much more emotional than he had ever felt at the loss of an inanimate life. He felt sorrow over having killed the flower—more than the rational mind could understand. He was a guest and didn't intend harm to anything in Katerina's world.

Katerina distracted him from his melancholy absorption, "Ian, would you like to see the symbol that is the name of the Sisterhood?"

He looked around to see her pointing to the front cover of the larger volume that was always on her desk. "Huh? Oh, sure," he mumbled. He wasn't really interested, but maybe it would distract him from his sorrow.

Standing in front of the desk, he noticed Katerina watching him, and he gazed into her eyes. A further flood of forceful emotions filled him, and he was still unable to identify their cause or justify their intensity. He was certain that what he was feeling at that moment was as irrational as a nervous breakdown, and just as impossible to control.

"Look at this," Katerina said. Her voice was gentle but commanding.

Ian followed her eyes downward until his attention fell on the cryptic icon in the center of the book cover. As soon as the image entered his consciousness, he felt himself completely released from the burden of magnified remorse and sadness.

The symbol looked like nothing he had seen before. It was contained in a ring shape, flattened on the top left. There were several disconnected lines inside. At first look, they impressed him as swirling flames rising from the image of an eye.

As Katerina pulled her finger away from the center of the book cover, Ian's eyes floated back up to her face. He saw a smile, and felt one spread across his own face. As quickly as they had come, the overwhelming and all-consuming feelings of unhappiness became foreign to him once again.

"Many of the Sisterhood enter in a lifelong bond with a partner," Katerina said, to continue their conversation from before the death of the flower. "Certain stages of learning and levels of commitment make being with a partner inappropriate or complicated. And there are some paths within the Sisterhood where a partner is not possible.

"I have been honored as the direct understudy of the Crone Mother and cannot enter into a partnership so long as I hold this position."

Katerina seemed thoroughly happy when she spoke of her honor. It saddened Ian that she was so content to be in a position that would deny them the option of becoming partners, despite the love he was sure they held for each other. Initially, Ian felt inclined to focus on his disappointment, but decided he would not allow himself to be as petty and selfish as to refuse to be glad for her, even if he was unhappy for himself.

Just then Katerina changed the subject. "I have to collect some things from the garden, Ian. Would you like to take a walk with me?"

He nodded.

As soon as they stepped out the door, Ian tucked his hands behind his back so he didn't inadvertently cause another living thing to die.

"You shouldn't be so hard on yourself," Katerina said.

"What do you mean?"

"Your hands," she replied. "What you're responding to is more than just the flower dying. The overwhelming emotion in response to the flower's death has to do with an increasing energy sensitivity emerging within you. It is unavoidable. Your experiences here are making you develop perceptivity to the fields of other entities and that talent will be carried back to your home also.

"The hypersensitivity is a little hard to deal with at first. I'm sorry that you don't have a brotherhood to help you with it."

"Not to worry," Ian said. "I have a good friend who I'm sure will help me if I have any problems."

They walked into an area of the gardens that Ian had not seen before, casually talking as Katerina selected things and placed them in her basket. Like other parts of the garden Ian had seen, this spot was an extraordinary natural shrine of herbs, flowers, trees, and small animals. Different paths took them by pools of water, arrangements of large stones, and grouping after grouping of beautiful plants. The layout was so exact that Ian began to believe it followed some scientific or artistic blueprint. The way this garden layout revered natural patterns reminded him of Vaastu or Feng Shui.

"Katerina, is your garden design based on some magical balance of harmony, specifically designed for an effect?"

"Yes," she answered, smiling. "Without training of The Nature, how do you know this?"

"I don't know. It just feels that way. Are all the Sisters' gardens like this?"

"Oh, all who have gardens will base the design on The Nature.

Every design is for a specific outcome, and not all gardens are intended for the same purpose. This design is for a specific focus of energy. This cottage is for who ever is the Crone Mother's understudy. That is why I live here now."

A couple of hours seemed to have passed while Ian and Katerina walked about. Though he had seen much of the garden before, this was the first time Ian was able to hear Katerina tell him the names of plants and the reason for their placements. Their meanderings would not have encompassed more than five acres, but there were times Ian had no idea where the cottage was. He was certain that no matter what the purpose of this garden design was, it was miraculous in its beauty.

They turned a corner and, out of nowhere, a green wall opened to bring them right back to the door they had used to exit Katerina's house.

"Do you have time to go with me to the Crone Mother's house, Ian? I have to deliver a basket."

Ian thought it was an odd question for her to ask. After all the time and effort it had taken him to get into just this situation, if Katerina had to make a trip, he was certainly not going to wait around her house alone.

"Sure," he said. "I think it would be interesting to see where the Matriarch of your Sisterhood lives."

Katerina looked at him as if she had not expected that reply. Ian had no idea why not, but it seemed that many of his responses were surprises to her.

She led him down yet another path of her garden, until it spilled through an opening in a high wall that surrounded the garden, out into something more like a street. It was amazing to see the landscape open up. Where Katerina's garden had given Ian the sensation of its being a solitary home in a lush forestland, before him now was a little community.

He had no idea there could have been this number of homes so close by. Though there was a wide array of designs, every house was built of what looked to be natural materials and blended well with the landscape surrounding it. Katerina stopped to let Ian get his bearings and catch up with her.

"What a fascinating village you live in," he said as he gained on her.

"Thank you, Ian."

"Where I come from, we don't tend to give so much consideration to nature inside our towns or communities."

"I am so sad for you," she said. "I don't think *we* could live otherwise."

He could tell by the tone of her voice that she was sincere. As they walked down the wide, stone road, they passed children playing, couples strolling, and people working in their own, less impressive gardens.

Katerina and Ian had been walking for some time before it dawned on him that he was not just another neighbor. The people they encountered spoke to them both. So the other people obviously saw him. Some called him by name. Yet when he had been there before, he had only seen children, and they hadn't seen him.

"Who do they think I am, Katerina?"

"Yourself, Ian."

"Yes, I noticed that. But who am I here? I'm not just your everyday resident."

Then a further complication dawned on him. "With this idea of physically materializing in other realities, Katerina," he asked, "why is it no one in any of my other destinations ever showed any awareness of my presence?"

"Whether you realized it or not," she said, "you chose to project as less than a physical form, or to drop into a host form."

Ian was silent as he considered her reply. They continued on their way, speaking to the occasional neighbor, but that bit of confusion was demanding more and more of Ian's attention.

"Why is it that the children didn't see me, though you could, during my first visits?" he asked.

Ian suddenly realized they had stopped on the doorstep of a majestic mansion similar to Tudor design, constructed of stone and timber frame. Looking back down the path, it was apparent he had been completely absorbed with the conversation for quite a while. Ian suspected they had not come to the front door, even though the cobbled road they had followed, and the gardening that lined it, could have been the proud front entrance of one of the grandest houses back home.

Leaning back, Ian looked several stories up the stone face of this wing—he could see the structure extended on to either side. If Katerina was living in the vicar's house, then this was undoubtedly the bishop's home. Gorgeous ornamental windows with wooden or lead mullions interrupted much of the deep, gray-green wall of stone. Statues were carved in the face of the wall in a number of places—not gargoyles, but kinder images that from this distance looked more like angels, fairies and saints.

Katerina stepped into the stone archway at the top of the steps, pushed open the heavy door—which displayed an excessive amount of ironwork—and went in. Ian followed. The doorway brought them directly into a huge master kitchen, undoubtedly not designed for cooking for a single person or family. He was correct in his assumption that this was the service entrance. In the center of the room was a large, heavy working table, about twelve by eight feet, with several people working around it. The stoves and counters that surrounded the enormous room were equally active.

More than a dozen people bustled at food preparation chores as Ian and Katerina entered. Others were coming and leaving in a hurry. The room echoed with sounds of knives chopping, heavy pans clanging against each other, and people calling out instructions and questions to one another.

Many voices blended, calling out, "Hello, Katerina" and "Welcome, Ian."

One young woman took Katerina's basket and delivered it to other women who began working with the contents. Friendly words were exchanged. Ian wasn't as at ease as he had been when he and Katerina started their walk, now that everyone in this world seemed to be so familiar with his presence. In so many of his visits he had longed to be acknowledged, able to interact. Now that he had his wish—was as real in this visited reality as those native to it—Ian was a little unnerved. He didn't know why, but he was.

One of the women came over to Ian and insistently engaged him in courteous small talk while Katerina moved away from the door and began talking about household business concerning the Crone Mother with another woman. He believed he heard that woman, who seemed to be the household matron, mention his name a time or two.

Katerina disappeared through one of the interior doors after the matron nodded her head in that direction. It was only a matter of minutes before she was back, in good spirits. The quick return was just as well. Ian was only seconds from asking the lady keeping him busy "Just who do you think I am?"

By the time they were headed back to Katerina's house Ian felt contented and relaxed—a little like he had enjoyed several glasses of good wine.

"Are you all right, Ian?"

"Sure, Love. In fact, I have had just about the most wonderful day of my life." It dawned on Ian that his time in Katerina's world had been one of emotional extremes.

"You may have to go soon," she said.

Ian didn't understand why Katerina would need him to leave, but said, "Sure, if that's what you want."

All of a sudden, Katerina was being rather serious. "It's not a matter of what I want, Ian. Are you feeling particularly relaxed? Like you're intoxicated?"

"Well, yes. Why?" he was feeling more and more tranquil.

"You'll be home soon. Please listen to me. You won't be able to come back right away, because your energy needs to regenerate. It won't take as long as it has before, because of the energy you absorbed from the garden . . . Are you hearing me, Ian?"

"Yes, Katerina." Ian could hear just fine, but he wasn't sure why she was so concerned. It seemed irrational.

"Promise me you won't try to force your return."

He didn't respond immediately.

"Promise for me, Ian," she repeated.

"Okay, I promise, Katerina." Ian was feeling almost asleep on his feet.

"Do you remember the *Sacred Vow*?" Katerina asked, raising her voice. He felt a little embarrassed because they were walking past another couple. The couple didn't seem to mind Katerina's loudness, but he did.

"Please speak a little softer," he said.

She lowered her voice and continued, "Do you remember the *Vow*?"

"Yes," he said.

"Whenever you feel ready to come back, meditate and repeat the vow. If you are ready, you will—"

Katerina went silent. Ian turned his head to see what the matter was, and found himself looking off to the side of his couch. The surprise of the location change threw him off balance. His muscles briefly cramped in response to the quick movement. Slowly pulling his legs from under him, he rolled over onto his back.

Lying there, Ian drifted through the day he had just spent with Katerina. It was both glorious and heartbreaking. A tear ran down his cheek. He recognized it was the beginning of the hypersensitivity Katerina had warned him about.

Spirit Mates

"Katerina, how many days have passed since I was here?"

She was opening a bundle that she retrieved from her doorstep. "It is the following morning." Katerina held up a pair of oddly designed shoes, which seemed handmade. "These are for you. The craftsperson worked late into the night."

"I'm honored, but what's wrong with my own shoes?"

"They are of your world," she replied, placing the shoes on the floor before him. "That hasn't been a problem when we walked about the paths and streets. However, you and I are going to spend the day trekking about. If you walk through the open countryside with your shoes, you'll leave footprints of dead grass.

"Are you comfortable enough with your energy field perception to wrap the shoes around your feet?"

The body of the shoes was split down to the toes, with little latches on the top. This allowed Ian to slip his foot onto the open shoe before pulling the sides into contact with the rest of his foot.

"No problem." Feeling quite confident, he reached around to get his now favorite little "attack stool."

Katerina had been right about taking the experiences of her world back with him. After Ian had returned home from their last visit, he noticed that he could, with a little effort, see and feel the aura of energy around numerous objects in his primary world. He had never been able to do such a thing before. Now he found that he needed to try only a little bit to locate energy fields here as well.

Sitting on the stool without any problem at all, Ian leaned forward to pick up one of the shoes.

"Though I spent the day with you last time, I found that only an hour and a half had passed at home. To make this all the more confusing, a week and an half has passed for me since I returned home from our last visit," he said, while turning the shoe in his hand for a good inspection.

"When I materialize myself in other realities," Katerina said, "I've noticed that the time frames never match up in the two worlds, despite the fact that their calendar cycles might appear to match. Even when returning to the same place, the time conversion is not consistent. It was one of the hardest things to get used to."

Ian slipped the shoe onto his foot ever so slowly, confident but not foolhardy. If fitting his new shoe went poorly, having his foot charged from all sides would provide a most unpleasant experience.

But Ian felt not even a pinprick. He tightened the latches on the top and stood upright, putting his weight down on his foot. Still no discomfort. A smile spread across his face.

Katerina clapped. "Bravo! I think you have the hang of being in our world."

Ian slipped on the second shoe, a little quicker this time, and walked about. "So, we're not going to confine ourselves to the city today?"

"That's right," she said, gathering some items into a couple of shoulder slings. "The Crone Mother has given me the day off from my duties, to show you about. We're going on a picnic, except we're not going to take food and drink because you can't take in substances from this reality."

"That's no reason for you to go hungry," Ian objected. "I wasn't hungry during the whole day I spent with you last time, Katerina. It seems that my hunger is still tied to my home location."

"Yes, that's true. You aren't here long enough, by your home time, for hunger to be a problem.

"As for me, I go through long fasts from time to time, Ian. I'll be just fine. Besides, I would not eat while my guest goes without."

Katerina handed Ian the shoulder strap of one of the slings she held. Paying too much attention to the conversation, Ian's hand slipped through the strap. The resulting shock surprised him and he jerked away. Katerina had also released the bag and it was falling to the floor. Without a thought, Ian leaned forward and grabbed for it. This time he caught the bag securely, without any unpleasant shock.

Rising upright from his feat, Ian looked up at Katerina and laughed. "Perhaps I need a little more practice in navigating surfaces in your world."

She just smiled and handed him some gloves. "Just in case you need to move a limb aside, or want to pick a flower."

Ian took his time and tucked the gloves under his belt. Their surfaces caused no tingling against his belly. His confidence was building.

"Why can't I learn to negotiate the field of other life forms, such as plants, so that I don't damage them without gloves?" he asked.

"You could, and may, but living things are a bit more complicated than nonliving entities."

Even after their previous walk, Ian was still amazed at the contrast between the environment within and outside Katerina's garden walls. The community that surrounded her garden was still comparatively quiet. It lacked the mechanical noises and booming stereos of his world, but it was very busy that early morning. A number of people were walking along the stone roadway between the lines of houses and gardens. Still more people were working or performing ritual motions in their gardens.

Just as before, people spoke to Ian and Katerina in a familiar and friendly manner. In fact, they treated Ian as if he was a cherished friend, returned from a long absence. He enjoyed their kindly attentions, but something about their genuine familiarity made him uneasy.

When he and Katerina came into a less populated section of the road, he brought up the subject.

"What were you saying last week—uh, yesterday—about how everyone knew who I was?"

Beautiful countryside spread out before them as far as Ian could see. In the distance there were a few clusters of trees and a lake-sized body of water. He and Katerina walked at a casual pace.

"Our community is very focused on the harmony of the Collective Consciousness. Anything related to maintaining that harmony is shared with every member."

Katerina veered off to the edge of the road, and leaned over to smell a particularly exotic looking flower that he had not seen in her garden. Ian waited for her.

"What does that have to do with me?"

Still bent down, she said, "Come smell this beautiful bloom, Ian."

He walked over to her and leaned forward, but his eyes were focused on Katerina, not on the flower. He came as close to her face as he dared without hitting the forcefield between them. She winked at him as he drew nearer to the blossom. A thoroughly foul odor overwhelmed his sense of smell. He stumbled back, unable to breathe.

"That's nasty!" Ian yelled, gasping for air.

Katerina pulled backward too, laughing while she also gasped for air. She had been holding her breath while pretending to smell the flower. Ian instinctively pushed out at her and the energy restriction knocked her over. She fell onto the grass lining the dirt road.

Appalled at his action, Ian reached to help pull Katerina up. She knew, though, that she wouldn't be able to take his well-intentioned hand. She waved his effort away, laughing so hard she could hardly speak. "No, no. You can't. I'm okay."

Taking her laughter as assurance that he had done her no harm, Ian stood up and put his hands on his hips. "How could something so beautiful smell so rank?"

Starting to calm down, Katerina sat up in the grass and said, "I grew up in an isolated area and always looked for another kid to move close by, to be my playmate. I used to imagine games I would play with my friend that never came."

"I'm so glad I could oblige. I'll be keeping an eye on Katerina the prankster from now on," Ian said, laughing.

Katerina brushed herself off. Ian handed her her sling, which had tumbled into the road. They continued on their way, but it took a while before Katerina could stop giggling. All would be quiet for a while, and Ian would think she had calmed down. Then, out of nowhere, another burst of laughter would interrupt the sounds of the scenery, birds, and small animals rushing through the tall grasses. It made him happy to spend time with another person who was equally at home in the ways of childhood and maturity.

Eventually, Katerina asked, "What was it you asked me before you found that flower?" She chuckled, but only quietly this time.

"You've made me forget," Ian said as he struggled to remember. "Oh, yes. What do I have to do with the 'harmony of the Collective Consciousness'?"

Katerina looked quite serious now. "Why do you think you have been visiting here?"

Trying to combine diplomacy with truthfulness, Ian replied, "Well, I had what I thought was a vision of you. From that first sight, I was possessed with a conviction that you and I shared something remarkable between us, something I had wanted to believe in but had never felt. I thought it was something beyond my ability to perceive. From that moment, no matter the cost, I wanted nothing more than to fully experience our connection."

"That was no vision," Katerina said. "You came here, to visit me."

"So I have come to realize since," he said.

"As a result, did you feel any motivation by an overwhelming commitment to something greater than yourself, Ian?"

Katerina's terminology sparked a bit of cynicism in him. "Only a commitment to you and the bond between us. I know of nothing greater, more worthy of devotion than such a love.

"If you are referring to serving the 'Collective,' I believe it is a greater honor to my Maker, or whatever you might title the Collective, to give myself wholly and happily to the truest inspirations of my core self, rather than to force myself into any high-minded abstractions."

Katerina stopped, and considered Ian with a puzzled look. He was a little concerned that her expression would turn to one of displeasure, but it went the way of a smile instead.

"True enough," Katerina said as she began to walk again.

Ever since Ian had regained consciousness on his return from the last trip, he had been eager to hear the Sisterhood's point of view on the *Vow* that Katerina and he used to contact each other.

"Katerina, one time when I came to visit you, you were at your desk. I don't think you knew I was there, and I couldn't get your attention.

"You had a piece of paper with the *Sacred Vow* on it, on top of your tome with the symbol that is the true name of the Sisterhood on the cover."

"The Crone symbol," Katerina said.

"What?" Ian asked.

"It's called the Crone symbol," she said.

"Okay," Ian said, and then continued where he left off. "When I was visiting that day, at one point you turned and looked me right in the face, before repeating the verse several times . . . Do you remember doing that?"

Katerina's look of surprise told Ian that she hadn't known he'd been present during such a recital.

"I've repeated the *Vow* numerous times. It's part of my function as the Crone Mother's understudy. I'm sorry I didn't know you were in the room. I don't know how that could have been possible."

"I wrote that exact verse down, Katerina, quite some time ago, after waking from a dream I could remember nothing about, except for the verse. Where did *you* get the V*ow*?"

"It was given through me as the medium in a Harmony Ceremony, with the Council of Crones."

"How long ago?" he asked.

"About six months ago," she said.

"My dream occurred much longer ago than that—several years, I think. I wrote down the verse and stored it away in my attic.

"I had completely forgotten it until I saw it in your house, and you repeated the verse to me.

"When I got home after that visitation, I dug through all my possessions until I found it . . . A friend of mine has repeatedly suggested that I find out why you and I are in contact with each other."

She cut in with a smile, "And you said there were no wise ones where you live."

"I was very mistaken about that. It's a good thing I have his help. It was his advice that kept me from getting totally lost, in the void, until you could redirect me from that very bad journey."

They walked in silence, and Ian thought of how thankful he was for Djalma, for Liz, and for Katerina.

"What's a Harmony Ceremony, Katerina?"

"It's a ceremony involving the Crone Elders, the Crone Mother, and her understudy. It's performed only for a specific need, so not many understudies ever have the opportunity. I've been very fortunate during my service to the Mother."

They continued strolling, stopping and starting again, looking at flowers, and wandering back and forth across the road.

"Can I ask the purpose of the ceremony?"

Katerina motioned to Ian to follow her onto a small, rough field path. Ian followed behind her.

"The ceremony is to allow the Collective Consciousness to communicate with the Crone Council through the medium of the understudy."

"What exactly are you referring to when you speak of the Collective Consciousness?"

"The supreme consciousness," she said. "The sum intelligence of all that exists.

"Do you believe in anything like that, Ian?"

"I believe there is a unified intelligence. I have heard it called by many names, and seen it used as the justification of many wrongs—as well as the motivation of some admirable humanity, I must admit. I don't claim to know this intelligence in any personal way. Not in any way that presumes I know what it needs or wants done."

"Wouldn't you imagine," she said, "that you are feeling familiar with it when you are in deep meditation, when you are particularly focused on nature, listening to certain music, in the company of special individuals, or anything that brings you a sense of serenity and expanded focus?"

Ian considered his experiences with such situations. "Yes. I do feel a profound connection with something that I might even call holy, but the thing is, I don't think what *It* wants necessarily translates into concepts my conscious mind comprehends, or would desire."

"Oh, I don't think it's as mysterious as that," Katerina replied. "I have every suspicion that whenever we feel the peace of our truest selves, we are experiencing the desires of the Collective Consciousness.

"Do you believe the universal intelligence is infallible, Ian?"

"That would depend on the connotations of the word *infallible*," he answered. "Most times there is an implication that *It* knows best, and therefore we must accept, perhaps even be thankful for what It has chosen. A natural disaster may be the best thing for the greater whole of nature, but I will always do my best not to be a victim of that kind of greater plan.

"Worse yet, such terms are generally used in context of the religious authorities being infallible in knowing best what *It* wants.

"I guess I would say I believe in the infallibility," Ian continued. "But don't accept that such intelligence expects me to blindly accept the first option that comes before me. The greater intelligence is also infallible in its having given me a means to choose."

The conversation was getting to a level of abstraction that made Ian a little uncomfortable. "Katerina, I'm fascinated by mystical, nature-based beliefs, but I have not spent a lifetime learning and living one. I am certain that 'to believe in the concept' and 'to know it with certainty, even to the core of one's spirit,' are very different realities."

Katerina didn't respond.

Ian didn't care much for the tangent they had gotten onto. He decided to change the subject.

"Are you getting tired of my questions?" he asked.

"Not at all, Ian."

Given permission, Ian gladly continued. "So, how did the Council know the Collective needed to communicate with them?"

"The Sisterhood is always in communication with the Collective. The natural ways of communication and healing are what we are trained for, all our lives.

"The Council understood that they needed to perform the Harmony Ceremony because they could feel the Collective was becoming increasingly out of balance."

"What if the Council was mistaken about their diagnosis, Katerina? My world has known situations where the religious authorities have invented an impending problem in order to validate themselves and justify exercising increased power over the populace."

"Such a mistaken or fabricated diagnosis has never happened here, but if it did, the Collective would not have responded through the Harmony Ceremony."

Ian's cynical nature continued, on a roll, and he spoke without considering what he was insinuating. "The only problem with that idea is the understudy could be part of the plot or, even if completely innocent, feel such pressure from the Council's preconception that she experiences a hysterical response corroborating the Council. She might believe she must surely hear from the Collective if she is at all competent as an understudy."

Katerina showed no hint of taking offense to his comments. Ian was initially unaware of whom his statement was accusing. The idea didn't come to mind until she gave him the warmest, kindest smile that he could imagine.

At first Ian was completely confused by her response. As he searched for what he had missed, he remembered just who the understudy was—and therefore who would have validated any incorrect assessment by the Crones.

Katerina's smile was all it took to wither his self-righteous rant. All things considered, Ian had to admit to himself that he wasn't worried about the integrity of the understudy during the recent Harmony Ceremony. Now his attention was diverted to concern over Katerina's reaction to his implied affront.

In what seemed a further show of her generous nature, probably knowing he was quiet only because of his embarrassment, but wished to continue hearing the entire story of Harmony Ceremony, Katerina didn't allow Ian to suffer in his silence for long.

"The only claimed knowledge about the problem in the Collective is there is an imbalance. If you ask the Crone Mother or any member of the Council what is the source of the imbalance, their response is 'It is not known,' which is also the standard, noncommittal answer given to any member who asks a question considered not to be within the questioner's scope of understanding.

"There is a legend, however, that every so often the life-force of the Collective begins to weaken because true bonding between couples—and people in general—is not being practiced throughout the infinite parallel worlds that make up the Collective Consciousness. Like all magic, when the magic of loving commitment is not believed in, or not being practiced, it begins to fade and die.

"Without devotion among the people, one to another, the Collective can have no radiance of life. It's said that the Council of Crones perceived the dwindling lifeforce and though they don't openly acknowledge the legend, they know the legend also says the Harmony Ceremony must be performed in such times to receive direction from the Collective.

"The Harmony Ceremony is one of very few ceremonial gatherings of the Council in which a member of the Sisterhood lower than the rank of council member or Crone Mother, such as an understudy, will ever be directly involved. In the Harmony Ceremony, the understudy is included as the psychic medium for the Collective. Few understudies over history have been blessed with receiving the message of the Collective."

"The Council, Crone Mother, and her understudy gather in a special location meditating and chanting for days, or however long it takes for the understudy to be moved by the Collective, whether by vision, voice, or other means. Once the understudy receives some message while in a trance, it is up to the Crone Mother to interpret the purpose within the message, and direct the understudy in the path to take after the Harmony.

"I received the verse of the *Sacred Vow*, and the Mother said it was to be chanted from within the cottage several times per day while I meditated. She said the vibrational characteristics of the verse would help to heal the bonding rift in the Collective, that it would help restore loving communication and commitment."

As Katerina went on with her tale, the little path wound its way up a grassy knoll, surrounded by some broadleaf, evergreen bushes. They crested the hill, and Ian was amazed to see elaborate stone formations on a flattened hilltop. It wasn't a singular ring formation of standing stones, as Ian had seen when traveling in certain countries back home. Although there was some circular distribution of the entire pattern, the arrangement was obviously made by several groupings of independent configurations.

The path they had followed to the hilltop split and headed into several different directions. The new paths connected all the minor groupings, and etched patterns of their own within the larger grouping. In the center of it all, there was a small mounded platform, a few feet higher than the rest of the hilltop.

Katerina waited for Ian to take it all in.

He finally spoke, "Is this our destination?"

"For now. We can stay here, or we can go on if you wish."

"I'd like to stay for a while, Katerina."

Ian followed her on one of the paths to the center mound. As they neared the center, the hair on his body stood on edge. The overall stone layout unquestionably focused energy toward this mound.

He turned to Katerina for explanation, "What is this place?"

"It's where I received the *Sacred Vow*."

Ian could see how one would be brought to some expanded state of awareness in this place. The air was still, yet he heard a roaring in his ears.

"You'll get used to the sensations in a moment," Katerina assured him as she spread a cloth on the grass in the center of the raised mound. "Let's rest a little while."

Ian's nervous system was getting a little more charged than he could stand. He felt a need to move from that particular location. Looking about somewhat frantically, he saw a stone grouping that made him feel comfortable on first sight of it.

Pointing to it, he asked, "Could we go over there?"

"Sure, if you want."

Katerina gathered her cloth and they made their way, following the most direct path available to that stone grouping. Once there, they spread the cloth again, and Ian sat with his back tight against one of the upright stones. It faced the sun and was angled slightly backwards, making an excellent backrest. Katerina sat beside Ian, just far enough away that neither of their forcefields pushed the other.

Silent and still, Ian was very comfortable, especially with Katerina so close. He could have sworn he felt some vibration in the stone when she leaned back.

He turned his head to look over at her. "It looks like we have come too far to get back to the village before dark, don't you think?"

"The weather will be mild enough for us to stay. We have sufficient wraps in our bags," she responded, turning to meet his gaze.

It wasn't the staying that concerned him. "But what if I have to go and you're here alone?"

"You won't have to leave tonight," she said, "not from this place. And if you did, I wouldn't be in any danger."

Ian had no interest in taking his focus away from Katerina's face, and she didn't look away. So, they watched each other's eyes for a time. She smiled and he mouthed a kiss to her.

As night approached, the shadows thrown about by the stones were surprisingly animated. A dramatically highlighted carving in one stone drew Ian's attention: it appeared to have moved. He hadn't really paid any attention to the carved patterns until now. It seemed that the placement of the stones and the patterns on them were intended to provide an illusion of movement.

"Katerina, is this movement of shadows on the stones something that I am imagining?"

"Not at all," she answered. "The patterns of the configurations, the shapes of the stones and their carvings are designed to manipulate light in times between day and night. The result is a three-dimensional mandala, a visual representation of the Collective."

Though Ian couldn't claim to know whether the mandala was an accurate representation of the Collective, the patterns that resulted had a consciousness-expanding effect all on their own.

He could imagine that a ceremony involving a number of spiritually progressed women, chanting away as the patterns changed, could have overpowering effects on a person.

"Does this stone or this grouping have a name, Katerina?"

She spoke reverently, "Every individual formation here has a grounding stone, in reference to the Motherworld, the world of the Sisterhood. The stone we are leaning against is the grounding stone for this formation."

"Not surprising," Ian said. As soon as he had touched this stone he had become calm, releasing the excited energy that had been building in him while they were on the center mound.

"This formation," she continued, "is the Onum Taar, in honor of Crone Tara. She was the first understudy to become the medium to the Collective during the first Harmony Ceremony, millennia ago. This is one of the oldest configurations.

"Would you like to know how the grouping is organized?"

"I would," Ian replied.

"The stone we are resting against, the second tallest of this group, is located at the base of the triangular configuration the group forms. It's opposite the longest side."

Ian leaned forward to look to one side of their backrest and consider the three stones. The angle directly opposite the longest side was slightly larger than ninety degrees, maybe about one hundred and ten degrees. Their stone leaned into the triangle's center by as much as twenty degrees. One of the remaining stones was shortest of the three. The third stone, taller than their backrest by at least ten percent, was perfectly erect.

"The other two stones represent two realities within the Collective," Katerina continued. "The smallest of the three stones also represents my home world in this configuration, as does the grounding stone.

"The tall stone over there," she leaned forward and pointed, "represents the Union reality."

Ian continued to look at the tall stone, even after Katerina repositioned herself against the grounding stone. "And what determines the Union reality?" he asked.

"That is the home of the second person to receive the communication from the Collective at any time of disharmony."

"The *Sacred Vow* verse was the Collective's communication this time, Katerina?"

"Yes," she responded. "It's not always the case, but the legend is that it was also the message received by Crone Tara during the first Harmony ceremony."

"So, why do you think I received the verse in a dream years ago?" Ian asked.

"Without being aware of what you were hearing, you were more sensitive to the needs of the Collective than even the Council of Crones. Years before the Harmony Ceremony, you were prepared to receive the Call. Without a doubt you are one of only two people identified by the Collective as being capable of helping resolve the fraying network of emotional bonds within the Collective.

"For all history of the Union, the complementary receiver of the Call—the receiver in the Union reality— has also been a member of a mystic order of a nature-based belief. It has always been believed that only masters in such a belief system are appropriately perceptive of the flow of energies in nature—therefore capable of becoming aware of the rift—and of the calls of the spiritual universe for assistance. That was why I thought you must have been teasing when you said you've never been a member of an order.

"Though the related legends in the Union orders have sometimes varied considerably from our belief, those orders were always familiar with the concept of the tear in the Collective. They also believed the coming together of two people selected by the Collective would provide a solution to the rift. Each culture had its own protocol and directions to follow once they were in contact."

"And I thought arranged marriages were contradictory to love," Ian said.

Katerina gave him a wary smile.

Ian returned to the topic. "That explains why everyone in

your village was so respectful to me and glad to see me," he said. "The only problem is, I don't know if I'm up to performing to their expectations."

"They all know the legends and are aware that the Council performed the Harmony Ceremony," Katerina said.

"How am I supposed to be able to help the Collective, Katerina, when I didn't even know it had a problem?"

Katerina didn't answer right away. She carefully weighed her words when she said, "*You know*. It's only that your cultural experience hasn't provided you with a means to express and understand what you know. You have already seen that you know much more than you consciously realize and are able to express in words."

"Katerina, my consciousness is manifesting me into your reality. But why could the children not see me before, and why can I not overcome the forcefield between us now?"

"As far as the forcefield goes: you, before me now, are as real and physical to all the people here as anyone else existing only here. The only difference in your physicality is that your form currently follows the definitions of your home reality, producing the forcefield that separates us. Because of the conflict in realities, there's some impact on your physical body in our home reality.

"Theoretically, we should be able to learn how to achieve full manifestation in multiple planes without conflict, even in realities that are not completely compatible. The Sisterhood accepts this as fact, but I haven't seen any documentation of successes in the archives.

"As for why no one saw you before, you were manifested to a much lesser degree when you were here before. Children aren't trained to recognize partially manifested energy fields, so they didn't notice you. Some people have trouble perceiving such fields, and find their presence disconcerting. Therefore, when I was in the company of others and you called to me from your tea, I projected myself to you rather than waiting for you to come to me."

Ian was glad Katerina had brought that up. Though it seemed irrelevant now, it was still an unanswered question for him. "So, why couldn't we have always visited at my location, so I wouldn't be in that state of a blurred image?"

"I could never properly manifest in your world either, Ian. And that was why we couldn't hear each other."

"Besides, it's the tradition for the Union courtship to take place on the Motherworld. The Council thought it necessary we follow tradition despite what seemed to be uncharacteristic circumstances in our situation."

"Courtship? Are you courting me?" he asked.

"Oh no," she said. "You are courting me." Her tone was playful, yet Ian knew she was serious about the distinction.

He smiled and nodded a single time. "Gladly."

As the darkness of night became deeper, their holographic mandala blurred. Bright stars in the sky were starting to provide a different show. Ian looked over at Katerina, who was still leaning against the grounding stone with him. She reached into her sling for a wrap. The temperature was dropping a little.

It was fortunate for Ian that Katerina wasn't shy about having him stare at her. His manners were better at home, but here her image was mesmerizing to him. Gazing at her gave him a sense of completeness within himself, and expanded perception of self.

"Katerina, it sounds as if you and I are supposed to come up with some solution to the weakening of the bonds of love in the Collective."

Katerina looked away. "That is true, according to the Sisterhood."

"Have you any ideas?" Ian asked.

"The legend is unwavering on one point: once two have heard the Call from the Collective, the discovery of the resolution is certain."

Katerina turned to look into Ian's face. Her fretful expression returned. It was clear to Ian that something about this conversation was troubling her.

Suddenly though, her expression softened and she said, "Have you ever heard a myth about the Rejoining of Spirit Mates?"

"Not that I know of. Please tell me the story, Katerina." Ian made himself comfortable, hoping that his relaxed responses would help her focus on less troubled thoughts.

"There is a belief held by some that, in human form, we are only half the persona we were in spirit—spirit being a nonphysical segmentation of the Absolute Intelligence into an individual consciousness. In spirit, we are both lover and beloved. This love felt by the spirit for its whole self is too pure, too perfect to be perceived by human senses or the human mind. This energy is too powerful to be contained in a single physical form.

"So, should this spirit choose to enter the physical realm, wishing to look into the eyes of love, to feel the touch of love, to know the longing of separation and the jubilation of rejoining, there is a price. When entering into the corporeal reality, they who have been forever one are thrown apart—sometimes across time, worlds, or realities.

"A thread that binds the two remains, but most of the time it isn't perceivable or comprehensible by the physical being's conscious minds. Sometimes awareness of the connection can be awakened by studies or activities that make one more aware of the core self. As is often the case, it's possible that the pair will not become aware—or if they do, they are unable to cross the distance between them. In these cases, their rejoining does not occur until both return to spirit.

"Therefore, any of these persons are only half the entity they were in spirit form. On those blessed occasions when one finds his or her spirit's true complement, he or she is rejoining their other half, becoming as close to whole as can be achieved in the physical form. The person has the opportunity to experience that which originally seduced spirit into physical form."

Ian rolled his upper body onto one side, so he could better face Katerina. The joy of what he was feeling kept him from responding immediately. Katerina turned her face to him.

"This is a *blessed occasion*," he said in a barely audible tone. "Yes, Ian."

Slowly, Ian raised his hand and traced the outlines of Katerina's face, "caressing" it without the benefit of touch. He kept his hand at a distance so there was no threat of initiating the forcefield that separated them. Katerina just stared into his eyes. When Ian slowly withdrew his hand, she raised her own, bringing it almost to meet his. With their palms facing each other, each staring into the other's eyes, they moved their hands closer, and closer. After a bit, Ian could feel the impending forcefield.

Katerina turned her focus to their hands. Ian followed her lead. They pushed their hands nearer each other by degrees. At some point, the increasing buildup of the forcefield caused them both to return their focus to each other's eyes. Simultaneously, they smiled silently, accepting that they wouldn't be able to grasp hands by force of longing. Reluctantly, they pulled their hands apart.

"It's good to see you again, Katerina."

"And you, my love, Ian."

For a time, they just stared at each other until Katerina spoke, "We don't have to find a solution, Ian. You and I are the solution."

"Now if all I have to do is to be with you, I can do that," Ian said, even though her tone let him know that something about that fact troubled her.

"This is just between you and me," she said. "For anyone else, we are feverishly seeking a solution, okay?"

"You can depend on that, Katerina."

"The Mother and Council would never tell the understudy the full story of the Harmony Ceremony. There are many things in the Sisterhood that the Elders believe better unknown to the Sisterhood body. I know some of the arcane details only because I've spent years studying the ancient texts, in the original language. It was Momma's hobby when she was the understudy, and she seems to have passed her fascination on to me."

Ian was glad to know Katerina didn't blindly follow all the

dictates and claims of the Sisterhood. He was also glad to hear that Katerina's mother had been an understudy. That implied that the position did not ensure a terminal absence of a partner.

"It's odd that the Council insists on that minor distinction," Ian said. "The difference between our finding a solution and our emotional tie being the solution hardly seems worth deception.

"So, how much of this Union mythology is just party line?"

"Party line?" she asked.

"Sorry. It's often a term about deceit, used a lot in my world. It refers to an official doctrine for the general masses, mostly absent of truth—at the very least, shy of the complete truth."

"Ah. The rift in the Collective is truth. Our being selected and brought together to correct that ill is truth. It is truth that the two come together on the Motherworld, enter into courtship and bond emotionally. Party line is this unique and sanctified love inspires the Union partners to find a solution that heals the Collective. Then they return to their separate realities."

"Except for the *returning*," he said, "it doesn't seem so bad. Why add the overhead of 'finding a solution'?"

"I don't, Ian. You have to remember, each person in the Union couple has historically been part of a society pursuing a purpose larger than the individual self. Perhaps the 'solution' was a means to divert the couple's focus from becoming completely lost in their affection for each other."

"Now that's starting to look like the basis of a party-line adjustment," Ian responded. "Control."

Katerina didn't participate in his disparaging indulgence. "It is truth that the Collective chooses two people, perhaps two who were one in spirit—if you so believe—but definitely who, at that time of need, are bonded through many lives within the Collective, and are known by the Collective to already have the strongest, most perfect union throughout all existence. They have always been in love with each other without knowing it. Being brought together by the Collective is only bringing together what their spirits know, though their conscious awareness could not perceive it.

"It has always been believed that by strengthening the couple's awareness of their bond all other emotional bonds throughout the Collective are made stronger. This *is* the solution to the rift.

"For me, believing that the Collective has infallible knowledge, I am greatly thankful for being brought together with my spiritual mate, or my spirit's complement."

Katerina's perspective completely diffused any of Ian's distrust of or resistance to the Union mythology. For the benefit of being brought to her, he could see why anyone would accept the rest of the belief-perpetuating ideology.

Ian didn't know how long he drifted in the radiance of his emotional response to Katerina's story. In time, his conscious mind fired up again.

"Do you need to sleep, Katerina? I assume that I don't."

"I don't need sleep tonight," she replied. "Neither of us will tire while we're on this platform. The energy flow here will not only maintain our needs, but also build up our lifeforce. After a time, the flow will become excessive, and we'll have to leave here. What we will have stored by that time will provide for our needs for days."

"A little nap and sharing a dream with you would have been fun," Ian said, "but I'm sure I have enough questions to talk the night away as well."

Ian slid down onto his back, spreading out over the cloth Katerina had placed on the ground, so his touch wouldn't kill all the grass in front of the stone. The moon was high and full.

Looking for You

Despite all the questions pressing in on Ian's mind, he was content to share a bit of undisturbed quiet, lying in the moonlight with Katerina. He may not have been able to touch the woman beside him, but he could "feel" her, her energy and her spirit. Since his first visit, maybe even before that visit, Ian had acknowledged her presence somewhere within himself. Undoubtedly, she was the one person who could make him whole.

"Katerina?"

"Yes?"

"After you received the *Sacred Vow*, and started to visit in order to look for the other person who knew of the *Vow*, did you encounter many worlds with manifestations of you and me?"

"I visited only realities where we had parallel lives," she said. "And I went specifically to our selves within those worlds."

"When we were not coming to each other in either of our

primary worlds, how do you suppose we visited only places where our parallel selves existed?" Ian asked. "And once in the reality, how did we specifically pinpoint their location?"

"Ian, I don't know how you were able to direct your destinations before the Vow," she replied. "For me, it was part of the information I received in the Harmony Ceremony."

"I find it hard to believe that I directed them at all!" Ian said.

"After the Harmony Ceremony," Katerina continued, "the Crone Mother said I was to enter into meditation in the understudy's cottage, and during the meditation repeat the *Sacred Vow*. Supposedly the use of the *Vow* is used to call to the Union partner who—also knowing of the *Vow* and the Union mythology—would respond to me. The meditator would then open a channel to allow me to visit his destination, or vice versa."

Hearing this, Ian again rolled over onto his side and propped his head up with his hand, staring down into Katerina's moonlit face. He suspected that he had been responding to her call long before she received the *Vow* in the Harmony Ceremony.

"During the ceremony, I was also provided the means to make a general search for your parallel selves. When the Collective delivers the means of communication—the *Vow* this time," she said, "it also provides the understudy knowledge of the general energetic resonance of the Union partner, and initial visions of the partner. This isn't enough to find the specific partner, but it can lead the understudy to any of the Union's manifestations. Because of the nonspecific nature, the understudy uses this information only as a backup connection. When there was no response to my chanting of the *Vow*, I began to search for you.

"Of course, none of the people that I encountered before I met you knew of the *Vow*, yet I continued my search. Except for my faith in the ways of the Crones, I would have thought the first trips pointless. I wasn't able to communicate with the people I visited, and they were unaware of my presence.

"I chanted the *Vow*, focused on the basic resonance of the

person I knew to be the Union partner, and followed my intuition to a connection. Sometimes I couldn't even enter into their world because I was blocked in transit. I could feel them there, but I couldn't coexist in their reality. Crone Mother said it was up to the spirit of each particular manifestation whether I would be allowed to enter his or her world, or how much I could communicate with people there.

"When you appeared, without my having heard your preliminary call to me with the *Vow*, I was amazed and joyful. I had begun to doubt I would be able to find you, and that was unacceptable. By my beliefs, I knew just how important you are to me, as well as to the Collective."

This woman was making Ian blush. Coming to the understanding that the definition of "his self" was much more than he had ever imagined, he yet again wondered what else about himself he was completely unaware of.

"Are the two receivers of the Call from the Collective always manifestations of our spirits?" he asked.

"Crone Mother said—"

He knew what was coming, so Ian piped in, "It is not known."

Katerina laughed at his irreverence.

Raising his hands in defense, he added, "No affront intended."

She just shook her head at him.

"Katerina, did you find it a little unnerving the first time you saw through another's eyes, realizing that the other person was an extension of yourself?"

"Not really," she said.

"Sisterhood training, I suppose."

She looked up at him and smiled. "That's right. There are many advantages."

"Do you think I could sign up?" he asked. "I could use some help in explaining some most unusual events in my life lately."

"No boys allowed, I'm afraid. But I might be able to provide some unofficial tutoring, personally."

"Better yet." Ian settled onto his back. "Does any legend

tell where the *Sacred Vow* came from originally, Katerina?"

In a playful voice, she responded, "Are you making fun of my culture?"

"Absolutely not, dear lady. I may not understand all you have introduced me to, but I don't disregard any of it. My own culture is very much in need of some defining legends and guiding rituals, without the distortion of political objective."

"Good," Katerina said. "It just so happens that there is a legend that says in ancient times the *Sacred Vow* was first shared between a wise King and his Crone Queen when they were about to be separated and did not know if they would ever meet again. He was to lead a group of his warriors into a spirit land, to subdue demons coming across the ethereal borders and stealing the spiritual essences of the King's people.

"None of our people, not even the Sisterhood had ever visited other realities at that time, and there was no way to be certain the King would be able to find his way back home. The Queen asked the Crone Council for a means to allow the couple to find each other no matter how far apart they might become.

"When either of the partnership calls with the *Vow*, the other will always hear."

"That's a wonderful legend," he said. "I think your culture is grand."

"Thank you, Ian."

"Could the King and Queen feel each other's hand when the *Vow* was invoked?"

"What?"

"You know, the part of the *Vow* that says 'expect me to reach beyond possibility and take your hand.' Could she feel his hand while he was off on his quest?"

Katerina was quiet before replying. "I don't know. It's never spoken of. That would make sense, if the *Vow* worked."

"What do you mean?" Ian protested. "Of course the *Vow* worked. I refuse to hear of a romantic legend with a magical chant that doesn't work."

She laughed.

"The King subdued the demons, came back to his Queen, and they lived happily ever after. Right?"

"I'm afraid not," Katerina replied. "The King had to stay forever in the Otherworld, keeping his people safe from further attack. The Queen and King maintained their connection only through the *Vow*, until each lived out their natural lives, performing their separate duties. Once both passed into the afterlife, they were reunited in the Land of Immortals."

"Hmmmph," Ian objected. "Maybe your culture could use some polish on the 'happily ever after' part of your legends.

"In my culture, when it appears a tragic couple will be forced to live out their lives separately until the afterlife, it is not unheard of for the couple to exercise a suicide pact, for a fast track to reunion."

"Oh, no!" Katerina so raised her voice in her distress that it made Ian jump. She sat upright in an instant, and stared down at him. "It is said, if mournful lovers take their own lives in order to reunite. Their efforts will end unhappily. Instead of bringing about reunion, their act may cause all their unions throughout the Collective to polarize and they will never again be together—anywhere!

"Such a tear in the heart of the Collective does a great damage to all. Our culture does not see such a pact as romantic at all."

"Katerina," Ian asked, "what do you believe happens to us after our death?"

"As you suggested when you spoke of a 'fast track to reunion,' I believe death is not a termination, but just another reality transfer."

"Since a person would be dead either way," Ian cut in, "why is it necessary that a lonely lover wait out his or her end in suffering, rather than help things along?"

Katerina's demeanor became sterner yet. "It is important that you await your designated time, for only then can you be certain that your energy signature will be correct to open the portal intended to carry you to your optimum destination, the return to your whole self. The body is dead, but not the person. The corporeal self of a single reality field becomes inert, finally altering its energy signature, and therefore the collective signature of the flanking area.

"You have manifested a body that sits at home, with a cup of tea while we visit together," she continued. "The energy signature is all that is required for this reality transfer to occur, but it is a vital part of the energetic mix. The signature of the body is required at the time of the reality transfer in death."

"It is a corpse, whether through suicide or natural death," Ian argued.

"But it would resonate differently," she stressed, "by the different experiences of the person."

"Yes, yes, I suppose I can see that the destination would be affected by the conditions of the environment," Ian replied, trying to calm her a little. "Many ancient cultures back home have processes by which the living will carry on a ritual to assist the recently deceased in their afterlife transference."

Katerina smiled. "Mine as well," she said. "And in that process they are helping to create a collective energy signature in the vicinity of the passing spirit that opens the channel for the individual's journey."

Ian was quiet for only a short while. Trying to further defuse the seriousness of the conversation, he said, "I'll say, your culture really knows how to do up the tragic love story."

His attempt at humor failed miserably. Katerina looked more distressed than before.

"It's not 'just a story', Ian. It's the way of things. All pairings between a couple and their parallels could be lost forever! And the result would not be just two lonely singles carrying out their lives elsewhere. Think about an empty eternity, never complete, without the hope of the sensation of the most fulfilling love. Complete and utter emptiness!

"No one capable of love would damn even their most hated foe with such a torment, much less someone with whom they shared love!"

"All right, all right Katerina. I promise. I understand, and I won't forget." Ian was maneuvering to sit upright, getting out from under her glare.

Katerina's fervor had driven the fear home for Ian. She so believed in this threat that he could not help but take that belief on himself, out of his affection for her.

"One other thing Katerina," he said. "When the King and Queen met again, were they in another world as compatible physical forms or as spirits?"

She went directly to answering the intention of his question. "The Union partners may become spirit, form, or a combination of the two; spirit is limitless. In either case, it is promised that the couple will be together, and compatible."

After a little while, the tension seemed to drain from Katerina's body. Eventually she reclined against the stone, and Ian followed suit.

They rested silently, looking at the stars. After thinking the whole story over a bit, Ian was ready to start his inquiries from a different perspective.

"Didn't you say the *Sacred Vow* is not always the direction received during the Harmony Ceremony?"

"That's right. Why?" she answered.

"After hearing the legend of the *Sacred Vow*, such an eternal commitment between King and Queen seems like the most perfect solution for the disintegrating devotion within the Collective."

"True," Katerina said as she slowly sat upright and began to put things into her shoulder sling. "Are you ready to walk again, Ian?"

"Sure," he said, and he rose to his feet. He hadn't realized it, but he was getting a little fidgety. "Have we had our full charge of energy?"

"I think so. And it's a good night for walking," she said.

The moon was so bright they had no problem seeing. In fact, Ian was glad he would be seeing some of the landscape in the moonlight. When they got down from the mound, it was obvious they were not heading in the way that they had come.

"Would you like to visit my parents?" Katerina asked. "They live in the opposite direction of my village."

"Sure. Visiting the prospective in-laws? That sounds like things are getting rather serious between us. Perhaps we should start looking for a home together."

Katerina just smiled his way.

"I'm not kidding," Ian said. "Of course, you'd have to find new work and move from your current residence—no partners allowed for understudies, and all that—I'd be glad to move to your world, even if I am never able to touch you. Being with you is enough."

Katerina didn't give him any response at all. She never rejected his flirtations, but she also rarely responded to them.

They continued their leisurely walk. It seemed there was no time limit on their objective. Some night bird sang a mournful tune. A long way over the horizon, Ian could now see the crests of a few hills, maybe even small mountains.

"Katerina, you said you used the *Vow* to open a channel to your destinations, and then your training helped you use the provided energetic resonance to pinpoint the location. Do you have any speculations on how I was able to visit you, and my other locations, before using the *Vow*?"

"I suspect the Crones would say that you have been developing the aptitude, even though you didn't realize it. Did you use some other chant to assist you?"

"No," Ian replied. "My learned friend Djalma claimed I first constructed a portal for the visiting, without being aware I was doing so. He also thought it was something I had been attempting for a long time."

"I'm not surprised that you found a way even without a brotherhood to guide you, Ian. Such a talent is either in a person's nature, or it is not. Not every female here becomes a member of the Sisterhood. Some aren't inclined, or find our ways and teachings incompatible to their true nature."

Speaking of the portal made Ian remember the days when both he and Katerina became ill. "Was there a time after you started to visit me, while our visits were still silent, that your health began failing?"

"For a while," she answered.

Ian was flooded with remorse that he could have harmed her with his feeble attempts to make contact. "Why didn't you protect yourself, Katerina, and stop the connection?"

She gently cut him off. "I was in no real danger. The Sisters cared for me. Besides, the connection was too important. By that time, I knew who you were, and I knew there was a purpose for the manner of your visits."

Regardless of her assurance, it took a while before Ian could let go of his regret. At one point, he caught a whiff of one of Katerina's little stink flowers. He chuckled to himself.

Then he began his questions again. "When I didn't use the *Vow*, I would end up anywhere, and I managed to go to no destination twice. How is it that using the *Vow* brings me to you?"

"I hear the *Vow* and respond to you by repeating the *Vow* myself," Katerina replied. "You must subconsciously use my repetition of the *Vow* to hone in on my location, opening your perception to the presence of my world and me. The Mother told me early on to reply by repeating the *Vow* whenever I feel the Union use it.

"Before you used the *Vow*, I could not make a full connection to your reality, whether I came to you or you came here. That was why we couldn't hear each other. Maybe it had something to do with the way your portal worked."

"Something went wrong with the portal," Ian said. "And it stopped working altogether. Djalma believed I then became my own portal, though he didn't understand how it worked. I had no idea how it worked either."

"That was a major accomplishment, Ian."

"Do you audibly hear me speak the *Vow*, Katerina?"

"Well, not exactly *hear*. It's more like I feel the vibration of it within myself," she answered.

"What if you're asleep?"

"I've always been awakened," she said.

They veered off onto a less traveled path. It was opportune that daylight was finding its way to them at this time.

"When you met our parallels, Katerina, were they always together, if they had partners?" Ian thought of the unfortunate Katerina who had fought to keep her child.

"Sometimes they're with other partners, and sometimes alone," she replied. "There are parallel lives where they both existed in the reality but were not together.

"I asked the Crone Mother why these two spirits were so frequently paired. All she said was 'It is not known.' She did say not all pairings are as prolific as ours seemed to be. It isn't the official perspective of the Sisterhood, but some speculate that such an abundance of pairings make a powerful union, and may be particularly helpful in balancing the Collective."

Katerina stopped to tighten her laces. Without thinking about it, Ian continued on the path. He was feeling a surge of playful energy. He felt like an impish kid, searching for some mischief to get into. As he heard Katerina come up behind him, he veered over to the side of the path, blocking her way.

"You!" Katerina responded and reached to lightly touch the back of his knee.

Ian felt a little shock. Of course, this made him quickstep down the path. "Hoo-hooo. That's not nice, Katerina."

"Then behave yourself," she said. "We're almost home."

"Our home? So you *do* care."

"My parents' home. Be nice," she scolded.

"Not until you agree to tell them we're moving in together," Ian teased.

Katerina tried to take the lead, and Ian cut her off again. There was no rationale to his behavior. He just wanted to play with her.

As Ian blocked Katerina's second attempt to go around, she didn't yield and used the forcefield between them to her advantage. When she leaned into him, Ian's body automatically withdrew from the initial charge, before he could override the involuntary response. They both started to laugh. As smooth as a trained martial artist, Katerina followed through by throwing her hips his direction, giving him a full jolt while simultaneously knocking Ian off his center of balance. His muscles jerked sharply and he went tumbling into the tall grass lining the path.

He knew some farmer or later traveler was going to be wondering what miniature alien spacecraft had landed here and killed this swath of healthy grass. Laughing uncontrollably, Ian just lay there, unable to rise.

"That's no way to treat the man you're bringing home to meet the parents. Now I will have grass stain all over my clothes." He looked about himself. "Or, dead grass stain."

Katerina stood on the path, laughing, with hands on her hips, victorious. "That will teach you not to be mean," she laughed.

Someone ran by Ian, bellowing at the top of his lungs, and snatched Katerina from the ground. She laughed and spun around and around, held tightly in the arms of a lean man with unruly gray hair. Before Ian could gather his wits and get up from the ground, another screaming runner went by, crashing into the two of them. This woman looked so much like an older Katerina that he suddenly knew these people had to be her mother and father.

Ian scrambled to his feet. No one seemed to notice his presence, but he didn't mind. He was vicariously enjoying the expressions of love and joy. He guessed that Katerina did not get to visit home nearly as often as she or her parents would have liked. He could tell her parents missed her dearly. She was well loved in this household.

After a while, Ian started to get a little uncomfortable about being ignored. His seeming invisibility made him wonder if perhaps he was already on his way back to the couch at home, but Katerina eventually brought him to their attention.

"Momma, Papa, this is Ian. Ian, these are my parents, Nola and Yannick."

Her father's arm shot out to greet him. "Welcome—"

Katerina was quick to step into its path. Yannick was obviously confused. Ian was even more confused when Katerina's parents found her explanation of him to be nothing out of the ordinary.

Did everyone in this place deal with people from other realities?

Yannick greeted Ian again, with a slight bow of the head this time. "Welcome, Ian. Thank you for kidnapping our Katerina from the Sisterhood and bringing her home."

"Papa!" Reprovingly, Katerina pushed hard against his shoulder. He swayed like a willow in the wind, breaking out in laughter, but he didn't move a step.

"I am honored, Yannick, Nola, to visit your home, and to know your daughter." Ian bowed his head in reverence, as one would honor a master in the Orient after instruction. He didn't know why he thought it was the right thing to do.

Nola welcomed him. "Please come into our home."

Katerina grabbed each of her parents by an arm and the three of them led the way to the door, side by side.

Her parents' garden was less elaborate than Katerina's or the Crone Mother's, but it was no less magically inspired. There was a beautiful balance in every element. The house was built of rustic stone and timber, but carefully crafted. Already Ian was charmed with the detail. He could see this was the work of a couple who loved their life together.

They were entering into a butler's pantry and mudroom. The thick exterior wooden door was ornate with carvings of symbols and adornment. Just inside, against one wall, herbs hung from the ceiling. Outer garments hung on another portion of the wall. Many shelves on the opposite wall held pottery jugs full of food.

Nola, Yannick, and Katerina removed their shoes and put them in a rack. Ian followed their example. One by one, Katerina and her parents disappeared through an interior door, about midway down the length of the mudroom. As Ian turned to go through the door, he felt the need to use the doorframe for support. Entering the kitchen, he saw an arrangement of flowers on a small, brightly painted dining table. He felt certain they were some of the same he'd seen just before smelling Katerina's "stink flower" in the field during the night before.

Stopping to take in the warm sights of the kitchen, he heard Katerina call his name.

"Ian?"

The rush came on Ian quickly. All he could say was, "I think I have to go now."

The calendar clock on the end table said Ian had been gone for three days. He had severe hunger pains, and he was noticeably weak when he tried to rise up from the couch.

Going Home

Going Home

Seeing Katerina with her family gave Ian a desire to be with his own. Not the family he was born to, but the family he was naturally drawn to, Liz and Djalma. Once his strength was back, Ian took off for the mountains. It had been quite a while since he had been in touch with them, and he knew they would be concerned about him.

Comfortable that Katerina was busy and cared for in her parents' home, Ian felt it was a good time for a road trip. There was no need to rush back to her. Besides, he needed confirmation from Djalma on some suspicions that he had developed.

The drive up into the mountains gladdened Ian's heart. Ian was going again to visit his dearest friends in this world. Liz and Djalma's support and love were always a source of comfort to him.

The beautiful countryside along the road reminded Ian of his recent walk with Katerina. Both areas radiated with the power and majesty of nature. Here in the mountains most of the residents seemed to honor the land appropriately.

Riding along, Ian had to laugh when he realized he was actually eager to announce his intention of commitment to Katerina. His visit to Liz and Djalma was complementary to meeting Katerina's parents, though Katerina could not be with him. He was indeed seeking Liz and Djalma's blessing for his union with her.

That would make his "father" little more than half his age, an under-thirty, culturally displaced Taoist hermit, and his "mother," a seventy-plus-year-old chatelaine and mystic. As odd as the arrangement may have originally sat on his conscious mind, Ian had to admit Liz and Djalma did watch over him to whatever extent he would allow. For all his days, Ian hoped he would be wise enough to take his guidance from whomever had the skills and the willingness to provide it.

When he pulled into the driveway of Liz's B&B, there were "Mom" and "Pop" on the second-floor deck. Ian laughed again, now solely from the joy of their friendship. He had not called ahead, but wasn't surprised they were awaiting him. It could have been coincidence, but Ian suspected that Katerina's Sisterhood had nothing on the magic of his own little "hood."

"The wanderer of realities has finally come home again," Djalma called out as Ian got out of the car.

"It's good to see you, sweetie. You pay him no mind," Liz said, scolding Djalma.

Ian went up the stairs and hugged both of them tightly. It was a glorious blessing to be able to wrap his arms around the ones he loved. As he moved toward his young friend, he saw a look in Djalma's eye that gave him a hint of what he had come to verify. He wouldn't have been able to read Djalma's unintentional reaction except for all he had learned in his recent visits to Katerina. Djalma would never impose his knowledge.

Now it was Ian's turn to walk with his own family toward the family kitchen. He looked forward to what he knew Liz would provide—the most comforting tea and sweets. How he had needed this trip!

"How is Miss Katerina, darlin'?" Liz asked as she was setting up the tea service.

"Thank you for asking, Liz." Ian never realized how much something he would have previously taken as trivial conversation could mean. "She's doing well. When I left her, she was at her father and mother's home in the countryside."

"Do you always return to her now?" Djalma asked.

"Yes, I return only to the Katerina of my tea visions. Meditating and repeating the *Vow* brings me back to her, wherever she is, every time. Somehow she's able to perceive my intended contact and assists my arrival—just as you suggested, Djalma. Katerina says that when she feels the attempt to contact, she repeats the *Vow*. I can then home in on her location."

"Have a seat at the table, boys." Liz grandly carried her tea service to the dining room. Ian had tried before to carry it for her, but she would get absolutely offended. The most she would allow anyone to do in return was to appreciate her efforts.

"Oh, Liz. I could stay with you and enjoy these teas forever," Ian said truthfully.

Liz's face brightened. "Or perhaps just between your visits with Katerina?"

They sat with their tea for several hours, and Ian told his family what he had experienced in his recent visits, what Katerina had taught him, and how he felt about it all. Liz and Djalma were affable and appeared to enjoy hearing his tales as much as he enjoyed recounting them. They laughed, touched each other's hands, and passed and ate the tea and sweets.

During the course of the afternoon, Ian felt his energy rise to levels much higher than it had been since his return from Katerina's parents' home. This visit, he felt certain, was part of his necessary rejuvenation in preparation of his next trip to Katerina.

"Are you going back today, Ian?" Liz noticed it was getting time for him to return if that was his plan.

Ian said sheepishly, "Well, if I can find a place to stay, I thought I would remain at least a few days."

"Place to stay? Don't be silly!" Liz's voice rose.

"I don't want to assume," Ian replied. "You might have guests booked in your suites."

"Even if I had a full house, sweetie, I always have my private living quarters. You could sleep on the couch if worse came to worst."

Ian reached over and squeezed her hand. "Thank you, Liz. I love you."

Liz blushed a bit. Ian thought he had never seen her even slightly lose her composure before. He was glad he had told her how he felt. It felt important.

Liz quickly recovered and gave Ian a loving smile. "I am sure Djalma would let you sleep on one of his benches if it had to be."

I'd feel safer in a sleeping bag on his porch, Ian thought. I'd be dreaming all night of a hail of books crushing me.

Looking over at Djalma, Ian saw he was receiving a bit of a teasing smile and nod. Undoubtedly, Djalma knew Ian's reservations.

"It so happens I have space for you to have a room of your own. A little later, you can get your things and I'll take you up."

"Thank you, Liz," Ian said. "Before it gets too dark, I'd like to take a walk with Djalma—as soon as I've helped you clean up." He looked over to Djalma. "If you have time."

"Sure, I have time, Ian," Djalma replied.

Djalma and Ian were able to convince Liz to let them wash the dishes after tea. She actually seemed to like having the two guys washing and drying the dishes. Ian and Djalma joked and talked, while Liz sat on a stool keeping an eye on them. Out of the corner of his eye, Ian once saw her leaning back with a big smile on her face, arms crossed. She looked like she couldn't have been more content.

Once their chores were done, Djalma and Ian went out the door.

"Any place in mind, Ian?" Djalma asked.

"No, just a walk, my friend," he replied. "I would be glad to walk to your house, or anywhere you need to go. I just need a little walk and talk."

Djalma didn't express any preference and merely followed Ian's lead. They headed toward the little cabin in the forest.

"I've learned a few things during my visits with Katerina."

"I'll say," Djalma spoke up. "You've been making some amazing progress during the short time I've known you."

There seemed little reason not to get to the point, so Ian continued. "I can often see energy auras now, Djalma—here in this world. And I know the latest trips to Katerina are taking a considerable toll on my energetic signature."

Djalma stopped and looked him hard in the face. Ian got the idea there was an implied "*and?*"

Ian smiled, reached out, and put his hand on Djalma's shoulder. "Am I right about the toll?"

The sternness of Djalma's expression melted into one of concern. "How do you feel?"

"I have to admit, I am no longer completely present in this world, Djalma." Ian dropped his arm and started to walk slowly toward his friend's cabin. It felt better for him to be active. An elevated heart and breath rate made him feel more tangible.

"It seems that each visit puts me in a position where I'm less bonded to this reality. I wouldn't mind it so much, except I see no indication that I'm acquiring any secure foothold in Katerina's world either. My guess is that I have a limited number of transmissions available to me. If I exceed that limit, my existence will be evenly spread between the two places, belonging to or existing in neither."

The two men walked silently for a ways.

"I don't feel bad," Ian finally said. "Except for the increased awareness I've acquired recently, I'd have no idea of a problem. I could just go on with my life.

"Unless I can find a way to overcome this limitation, I think I will soon see Katerina for my last time. The idea of eventually being stuck here, never able to return to her again, makes me feel deathly ill. I'm almost more inclined to accept being lost in the void."

Djalma spoke softly, sympathetically, "But you know it's never that simple."

"Do you know anything that might help me?" Ian asked.

This time Djalma rested a hand against Ian's shoulder blade as they walked. "I'll look for information, and I'll do everything I can to help, Ian. But, I suspect there are few people in this world who would have any idea how to cope with this experience."

Feeling a resurgence of hopelessness, Ian lowered his head.

Picking up the tone of his voice, Djalma patted Ian on the shoulder. "Not to worry. We'll find something. In addition, we have Katerina on our side. I suspect she knows a thing or two about such mysteries."

Audience

That night Ian found out what would happen if Katerina was not available to return his call of the Vow. At least, he found that he would no longer drift off into some indiscriminate parallel existence.

He was trying to visit Katerina, but instead was surprised with the sensation of dangling near the high ceiling of a massive ceremonial room. It was rather dark, but Ian could tell he was facing a flamboyant throne on a platform, with lesser thrones on either side.

Ian just floated there, sensing that he was invisible.

The main throne became illuminated, and so did a runway leading from the door in front of the throne. A regal woman in flowing robes came through a concealed opening behind the largest of the thrones. Several attending women followed. Once the stately woman sat, the attending women adjusted her garments and her headdress.

The sound of an opening door and footsteps from behind him caught Ian's attention. He looked to see Katerina moving toward the throne. As she passed under him, Ian and Katerina began to move forward simultaneously. As Ian moved forward, he was moving closer to the floor. Katerina lowered herself to her knees once she was immediately in front of the dais. Ian floated about fifteen feet above her.

This woman on the platform has to be the Crone Mother, Ian thought. He was sorry to see that Katerina had not remained with her parents.

Though feeling the need to protect Katerina, his old predicament of being merely a spectator made that impossible. In this case, however, he felt certain his invisibility was probably to their mutual advantage.

"Highness," Katerina said.

"Rise, child, and face your Mother."

Katerina rose from the ceremonial bow. Though standing, she did not look into the face of the Crone Mother.

"I apologize for having not realized the way to mend the Collective, Crone Mother."

"It is not necessary that you realize the solution. The Collective moves all those involved in the way it desires. Whether it is apparent to you or not, you have done all that the Collective requires of you."

"Yes, Crone Mother."

"Where is your Union partner, Katerina?"

"I think he recovers in his world, Crone Mother."

"He is slow in his returns to our reality," the Matriarch said disapprovingly. "This process should not have taken months. In all of our history there has never been such a prolonged bonding."

"Ian—" Katerina started.

The Crone Mother interrupted, "That is his name, Ian?"

"Yes, Crone Mother."

"Relax, child. This is not a formal audience."

"Yes, Mother. Ian is without instruction and training. He is without the support and benefit of belonging to an order. This has never been the case in any Union before."

Ian didn't know why Katerina put so much importance on his not being part of an order. Apparently, the Crone Mother did not find it so important.

"Yet he is the one who heard the Call, who heard the *Vow*." By her tone and her mannerisms, it seemed the Crone Mother almost considered him an unsuitable Union for Katerina.

"Yes, Mother. But what if he needs the support of an order after the bonding?"

The Crone Mother looked Katerina over suspiciously, as if believing by sight she could discern some added meaning in the question.

"Why would he?" the Crone Mother asked.

"He may not," Katerina said, "but what if he did?"

"That is not your concern, Katerina. The Collective chose Ian, so he has obviously had sufficient instruction. The Collective is the definition of all reality; it is incapable of mistake. The bonding will proceed, and we can only accept that what happens afterward is the design of the Collective."

Katerina played her part as expected. She gave no indication of knowing the true solution to the Collective rift.

"But, Mother, I have . . . we have, Ian and I . . . have not been inspired with a solution," Katerina pleaded. "We have been together only for a few days."

The Crone Mother raised her voice impatiently. "The Sisterhood does not define the timeline. It will not be extended!"

Katerina lowered her head in response to the reproach.

Then the Crone Mother softened her tone. It appeared to Ian that the Matriarch realized that the emotion of her response revealed more than she intended.

"Don't worry, Katerina. You have never failed in your duties to the Sisterhood. It will be the same this time. It is impossible for you to fail."

The Crone Mother looked about the room, as if she had lost something. At one point, she looked up. Ian could have sworn she looked right at him. If she was indeed looking intentionally in his direction, she gave no indication that she recognized his presence.

"You were visiting your birth mother recently?"

"Yes, Mother."

"How is my old understudy Nola?"

"She is well, Mother."

"And her . . . partner?"

The broken pattern and little twist of the head as she said "partner" made it evident the Crone Mother had no particular affection for Katerina's father. Ian was glad to see he was in good company with the Crone Mother's disdain.

The Crone Mother drifted off into distraction, looking about the room again. "You are the only understudy in the history of the Sisterhood who has been even more talented than your birth mother, Katerina."

"Thank you, Mother." Katerina spoke softly. It was evident she was well experienced in soothing this sensitive issue with the Matriarch.

"Not every understudy progresses to lead the Order," the old woman said. She was silent for a moment before continuing. "But Nola could have been Crone Mother, and I would have taken my leave before now."

Katerina interjected softly, smoothly, "She will forever love and serve the Sisterhood faithfully."

The Crone Mother continued absentmindedly, "She has the knowing of The Nature . . ." The Matriarch stopped abruptly and looked down at Katerina. "Not so much as she loves her man from the Stone Mountains!"

"Thanks be that the Sisterhood allows for both," Katerina said defensively. "My father is wise, kind, and loving to my mother. She is happy. And it is written that true joy serves the Collective best."

The Crone Mother continued to stare at Katerina, admonishing her for the implied contradiction. "He is a strange man from a strange people."

"But, Mother," Katerina responded, "I have heard members of the Sisterhood say my father's people also know The Nature."

The Crone Mother's reply was sharp and quick. "Their ways are not our ways!"

Aware that this part of the conversation was over, Katerina dropped her head. No other sound was made until the ring of the Crone Mother's retort faded from the hall.

The Matriarch looked about the room, and then made an obvious attempt for a more positive focus. "But that is of no matter to me now," she said as she waved her hand to one side in the air. "From that joining, I have had the most talented understudy ever known to our order." Her words trailed to a barely audible level by the end of the sentence. She was silent for a moment. Without looking at Katerina, the old woman quietly continued, "You would have made an excellent Crone Mother."

Katerina responded in a reverential tone. "I still hope to have the honor of so serving the Sisterhood one day, Mother."

Apparently lost in her own thoughts, the Crone Mother was slow to respond. "What? Oh, yes. And we all hope that for you, my dear."

Ian got the impression the Matriarch was not being forthright—perhaps because everything surrounding the Union arrangement to that point had been less than straightforward. How he distrusted that old woman!

In a kinder tone, having regained her focus, the Crone Mother spoke. "Why have you asked to see me officially today? What can I do for you, my dear child?"

Katerina rose fully and looked into the Crone Mother's face.

"I have come first to petition the Council on Ian's behalf."

"Let us hear your petition, Sister." The Crone Mother's voice and demeanor became rigidly ceremonial.

Whether it was always required in a petition, or was in response to the Mother's behavior, Katerina spoke formally: "I, Sister of the Knowing rank, Katerina, understudy to the Crone Mother, receiver of—"

The Crone Mother waived her hand upward to cut short Katerina's reminders of her achievements.

Katerina continued, "I petition the Crone Council for their energetic healing and support of Ian, Union in the mending of the Collective imbalance this year of the History of the Sisterhood."

"Why do you believe this is necessary, Katerina?"

"Because, Crone Mother, even after we spent six hours on the Mound during his last visit, Ian was forced to retreat to his world less than three hours later."

"The time on the Mound should have been vitalizing enough to serve him for days at least. Only three hours?" the Crone Mother asked, surprisingly concerned.

"Yes, Crone Mother. The resonances of our realities have proven very incompatible, except in marginal interaction. When I visited his homeland, only the support of the Sisterhood allowed me to avoid toxic consequences. As I pointed out before, Ian does not have an order to assist him in such ways. So it is even harder on him than it was on me.

"If the Council performs ritual Cleansing Ceremony in Ian's behalf, he would be able to extend his stay."

The Crone Mother leaned back into her chair, surprised by the request. "That is a very demanding, and possibly dangerous, ceremony, Sister."

"Yes, I know, Crone Mother."

"Why do you think the Union needs to spend more time in our world?" the Mother asked.

"So, Crone Mother, Ian and I can perform for the Collective the task for which we were specifically called together."

Ian did not like the furtive look on the Crone Mother's face.

"The Collective ensures that the Union remains in the Motherworld no longer and no less than is required for the mending.

"Your petition is denied. I assure you, as your Crone Mother, that the Collective mending is almost complete. The process has no need of an extension in his stay."

"Then I make the request as part of my second petition, Crone Mother."

Staring hard at Katerina, the Mother seemed to defy her understudy's audacity.

Without any show of any disheartenment from the first denial, Katerina stood tall, and daring. "I, Sister of the Knowing rank, Katerina, understudy—"

Again the Crone Mother cut her short with a wave of the hand.

"—petition the Crone Council on my own behalf, for the ritual Cleansing of the Collective Union, Ian, so that he may—"

"What do you think you are doing, Sister?" bellowed the Crone Mother, but Katerina did not falter.

"—remain in the Motherworld until a way can be discovered for him to reside permanently here as my committed partner—"

Her words were drowned out by the screeching Mother "Be very careful, Sister!"

Up on her feet, fingers digging into the armrest of the throne, the Crone Mother looked as if she were about to jump on top of Katerina.

"Don't make the same mistake your mother did, girl."

Katerina was unwavering but respectfully silent. She had made her petition and knew there was nothing to do now but wait for the response.

Still bearing down on Katerina, the Crone Mother said, "I am giving you this opportunity to withdraw or reword your foolish petition. What say you?"

Without raising her voice, Katerina said, "Crone Mother, I reverently ask that you consider my petition as originally presented."

"He is the Union of the Collective. If the Collective had ever desired or required any Union partner to remain in the Motherworld, it would have made information to allow such a thing available to the Sisterhood by now."

"Perhaps the Collective has already provided the means to allow the Union to stay in the Motherworld," Katerina said. "But we have never utilized the resources because the possibility was precluded by our fixed perceptions."

"You are bordering on heresy, Sister! You would do well to

reign in your emotions. I suppose your obsessive concern for this Ian is to be expected. It is regrettable, but not surprising. For that we will absolve you of your trespasses."

Ian wanted to yell to Katerina, "I don't need or want their help!"

"But Mother," Katerina said, slipping from protocol. "If Ian and I are called by the Collective to mend the rift, would it not be to the benefit of that purpose for the Sisterhood to offer the support other Unions would otherwise have? This could be just the assistance needed to acquire the solution we have been searching for."

The Crone Mother's anger overcame her diplomacy, which to Ian confirmed the Sisterhood's intentional deception.

"You cannot convince me that you are as naïve as you present yourself, Sister. He is not allowed here to help you search for a solution. You and he *are* the solution. The pair of you have always been committed to one another. You have been allowed together to symbolically finalize the Union. And I can see by your devotion to him that the Joining is complete!

"This is The Nature of the Collective healing: two realities come together to bond, and then return to their separate worlds. Only by the tie across the separateness is the rift mended."

The Crone Mother turned quickly away from Katerina and her robes flew about like a great tempest as she rushed off the platform, screaming, "The Union will not be allowed to remain in, or to revisit, the Motherworld!"

Ian did not remember returning home, but he was awakened from sleep with Djalma pounding on the door and calling out to him.

"Wake up, Ian. Are you still dreaming? Wake up," Djalma was yelling. "I think we may have something to work with. I have just had a vivid dream about a white-haired man named Yannick."

Making Plans

Despite the Crone Mother's words, Ian was determined to try to return. If she proved able to enforce her decree, then he hoped Katerina would be able to come to him. Maybe Katerina's visitation to his world was outside the old Matriarch's domain.

He appeared back at Yannick and Nola's house. Ian was happy to see that Katerina had returned there also.

Ian heard the words, "This time I'm not letting you leave before I know your intentions for my daughter."

As visual clarity came to him, Ian realized he was sitting in a chair, and Yannick was sitting in front of him, smiling widely.

After giving Ian enough time to become fully cognizant, Yannick said, "Welcome back, Ian."

He heard two women laugh and recognized one of the voices as Katerina. Ian looked around for her and saw her standing just behind him.

"How are you doing, dear one?" Katerina asked.

"I could just kiss you, Katerina."

She replied only with a smile.

"Now, look you, Mr. Ian." Yannick regained his attention. "I believe you to be an honorable man, but I must know just what you have in mind with my daughter."

Ian looked Yannick squarely in the eye, and was happy to play along. "I am, sir, an honorable man. And I respect your family's virtue. I cannot offer you my hand as a seal—"

Katerina and her mother chuckled at that reference to the incompatibility of their worlds.

"—but I give you my word," he continued, "when I ask for your daughter in a most committed bond." A few more words forced themselves from him, almost of their own volition ". . . for all time."

Behind his chair, Katerina and Nola were talking between themselves and laughing. They acted like very close sisters more than any mother and daughter he had known. Ian turned his head to look back. Yannick leaned in to speak near his ear.

"That is a most acceptable offer. Welcome to the family, Ian."

When Ian turned his head, he was careful not to move toward Yannick too quickly so the forcefield between their worlds did not jolt them both. Looking straight into those soft eyes, Ian had to agree with Katerina. Her father was a wise and kind man.

Ian and his new family had an old-fashioned betrothal ceremony. There was much dancing, but no touching between the new couple. They all sang, sometimes together, sometimes individually. They told jokes and laughter rang out, lots of laughter. Katerina's parents drank quite a bit of wine; Katerina, drank a little, and Ian, not at all.

Of the whole festivity, Ian liked best Nola and Yannick's sharing of tales of their courtship and life together. He could see that the couple loved each other with a passion, far more than each loved him- or herself.

What kind of fear, Ian wondered, could bring any mind to imagine that such an abundant sharing of love could in any way threaten the Sisterhood? Nola and Yannick's joy in each other was life at its best.

In time, after her parents retired upstairs, Katerina asked Ian to take a walk around the farm in the night air with her.

"I'm sorry my father was teasing you about your intentions. You're not obligated," Katerina said.

Quickly swinging round in front of her, Ian looked into Katerina's face. "I make my vow to you and you alone. Will you make such a commitment to me, Katerina?"

She smiled. "And I, to you alone."

After a few minutes of shared silence and smiles, they continued to meander along.

"I know the Sisterhood will not let me stay here, Katerina. I had a reality transfer, and came to you while you were in audience with the Crone Mother—what a wicked creature!"

"I don't agree, Ian," she objected. "The Mother is not bad. She wears the yoke of millennia of tradition and the needs of the Collective. If you would judge her, it should only be for not having the strength to reach beyond the boundaries that were handed down to her."

"I suppose," he admitted. "Anyhow, I managed to be present in your meeting with her."

"I'm so sorry you were left drifting there," Katerina said. "I heard you call, but couldn't respond completely because I was about to come before the Crone Mother and couldn't delay. If I had fully responded, you would have materialized in the audience chamber."

She shuddered, and Ian broke out laughing.

"Poof! There I am, appearing out of thin air. Beg your pardon, Mother dearest," he said.

"That would not have been helpful, Ian."

"Oh, I know, but I would have enjoyed the startled look on her sour face, Katerina.

"Why did you go to petition her? I don't need their help. She cannot be trusted." It took all his reserve not to directly mention the Crone Mother's admission of duplicity. He knew it would have only been pointless insensitivity on his part. Katerina knew the truth, but obviously she wished to believe in the higher ideals of the Sisterhood.

"When you had to leave so quickly after so many hours on the mound, I knew your remaining time here was becoming very short," she said. "The Sisterhood has the resources necessary to give us more time together, but the Crone Mother would have to approve it."

"So how are we able to get together this time, when she said I was not to return?"

"I don't think the Crone Mother really meant you could never visit again. She was just angry and hurt that I might choose to leave her service. Anyhow, I requested some time to come back home, knowing she would grant it. As long as I'm here, she can't affect my activities, even if she desires to do so."

The subject of the Crone Mother's effect on them and the restrictions of the Sisterhood were depressing Ian. He decided to change the subject. "Did Yannick visit Djalma recently, Katerina?"

"Yes," she responded with delight. "Papa is not of the people of the Sisterhood. His family comes from the mountains. They are a people of The Nature as well, called the Tolen.

"They have a method of calling a person forth, while that person dreams, or coming to another within that person's dreams."

Immediately, Ian saw possibilities outside the control of the Sisterhood, "Is that something Yannick can teach us to do? Dreams are unlimited. We could come to each other, and have the sense of touch between us. This could solve our separation!"

The look on Katerina's face made it evident to Ian that his suggestion was something already tried and failed more than once.

"Papa has attempted to teach Momma the dream calling during all their years together. Many times he has tried to give me the gift. I have proven to be even more of a failure at it."

"Maybe I could learn to—" Ian started to say.

Katerina was already shaking her head. "I don't doubt that you could learn the calling, Ian. But even the best of Papa's clan take years of dedicated daily instruction from their masters to learn the way. And their lineage has come from a long history of active dreamers. We must accept that you and I do not have sufficient time here on Motherworld to learn the talent."

"No!" he shouted.

Katerina put a finger to her lips to calm him.

"I cannot accept being restricted to our separate worlds alone, Katerina. I cannot live never to be able to see you again, knowing you are forever in the space just before my eyes, but forever invisible to me."

"Nor can I, Ian."

Ian took a deep breath and intentionally changed his focus.

"Do we even know if our suffering together has provided any benefit, other than to validate a ritual?

Katerina looked at him in dismay.

"Oh yes," he added. "Let me further introduce you to another key component of my culture. Cynicism."

Katerina responded, "Legend says benefits are experienced not only in the present and the future of the Collective pairings, but are retroactive as well."

"Yeah, right," Ian said. "But does anyone verify this benefit? Or do we just take the word of those in power who have a vested interest in their little ceremonies?"

Frustration was getting the better of him. Katerina defused it a bit with a little laugh.

"We have a little of your cynicism here as well, mister. I was wondering the same thing during a period of my own mistrust and doubt. So I visited a few of the people that I encountered before finding you.

"We can be happy that, in every case, they seemed to have more of a zeal for living. Even where there had been the most suffering, some sense of hopeful expectancy had been revived.—As long as there is hope, there is a future—In some cases their lives had so changed for the better that I had a hard time believing I had arrived at my intended destination.

"I don't believe our union will create your 'happily ever after,' but it gives me some optimism. The improved circumstances of our parallels, and all other people, are evidence of the improving condition of the Collective."

"I pray you're right," Ian said. "There is one 'Katerina,' whose child was being taken from her. I want to believe she's better off for our effort."

"Is she the one you visited just before you came to me when you were so injured by the void, Ian?"

"Yes," he said. The memory of it brought tears to his eyes. "It was my overwhelming compassion for her pain that caused me to foolishly attempt to spring back into her reality. I hoped to help her. But as you know, the effort landed me in the void."

"After I sent you back home that day," Katerina said, "I went to visit that location by retracing your path. I wondered what could have caused you to chance such harm. I found her. Yesterday I went back, after returning from my audience with the Crone Mother."

"Are they together?" he pleaded.

Katerina smiled. "She has the baby, and the little girl has a loving father."

Sheepishly Ian asked, "Is the father one of my parallel identities?"

"No, it is another man and he is bonded with the mother. Their lives are a hard path, but their companionship makes it far better than before."

Ian and Katerina walked in silence for a long time before he could accept that comforting thought. Then he returned to the current problem that he and *his* Katerina shared.

They walked to a large outcropping of stone, and decided to sit for a while.

"If this union causes changes to the future *and* the past of

Making Plans

the pairings in the Collective, I wonder how our relationship here has already been redefined by our continuing actions," he said.

"I am afraid that we won't be able to know that, Ian, since we don't have the ability to view our lives from outside of our immediate perspectives. We'll just have to have faith that our bond is becoming stronger with our efforts."

A gentle breeze blew. Long grass in the field swayed.

"Katerina, in your audience you mentioned a Cleansing Ceremony. It sounded like if the Council would do one I would be able to extend my visit. Is there no way we can bargain with the Crone Mother to get them to perform the ceremony? Can anyone else do it?"

"Only the Council would have the collective talents to perform the true ceremony," she said. "They would never perform the Cleansing without the Mother's direction. And it's certain, she won't permit it."

"Hateful woman!" he blurted without thinking.

"I thought so at first, but Momma says even though the Crone Mother is not making her choice for our benefit, the Mother's path is very likely the best choice to secure our future together."

"How so, Katerina? Our future together—apart?" Ian's voice trailed off into dejection. "And your culture doesn't even provide divided lovers the option of hastening their return to each other."

Katerina turned to look sternly at him. "You remember that, Ian. Do not do that to me! Do you hear me?"

"I have promised you, Katerina, and will not take that pledge away from you. This promise *is* mine to make."

The instant change in Katerina's expression made it obvious that she was certain of the harm that could result from disregarding one's own life. It would be a long, hard promise for Ian to keep. But he would force himself to keep it.

"Although I am not thoroughly convinced," Katerina continued, "Momma is of the opinion if the Council performed the

Cleansing, and you stayed in the Motherworld, the result would eventually take us away from each other forever. We would even lose our memories of each other."

Ian stared at her, completely confused and disbelieving. This is *truly* the world of tragic legends, he thought.

"Momma cried for us much of the first night that I returned, after I told her and Papa about our situation. The three of us talked through all the ancient legends we knew from both peoples. Coming from two realities, fusing into a single heart and bonding the rift in the Collective, this is what fortune defined for us.

"If we force a path outside the Collective's intended plan, we may cause the disintegration of all our pairings throughout existence."

"Let's say I accept this idea. Are you so certain that the Sisterhood is infallible in their understanding of the Collective's intended plan for us?"

Katerina seemed a little dispirited. "*They* are certain."

"I have no doubt that *they* are certain, but do you agree with them, Katerina?"

"I don't know. It's not something to regard lightly. The cost—if I am wrong—could be a price that I would be least willing to pay."

Ian took a slow, deep breath. He was beginning to feel completely numb to the pain of the situation. His sense of defiance, however, was not diminishing at all.

"There is something far more popular in my culture than the occasional fatal pact between star-crossed lovers," he said. "We have an affinity for defiance, rebellion against overwhelming odds.

"I can understand that you've spent your whole life believing in, and following, this belief system put forth by the Sisterhood. I wish for you that it were possible for me to have such faith. It's selfish and petty on my part, but I would feel more assured about the survival of our love, Katerina, if I knew you weren't willing just to let the Sisterhood take everything away from us without a fight, without taking any chance at all."

Suddenly charged with animation, Katerina arose and stood

firmly on her feet. The look on her face was a complete reversal of a moment before. With determination, she said, "I'm glad to hear you're willing to fight the odds. There's something that might allow us at least to stay in contact, until we can manage more."

Ian's heart began to race. Automatically, he started to stand, his arms reaching out to hold her. He quickly stopped himself and lowered himself back onto the rock. "It's times like this that it's so hard not to be able to hold you in my arms," he said. "What will we do?"

"You may not think it's a good idea, Ian, once you've heard it. There's danger involved."

"I don't care. What are my options?" Then something crossed his mind. "Danger to us both?"

She nodded.

The idea of danger to Katerina was another issue altogether, as far as he was concerned. "How is it dangerous to you? What are you thinking?"

"It's something you brought up about the first *Sacred Vow* something that allowed the King and the Crone Queen to always be in touch."

"Katerina, I'm remembering that was a tragic legend."

"Not as tragic as the tale the Crone Mother is weaving for us," she replied.

"True. Tell me about the danger," he said.

"I got to thinking when you asked me about the line in the *Vow* that says 'expect me to reach beyond possibility and take your hand'. According to all the ancient texts I could find, and the ones Momma knows from her studies, not since the original King and Queen has the reference of touch between the Union partners been taken literally.

"The earliest archive texts, however, undeniably refer to the *Vow* as more than a romantic commitment. It was the performance of a charm to allow physical contact across time, space, life, and death itself. The charm is performed, the *Vow* is exchanged, and when contact is made between them, the fusion of the two individuals remains intact for the duration of all time.

"We might be able to have this same touch between us. It's an exchange you and I can experience for the rest of our lives, until becoming Immortal. And this would be a union the Sisterhood cannot deny us."

Ian's spirits were dashed. Surely, he had misunderstood something in her plan. Haltingly, he pleaded, "We cannot . . . make contact here . . . or in my world. How can this part of the *Vow* provide us any hope?"

"The Tolen have kinsmen in a parallel realm where the resonance is so contrary to their own that visitation of either people to the other world would mean instant death to the visited and visitor. Their close ties developed before this incompatibility became the case. As they realized the change that was taking place, the priest caste of their worlds learned a way to allow the Kings and high priests to continue to meet, in order to make bonds and negotiations between their peoples. It is called the Menchune Rite."

"Can we go to Yannick's people and petition for their assistance?" Ian asked.

"It's a high crime to perform the rite except for the needs of the King, but my parents value a true bond between couples, so Papa will do it for us. He was a priest of considerable achievement before he and Momma met and gave up everything to be with each other."

Katerina's voice told Ian that this solution was not free of trouble.

"It sounds as if this rite could take us to a place in between both our worlds, Katerina. Do the Tolen Kings make physical contact with their brethren during the Menchune?"

"Papa says he has never heard anyone confirm or deny that contact has taken place during the rite, but he knows there's been no such contact in recent history."

Ian just looked at Katerina. He was hoping she would bring all these pieces together into a plan at any moment.

"The Tolen and the people of the Sisterhood, the Aronkar, were one people in the time of the ancient language in which the oldest archives are written. The basis of most of our separate rites and ceremonies can be found in the common ancient ways.

"Because my parentage is from both cultures, I have always been interested in the universal legends and traditions. Being the Crone Mother's understudy has provided me free access to the archives. My curiosity and enthusiasm for the ancient language has come in handy."

Ian stood and started to walk slowly in an arc around the rock. It helped him to take in all Katerina was saying.

"Several years ago," Katerina continued, "I mentioned to Papa that I'd found an archive of a reference to a ritual that translated into something like 'Commoning.' We both felt it referred to the original Menchune. The particular text was focused on how the priest or King could be protected from any treachery of assassination during contact in the common space.

"After our trip to the Mound, I remembered seeing that text, and I went back to the archives to look closer. If the ancient priests needed to be concerned about the physical well-being of the visitor while in the common space, it had to have been possible to make contact there."

Ian was starting to understand Katerina's focus. "So, when Yannick performs the Menchune, we'll be in a place where we can touch? You and I will make contact, exercise the *Sacred Vow*, and always be in touch thereafter?

"The first thing I'm going to do when we get into the common space is give you such a kiss and a squeeze as to make everyone in the ceremony blush."

Katerina gave him a momentarily coy look. Then her expression went right back being solemn.

"Okay, I'll be serious," he said. "What else?"

"While I was in the village, waiting for my audience, I searched through the ancient texts of sacrament, to find the rite originally referred to in the old tale of the *Sacred Vow*. I'm sure I've found some of the original pages, but sections of the manuscript have disintegrated. I found several later translations, but I don't trust them. Much of their translation work for the available pages is sloppy.

"The tale in the original manuscript speaks of something called the Clutching Rite. I searched for a long time and finally found a document that actually explains how to perform it. It follows the same format as is standard for ritual codices throughout the rest of the archives for the same time period. If I'm to believe the authenticity of this text, there would be reason to suspect that before this older translation took place some of the warnings, preparations, and possibly a portion of the basic chant had already been lost in the damaged original. And, again, I have found no reason to trust the more recent translations."

"It sounds like we have to perform this rite in order to truly retain some perceivable bond between us after we are forced to part," Ian said. "Katerina, do you think it's something we should chance?"

"I'm willing to do so if you are, Ian, because we have nothing else. What are your feelings about it?"

Ian stopped pacing to look into her eyes but said nothing.

"I must tell you," she continued, "that if we choose to do this Clutching Rite, we need to clasp only one hand between us. The available text makes some emphatic warnings about the damage that can be done to the body at points of contact if we do not follow all the precautions and procedures precisely. Should we incorrectly perform any part of this ritual, we could be left with nothing more than a crippled hand each."

Each time a question of danger arose, Ian was bold enough to go forward until he remembered that Katerina could pay an equal price. He didn't doubt she had the same feelings concerning him.

"I must agree with you, Katerina. We're not being given any choice. How soon will we be able to perform the rite?" he asked.

"There are many preparations that must take place first. I have to resume my duties in the village—"

"Katerina! Even after all the selfish deceitfulness the Sisterhood has imposed on us, you're still going to remain faithful to them?"

"I have never been blindly allegiant," she assured him. "If I had, I would know nothing of the common heritage of the Tolen and Aronkar, or the ancient texts that tell of the rite we're planning to perform. There have always been members within the hierarchy that become too obsessed with the rule of the belief. This doesn't, however, mean the core of the belief is stifling or unworthy.

"Besides, if I walk away from the Sisterhood, I only exclude myself from the benefits it can otherwise make available to us. In the future, the ancient texts may provide a way for us to return to each other. You never know, the Crone Mother may be replaced with someone who thinks of the matter differently.

"Part of the reason I'll remain is hope for our future together."

Katerina's words shamed the defiance right out of Ian. "That's the kind of wisdom I need to take back home with me. What do we need to do to prepare?"

The beautiful reddish purple of dawn was coming over the horizon as the couple began their return to Yannick and Nola's farmhouse. A faint light in the far off windows told Ian that Katerina's parents were already busy with the day's chores.

"Oh yes, I forgot about Djalma's dream," he said. "He said it was rather a strange thing. A white-haired man appeared and introduced himself as your father. He was very courteous and friendly. Djalma said they just talked about some esoteric subjects, none of which were particularly abstract, and then Yannick asked if Djalma would be willing to help do something for you and me. What was all that about?"

"Papa tells me that you do indeed have a 'wise one' back at your home. He is very impressed with your friend Djalma. I mentioned that you spoke of such a friend and Papa sought him out, through your connections to him.

"Djalma has agreed to help us with the Menchune. You and I will require 'seconds,' to keep us connected to our respective worlds—Momma will be mine. They'll be our psychic lifelines during the ceremony. You know full well the impact of spending too much time between parallel realities."

"Are we endangering anyone other than ourselves with this endeavor, Katerina?"

"It's not without degrees of danger to everyone involved,"

she said. "No one around us is willing to let us lose what we have found, though. We are much loved.

"Papa will leave today, Ian, to go visit his brother priests. It's been a long time since he's been to the cloister. He must perform the required atonement, study, and make the dedications necessary for a priest to perform a rite, especially one as demanding as the Menchune.

"Though he can't tell any of his brotherhood what he intends to do, Papa will appeal to his closest brethren for their renewed support as one of the priesthood. He'll need all the energy and spiritual support possible.

"The Menchune would normally involve two overseeing clerics, one based in each of the participating worlds. They're the directing forces of the rite. Papa says it is possible to perform the ritual with a single cleric, but it would be very demanding on him and would require every other participant of the ceremony to be completely prepared."

"Would it be possible," Ian asked, "for Yannick to teach Djalma to perform the part of the second cleric?"

"It requires much more than merely learning a sequence of procedures. The function is based on a lifetime of rigorous achievements. Djalma may already have some of the necessary talent, but to ask Papa to so violate the code of his faith would be very offensive."

"I'm sorry to have been so thoughtless, Katerina. It's true that I don't always understand such dedication to a larger philosophy, but I mean no disrespect. You and your family are very dear to me, and such a dedication is obviously what makes you who you are. I sincerely apologize."

"I know you mean no harm," she replied. "Papa assures me that with the proper preparations, he can perform the rite alone. He asks only that we be equally dedicated to preparation."

It was full daylight, and they were nearing the house.

"How exactly will this variation of the Menchune Rite work, Katerina?"

"After the necessary preparations, Papa will go to the ritual altar he maintains here. Several days before the ceremony, he'll consecrate the altar especially for the Menchune. At the altar, he'll enter into a state that will allow him to reach out and contact all the participants, you, our seconds, and me.

"We will each be in our separate worlds, in a special place that each of us has prepared for the ritual, where we can be certain that we won't be disturbed during the process. I'll be here, at home, with Momma. You and Djalma must find some place where you won't be disturbed. This is very important.

"You and I should be reclined, completely relaxed. Our seconds should be seated, in a relaxed position, near our heads, where they can contact us and speak the Calling to keep us grounded to our worlds. It is a repetitive chant that we'll hear subconsciously, keeping us linked to our seconds, but it is designed not to intrude into our consciousness, and so we're able to perform our own rite in the Common Place.

"After Papa feels secure in his contact with each of us, we will become aware of a series of ritual functions that he'll perform as if we were physically doing them ourselves. We'll see through his eyes. Then we'll hear his voice as he begins an elaborate chant in the liturgical language. The rhythm of the language will start to bring us to a necessary state for the transfer. This ritual allows the cleric or clerics to be certain of their connections, as well as to verify that all the participants of the ceremony are prepared."

Katerina continued "Once Papa's voice moves to the background in everyone's mind, our seconds will lay hands on our foreheads and chests, and begin the Calling chant.

"Our energetic bodies—our personal energy fields—will move to the Common Place, which is a place that Papa, as the cleric, will define to us at that time. The cleric will become silent, maintaining the sanctity of the common space within his consciousness. You and I will stand before each other and speak the Clutching Rite—which will allow our contact—as it was in the earliest Menchune. At the end of the Clutching Rite comes the part none of us can be sure about.

"Still facing each other, you'll raise your right hand and I will raise my left into the air. We will begin to speak the words of the *Sacred Vow* while slowly moving to take each other's hand. At the moment of the last word, we should firmly grasp each other's hand. From what my parents and I can tell from our readings, we'll probably able to hold the contact for only a split second. Most likely our hands will be thrown apart.

"This is the part that could be a problem. Papa says he can't anticipate what impact the introduction of the additional rite of the *Vow* will have on the Common Place. We both agree that the nature of the fusion of two realities could create quite a disturbance. In addition, I can't be certain of how much of the translation of the Clutching may be missing due to the damage to the original manuscript. Even if none of the document was missing, it sounds as if the original, unaltered ritual of the Clutching was always a gamble."

"I love you," Ian replied. "I'll do whatever I must to be able to hold on to you, Katerina, or to have as much experience as I can of growing old with you, no matter the gamble. There's nothing more important to me than our success, and I couldn't have any better fortune than to be dependent on the group of people who are involved with this. What do we need to do to prepare?"

She smiled. "I feel the same, dear one. I love you, and I always will.

"Papa will give you some instructions for physical, psychological, and spiritual preparation before you go home to your primary reality. He'll also deliver further information to you and Djalma after you are home."

They were almost on the doorstep. A large backpack and sleeping roll were leaning against the house. Yannick was ready for his trip.

Katerina's Papa stuck his head out of the door. "Come in the house, son-in-law. There are some things I need to tell you, and I must leave very soon."

Nola

Yannick laid out further details of the Menchune Rite, explaining how each of them would need to prepare. He and Nola asked Katerina specific questions concerning the Clutching Rite, and made suggestions of possibly related archives that might be worth searching. Ian felt like he was in some ritual think tank. Yannick wasn't able to leave to visit his brother priests as early as he had planned, but by the time he was ready, all of them felt they had done what was needed.

Before Yannick started his trek to the Tolen capital, Katerina surprised everyone with a request to go along, without Ian, on part of the journey.

"I need to go over a number of specifics that I'm uncertain about before I return to scour the archives," she explained.

Yannick couldn't suppress a little smile, but said with concern, "That will extend your journey quite a bit. Aren't you expected back to the Crones' service?"

"Oh yes. I must present the Crone Mother with the appearance of proper repentance for my emotional indiscretion, but

I don't want to waste time on futile searches in the records. There are things about the Tolen history I think might help me succeed in finding what has escaped me so far."

Katerina turned to look at Ian. "Is that all right with you, Ian? It probably won't be long before you'll be going home."

Actually, it was not all right with him, but Ian could tell she wanted time alone with her father. "Sure. I'll visit with Nola until then."

Katerina got her gear. Nola and Ian began to say good-bye to their beloved travelers. The strong hugs and warm kisses Nola and Yannick shared made Ian envious.

Denied touch, Ian focused his attention on Katerina's face. He felt their spirits begin to intermingle, like the flicker of flame tickling his soul. Rather than "falling into her eyes" as when she first recited the *Vow* to him, he had a growing awareness of becoming a single spirit with her.

Though he couldn't think of the words to explain properly, Ian needed to make sure Katerina knew what he was feeling. He opened his mouth to speak, but words escaped him.

"I know," Katerina said in a sedate voice, barely above a whisper. "I feel . . . you, too."

When they released their gaze, Katerina and Ian realized that Nola and Yannick were watching them, awaiting their "return." The younger couple mouthed kisses from a safe distance. Katerina and Yannick then started down the path to the Tolen capital. Nola and Ian stood in front of the farmhouse, watching them disappear into the distance.

Suddenly the benefit of time alone with Katerina's mother hit Ian and he asked, "Nola, have you ever regretted leaving the Sisterhood?" His question pulled her from watching her family move toward the horizon.

"I've never regretted my choice. Not when leaving was my only way to have this life with Yannick, or to know Katerina."

"I wish you could talk your daughter into following your example," Ian said.

Given her personal experience, Ian thought Nola would be

sympathetic to his purpose. Instead, he was surprised with her look of shock.

"I'd never be so presumptuous as to voice my opinion on such a thing. A person's path is her or his choosing alone. Only the individual can be certain of the appropriateness of the choice."

"I can understand that, but the Sisterhood would have kept you and Yannick apart," Ian said. "And now they are doing everything they can to see that Katerina and I are separated. I'm afraid I can't hold allegiance to a belief system that is fearful of love between couples, just because they're from different worlds and their union disturbs the Order's carefully defined perspective."

"It is not the Sisterhood's belief that is fearful," she said. "Fear manifests itself in the way some choose to practice the belief."

"So Katerina could keep the faith and remove herself from the restrictions of the Order's misrepresentations. I wish Katerina would free herself, as you did."

"There are other things to consider, Ian."

Certain that he had considered all possible viewpoints in this issue, he continued. "I do not mean any disrespect, Nola, but what more is there to consider? The Sisterhood has proven themselves to be secretive and self-serving in this Union ritual. They refuse to give us any assistance, so why should Katerina subject herself to their continued scrutiny and interference? It only seems to help the Order work against us."

Nola looked into his eyes but remained silent. Ian got the impression that she was debating how to respond and did not rush the conversation. When she finally spoke, he was disappointed to hear her only repeat her previous point without being any more specific.

"There is more to Katerina's remaining in the graces of the Sisterhood than you realize, Ian."

"Please help me understand, Nola. I am trying to appreciate Katerina's choice to stay with the Order, but I just cannot comprehend. I'm afraid of how their intentions will affect us both."

After another period of silence, Nola said, "Come with me while I tend to the farm."

As they started to walk toward the animal shelters and pens, Ian felt he was beginning to lose his hold in their world. Soon he would find himself back home on the couch. Focusing on Nola, he tried to cling a little longer, at least until hearing what she seemed to be thinking about telling him.

"Katerina has become one of the wisest women I have ever known, Ian. You needn't fear for her, or for your relationship when it's under her watch. The Sisterhood has never deceived her and will have no better luck in doing so now. She returns, not on their command or for their benefit, but for what she believes in and cares about."

"Oh, I know she has a spirit and a mind like no one I've ever known before. And, I'm certain she has good reason for her choice. That is why this decision so confuses me. Either her continued allegiance is completely out of character, or the reasons she's giving me are not to the point."

Nola picked up a pail of grains and handed Ian an empty basket. She started feeding the fowl and small animals in various pens. Once finished with the animals, they walked through the garden, where she picked ripe produce and began filling the basket that Ian carried.

"Katerina hasn't told me any more than she's told you, Ian. She's convinced she's protecting us all."

Ian could tell Nola was softening to his request. Once he dropped his forceful certainty, she dropped her defenses. He heard something in her tone that assured him that she knew more about what Katerina was not saying.

"You know why Katerina feels she must remain with the Sisterhood, don't you, Nola?" Ian asked aloud, but said to himself, so what is it that you're not telling me?

"It's true she's told me no more than you, Ian. She didn't tell me, and she doesn't know that I know. I wasn't going to pry unless she wanted to talk about it. Besides, there's nothing I can do to help."

Ian hoped Nola had some information that would alleviate some of his fears for Katerina. Instead, her words were only making him more distressed.

Please hurry, Nola. Tell me what you know, he thought. I'm certain I'll slip away very soon, and I need some further assurance about what Katerina is subjecting herself to, and why.

Nola had been walking in front of Ian. When Nola turned to speak to him again, he saw that tears streamed down her cheeks. It looked as though she had been silently crying all along.

"I'll tell you what I think I know, only because these concerns of yours are coming between you and your total connection to Katerina. She needs all of your support now, Ian.

"She is returning to the full service of the Sisterhood for your sake."

The recurrent assumption that the Sisterhood had something to offer him, despite the Order's manipulative interference, was frustrating Ian beyond his tolerance. He started to object, "She knows I don't need—"

Nola raised her hand to give him pause. The look in her eyes completely silenced him.

"Katerina doesn't have any idea that I know, but I'm certain she's found something in the ancient texts that gives her no choice but to use every resource available to her to help the two of you. I found the same thing years ago.

"When she first sent word to us that a Harmony Ceremony was going to take place, I cried for days. I was glad she hadn't come to tell me in person. I thought I had become strong enough to hide my reactions by the time you and she first came to visit us. Despite my efforts, I cried all night. I don't think she realized why."

"She told me about your crying," Ian said.

"As you have found out, the power structure of the Sisterhood does not always present the full story behind their ways and reasons. 'It is not known' is sometimes more accurately 'It shall not be known.'

"Katerina isn't the only one in this family who has loved

exploring the ancient archives, especially those particular volumes that seem almost off-limits and untouched. It is not something the Council sanctions. With a little discretion, being understudy to the Crone Mother allowed each of us, in our own time, to go into those archives that were considered unsuitable for the general body of the Sisterhood."

Ian had a growing sense of doubt as to whether he would be able to stay long enough to hear Nola's whole story. It was obvious that she needed to talk this out at her own pace. She had held what she learned secret, in deference to Katerina.

"I don't know if Katerina has told you, but the history of the Harmony Ceremony always speaks of the Union from the complementary world as coming from a mystic order, and that order is also aware of the periodic disharmony in the Collective."

"She did," he said.

"Katerina couldn't accept that you didn't need the support of such an order because in the cultures where the previous Unions have come from, it was a great honor to be chosen as Union. The individual was seen as having played a vital role in saving the Collective, the many universes. Those individuals had the general support of their culture, and more specifically the support of their order, which provided any needs they had after the ritual.

"They also had a historic understanding of their fate. They saw themselves as being brought to their perfect spirit mate, whom they would never have otherwise met."

"So I understand," Ian said. "Even without an order to tell me so, I can see that Katerina is the complement to my spirit, without question. And I'm thankful to the Collective, or whatever, for introducing me to her."

Ian got the uncomfortable impression Nola was giving him an "oh, you poor unknowing child" look. It wasn't helped by the increased flow of her tears. She dabbed her eyes and continued.

"But how will you feel, living the rest of your life alone, once you have known this intense love and then are denied access to the one you so love?"

"We're not going to let that happen," Ian replied.

"For all the previous spirit mates who came to know their great love this way, a complete separation has been their final end," Nola said. "If such a fate can be defeated, Katerina will find a way. But to do so, she must have the resources of the archives and whatever else she can secure from the Sisterhood, no matter how unwilling they are."

With Nola's pail and Ian's basket now full of fresh produce, Ian followed her toward the house.

"Those chosen by the Collective are honored for more than just saving all existence. There is a great sacrifice in being chosen. 'From those to whom much is given, much is expected.' Being the two in the Union Ceremony is considered the greatest sacrifice for the greater good. To be emotionally quickened by being introduced to your perfect spirit mate and taken beyond one's previous imagination to feel true love is their only reward. So far, you have only experienced the positive side of the Union, still able to come to Katerina. Consider those poor souls who were eventually forced to live the duration of their lives aware of such a love, yet having no further contact with the person so loved due to the restrictions of their belief system? Being parted like that makes for a hard and lonely life.

"Of course the romantic lore claims that these lovers develop the sensitivity and perceptivity of saints. You and I would probably agree that the espousal of this idea is for the benefit of the belief system, not for the Union partners."

"I can understand the need for the bonding," Ian said. "But I can't believe that an intelligence capable of creating infinite simultaneous realities desires or requires such cruel suffering."

Nola continued, "Neither does Katerina. She believes the Sisterhood's handling of the Union is a misinterpretation of the desire of the Collective. The Sisterhood has always been convinced that because some of the spirit mates called for the Union have been physically unable to stay in the same world afterward—who knows if all, since none have ever been allowed to attempt to remain in contact—this means the Collective desired the two to remain forever out of contact after the quickening. The modern Crone Order assumes that the Union relationship must fit into these preconceived molds.

"Katerina is certain that if talents can be realized to allow a continued connection between the Union partners, then that's proof the Collective so desires that continued connection. She believes the Collective might need the benefit of a love reaching across realities, but she doesn't believe this dictates that the partners must live exclusively in their separate worlds."

That's just what I've told Katerina, Ian thought. But, she had never hinted that she agreed.

"Why didn't Katerina ever tell me," he asked, "rather than letting me pointlessly rail against her choice?"

"She anguished over the fact that she had the support of both her life beliefs and her love for you. You, on the other hand, were responding solely to love.

"I believe she has always hoped to find an overlooked solution to allow you two to remain in contact. She can see that simultaneously manifesting yourself in two realities is wearing on you. She didn't want to add worry as long as she had any hope. Now she's come to a more complete understanding of the *Sacred Vow* and found the Clutching Ceremony. I am sure she feels within reach of being justified in that optimism."

"I hope the Clutching works for us, Nola. I want, more than life, to remain in contact with Katerina if I cannot remain here with her. If it were not for Katerina's concern about harming oneself, I would continue to come here until it took my life."

The cold, sharp look Nola gave him left no doubt she shared Katerina's ideas about disregarding one's own life.

"I know, I know," he said. "Don't worry. I've promised Katerina that I will never purposely endanger my life."

Nola gave him a satisfied smile.

"I feel bad about pushing Katerina to separate herself from the Sisterhood," he continued. "I believe she'll find the information we need to make the Clutching Ceremony work. But if we fail, I believe the result will be heartbreakingly sad, but not mortally tragic. I wish she hadn't kept me in the dark about her concerns. It's something we could have supported each other through. Instead, I put the issue between us."

"She understood, Ian. Don't blame yourself. You're wrong, however. Failure is mortally tragic. And Katerina knows it, but she didn't intentionally share her awareness of it with me, not wanting me to worry. It's what she has discovered about the life after the Union that scares Katerina about your being without the support of an order.

"I know she knows because she made reference to some text that I happen to know is contained only in the same tome that holds the well-hidden secrets about the lives of the understudies who experienced the Union."

They entered the house, and Nola started to wash the vegetables as she talked. She didn't notice that Ian was holding himself up by leaning on the table. He was just about to return home, still hearing but physically unable to speak in order to ask her to hurry.

"Living life without your spirit mate, once quickened to their reality, is so hard that no understudy experiencing the Union ever became the Crone Mother, despite the fact that they had consistently been some of the most achieved members of the Sisterhood. Those women invariably lived much shorter lives than their peers, encountering extensive and mysterious health problems. And this particular thing—I believe you can appreciate the implication now fully understanding the Aronkar belief on the issue—"

The last thing Ian heard Nola say seared deep into his heart and mind as he was forced to let go of their world once more.

". . . In many cases, those who experienced the Union later required continual guard to keep them from committing suicide because they were tormented into madness by the separation from their spirit mate."

The Menchune

No matter how the rite would turn out, Ian knew his life after the Menchune could never be the same. He collected his most personal belongings from his house—the teapot, of course, but only for memory's sake—stored away a few other less treasured small items, and put the house up for seasonal rental with an agency.

It was amazing that he had spent so much energy collecting perceived treasures over the years: and now they were completely without meaning. It seemed Djalma was right, that all the collecting was just energetic alchemy. Now that he no longer needed the items to achieve their purpose, they weren't important anymore; they were merely possessions again.

Ian knew it was unlikely that he would ever return. He took an extended leave of absence from work, and told his friends he was going to do some traveling.

It was late spring and Ian could not find a place to rent near Liz's B&B. Fortunately, the basement to Liz's house had never been remodeled for rental. Most of it was used as gardening storage and a workshop, but there was a small room in a back corner with a very old sink and toilet. With a little work, Ian was able to make this a suitable living space.

At first, the location seemed a little dreary. It had no natural light, and Ian had to make a path through all the boxes of storage, around a wheelbarrow and the gardening tools, and by the potting table to get "home." Because he spent most of his time meditating, fasting, and memorizing everything he needed for the Menchune, however, this little hideaway proved to be perfect. When Liz was in and out of the basement for gardening tools, he heard nothing. He heard none of the guest activity, outside or upstairs, either.

After his conversation with Nola, Ian became obsessed with flawlessly performing the tasks Yannick had assigned him. At stake was, as Katerina had said, a price that he would be least willing to pay. For over a month, he completely focused on the daily and weekly rituals and chores he had been assigned. He missed Katerina dearly, yet he knew they were committed not to visit each other during this time of preparation. They had to build up their psychic signatures and retain all their energies for the task ahead.

Each person to be involved with the Menchune understood there was no set time for when the ceremony would take place. It would happen when Yannick felt everyone was sufficiently prepared to achieve his or her goal safely. There was also some question as to how long it would take Katerina to extract enough information from the archives to feel comfortable with their use of the Clutching Rite. Even once she found the related texts, translation from the ancient language was a slow process. The statements had to be understood in the context of the culture.

Additionally, she had to avoid raising the suspicion of the Crone Mother. Working in such areas of the archives was not normally part of her duties, and it would seem all the more suspicious considering Katerina's recent *crisis of faith*.

Yannick visited Ian's dreams a few times, but only long

enough to convey specific information or to ask about the state of his training. He was kind enough to convey short messages from Katerina, saying she was well and looking forward to being with him again.

Yannick made longer visits to Djalma, exchanging information and giving instructions on how to collect and prepare herbal mixtures for Ian and Djalma's conditioning for the ritual. Of course many of the plants found in Ian's world were different from those generally used, but Yannick told Djalma the characteristics of the plant needed, or what effect was expected, and Djalma was able to find substitutes. In several cases, however, it was necessary for Djalma to order herbs from China to fulfill the need.

Yannick had Djalma and Ian perform several psychic fusions. It was generally required between the visitant and his or her second, to ensure that the visitant's connection to his or her home world was sufficiently strong before participating in the Menchune. With Nola at the farm and Katerina back at her village, Ian wondered how they would perform their psychic fusions, but Yannick assured him that, without question, mother and daughter were already properly fused. Nothing during the rite would be able to pry Katerina from Nola's hold should complications occur. Ian took great comfort in the reminder of their closeness.

Even with all his studies and preparations, Ian had plenty of time for helping Liz with her gardens and guests. One of the prerequisites for participating in the Menchune was to bond strongly with the life he was leading. When floating in-between his world and his destination during the ritual, his subconscious would rely on these bonds as an anchor, especially in the time when he and Katerina were not together. He was thankful for this time and glad to be there to help Liz around the B&B. She was not as strong as either she or Ian wanted to believe.

Djalma and Ian became closer during the preparations. They did the required meditations together, took walks to bond to The Nature of their world, and practiced the defined procedure that would be the initial steps of the Menchune. Ian suspected Yannick just wanted them to spend as much time together as possible. Though they had grown close quite quickly, it hadn't been a year since Ian's first visit with Djalma. For Ian's part, the month they trained together further convinced him of the remarkable spirit of his dear friend.

Ian noticed changes taking place in Djalma. When they took walks up the mountain, he responded to everything they encountered with even more reverence than Djalma had had in the beginning. He touched stones, plants, and even the soil in certain places, and he seemed to become overwhelmed with what he perceived. Ian took this as evidence that Yannick had been teaching his friend. Being the well-prepared pupil that Djalma was, the short dream sessions he shared with Yannick were enough to allow him to make significant progress.

One day Ian arrived at Djalma's cabin to find most of the books removed from the shelves. Almost all of the speculative philosophy texts were gone. Taoist and other naturist poetry, texts about plants and animals, and a handful of highly esoteric texts were all that remained. The shelves looked unusually capable of supporting their meager load. Djalma didn't say anything about the change, so Ian didn't inquire.

They searched for an isolated place for the Menchune. They would need absolute concealment. Once they entered into the Menchune, they would be physically and psychically defenseless. Though malicious threats didn't worry either of them, there was still the possibility of being unintentionally torn from the process by some unknowing intruder.

Each participant in the ritual had to remain secure in his or her function for the safety of the group. If any member were suddenly roused from the appropriate state, balance would be destroyed, threatening the rest with being psychically battered about like a flag in a cyclone.

Ian's new room looked to be the best place available. Even an isolated spot on the mountain top would allow the infrequent hiker to stumble onto them. Hidden back in the unexposed corner of the basement, with Liz as the guardian to the basement door, Djalma and Ian were certain to be secure.

After a time, Ian became adept at focusing only on his present task at any part of the day. He would be glad when he could next look into Katerina's face, but that desire didn't distract him from whatever he needed to be doing at any point in time. Each day he rose without anticipation, and retired without regret.

It was the middle of the night when a rhythmic drone awoke Ian. In a little while he recognized it as a chant in some unfamiliar, guttural language. Though the tone used in the chant made the voice unrecognizable, Ian knew this was Yannick. The Menchune had begun.

Without a thought, Ian responded just as it had been drilled into him day after day. Pushing his mattress to the center of the room, he moved everything else to the wall. He placed the meditation mat and pillow Djalma would use to the right of the head of the mattress. The well-rehearsed sequences were reassuring; Ian had no worry of forgetting. The only thing that was not part of Ian's training was the little whisper he directed to Katerina, somewhere near Yannick and Nola's farm: "I will be with you soon, dear one."

Ian was lighting candles and incense as Yannick had requested when Djalma opened the door.

"You hear it too?" Djalma asked.

"Yes," Ian said. The chant was getting louder by minor degrees, remaining steady in rhythm.

"I'll go get Liz," Djalma said.

For whatever reason, Ian had been told to wear a light, loose gown—not pants and a shirt—during the rite, so he changed for the occasion. By the time he had drawn a pitcher of water and placed it with a washbowl near Djalma's mat, Djalma had returned with a plate of cut fruit and bread for later.

In Ian's head, the rhythm and the volume of the mantra was

increasing. With the hypnotic effect this was having on him, it was a good thing that all of his actions had been so practiced as to become second nature.

Liz stuck her head in the door. "You will not be disturbed this night," she said.

Lowering himself to the mattress, Ian looked up and said, "Thank you, Liz."

She smiled, nodded, and pulled the door closed. Ian could barely hear her footsteps toward the outer door. The chant was taking over.

Djalma sat on a pillow and crossed his legs, reaching one hand to touch Ian's forehead and the other to touch his shoulder. They smiled at each other and closed their eyes. About that time, the rhythm broke. After a momentary silence, a new pattern started up, louder, faster, and more intrusive within the mind. Ian was feeling a sensation of being pulled into a trance. He was losing the awareness of his body.

Now Ian saw only what Yannick saw, moving through the initiation of the Menchune. His father-in-law's sacred place was outside somewhere. There were piles of stacked stones with flat tops placed evenly about. Ian noticed that each stack seemed to be of a different type of stone. Each platform had some kind of ornamentation: sometimes statues, sometimes pots, sometimes altar objects or incenses.

Yannick sat on a large, flat boulder in the center of stacks of stone, surrounded by small ritual lanterns, and clusters of smoking herbs. He had drawn patterns on the stone beneath him. As he chanted, he moved his arms, rhythmically sprinkling concoctions about, sometimes onto the flames, which caused colored smoke to rise.

Ian's consciousness began to be pulled into another place, separate from Yannick and separate from where his body was. In his past reality expansions, there was always the shift from one place to the other. The movement between locations did not have a real physical sensation. This was different. Ian felt as if he was being physically "taken" to a location. Forces were carrying him.

His presence was deposited into a place without physical form, where light was just beginning to unfold. He materialized in midair of that lighted expanse.

At the same time, he started to see Katerina before him. Seeing her again gave him tremendous joy. Fortunately, the domineering chant kept Ian's mind sedated enough that he did not forget their purpose. He let the emotion pass and continued on with what he knew he had to do.

He and Katerina floated face to face. Then the chant abruptly stopped. The sudden silence was shocking. Ian was not distracted, however. His training had told him that he would not hear Yannick continuing the chant, which would maintain the Common Place that had been created for him and Katerina, the place where they were now. He would hear nothing more from Yannick until the cleric began to bring them home.

Ian also knew that Nola and Djalma were executing their grounding chants, to keep him and Katerina connected to their respective realities. Though he couldn't hear either of them, he was secure that he and Katerina were safe in their seconds' care.

There was no sense of time, no way to know how long they just stared at one another, each drawn into the other's eyes. In response to their training, each held the other's attention, enabling them to avoid drifting away and becoming permanently lost in their blissful state.

Their Clutching chant began on queue. Ian had no idea what they were saying. Even after Katerina had provided the translation, he could make no sense of it. But he trusted that the chant would synthesize physicality in a nonphysical place.

Ian didn't know if it was his induced state of mind, or just the vision of Katerina, but in this place he felt defined only by their joined voices. He felt no sensation of breath, or of rushing blood. He perceived only the divine rhythm of the Collective. The sensation was painfully exquisite.

Their chant complete, a moment of silence passed. Then they slowly raised their hands: Ian, his right and Katerina, her left. Moving their raised hands closer, ever so slowly, they stared into each other's eyes. In that nonphysical place, he could for the first time feel energy that radiated from her, not as a threatening forcefield but as the warmth of a woman's hand.

Each on the verge of their love's first touch, Katerina and Ian began the crucial verse of their ceremony.

> *I offer this Sacred Vow to you alone. If ever you are in need, expect me to reach beyond possibility and take your hand. As you feel the warmth of our bond, know that you will never be forgotten, never be alone, and never be without this one enduring love.*

Finally their hands touched. It was extraordinary. Though only instantaneous, Ian felt the fusion to Katerina, right down to the core of his spirit. His hand would never again feel like his alone, and Katerina would never be apart from him again.

As exquisite as that moment felt, as soon as contact was complete Ian and Katerina immediately understood why the scraps of the ancient manuscript had spent so much time in warnings. Simultaneously with the bonding, they were repelled from each other so powerfully that Ian thought his hand had been blown off. The pain that followed was excruciating. A blinding flash of light left him unable to see if Katerina had been injured. Wind roared and Ian was being thrown from the Common Place at a tremendous speed, completely out of control. Still blind, and hurtling through a vast space that he couldn't identify, Ian seemed to hit several objects, careering into different directions

Suddenly Ian felt a kind of net seize him, quickly reducing his speed. He began to hear Yannick in his head again, and realized it was the exit chant. The voices of Nola and Djalma joined in. Ian knew he was going home. He hoped that Katerina was going home as well.

Regaining awareness of his body, Ian heard Djalma's chanting with his ears now; the sound was no longer coming directly

into his consciousness. Pain shot up his arm from his hand. Djalma jumped up from his mat as Ian rolled over, bolted up onto one knee, and screamed, "Bloody hell!"

Then Ian burst out laughing, thinking about the first time he had tried to hug Katerina. Djalma was squatting, a few feet away, looking at him as if he were crazy.

The hand that Ian had been so sure he had lost was just fine. It felt rather tender, but it was intact. Seeing it gave him reason to believe Katerina was well also.

"What's so funny?" Djalma demanded.

"Quiet boys, it's still early," Liz said, coming through the door.

Ian lowered his tone. "My hand hurts like hell, but it's still here." He continued to laugh, almost uncontrollably.

Djalma just stared as if Ian had left his wits in the Common Place. "And you find that raving funny?"

"No, Djalma. I'm just happy. The first time I tried to hug Katerina I got a jolt, and introduced myself with the same exclamation."

"Oh, okay." Djalma gave a look of confused acceptance. "Welcome back, Ian."

Ian took a deep breath and smiled broadly at Djalma and Liz. "Thank you, my dear friends. That was amazing. I actually experienced the touch of Katerina's hand!"

Thinking of Katerina, Ian closed his eyes and slowly squeezed his throbbing hand, ignoring the pain. He could swear he was physically grasping Katerina's hand in his. He felt his fingers slide between hers; he felt the warmth of her palm. The sensuousness of her soft touch—defying any space between them—completely overwhelmed any other sensation from his body.

Reluctant to release that contact, Ian finally returned his attention to his friends and rose to his feet. Looking over to Djalma, his wide-eyed gaze became frozen on the young man.

"Is there a problem?" Djalma said.

"Look at him," Ian said to Liz as he pointed to Djalma's

head.

"Oh, my God!" she cried.

Djalma was looking bewildered. "What are you two going on about?"

"You're a wise old man," Ian told him.

"You are too kind," Djalma said, shaking his head and giving Ian a wary look.

"No, I'm serious, Djalma. Look in the mirror!"

When Djalma turned to see, his knees buckled. His head of braided, blond hair had turned pure white. Never again would anyone have reason for complaining that he did not look the part of his wisdom.

Into the Mist

Not long after that day, Ian found himself wandering through a massive dream world hallway. It had very high ceilings, a wooden floor, and thick, old doors with glass transoms above. To him, the place had the feel of an old schoolhouse.

People were moving about rapidly down the hall, in and out of the doorways. Ian was just walking along, curious to what this place was. As he peered into the open doors, he found classes taking place inside some of the rooms, while others were living quarters. Just as he was about to look into another door, Yannick appeared in it.

"Welcome, Ian!" he said.

"Yannick! It's so good to see you!" Still in the daze of a nonsensical dream state, he moved to hug his father-in-law. "How is—" Ian began excitedly to ask about Katerina.

Yannick cut him short. "Come inside, Ian."

Ian entered a large space, which seemed to be a mix of open

outdoors and interior living quarters. His focus was diverted to the peculiar mix. "I like what you've done with the place."

"It's what *you've* done, Ian."

Ian studied Yannick, not understanding his humor. Then he realized he was being serious.

"We're in a dream, aren't we, Yannick?"

"*You* are. I've come to visit."

"So I have created this room?" Ian said.

"Yes, you."

Ian scanned the room again, watching birds fly over interior furniture, looking at grass bordering an Oriental rug. "Well, I like what *I've* done."

His tranquil state broke as Ian remembered whom he was speaking with. "How's Katerina? Did she make it back without any negative effects? And how's Nola?"

Yannick laughed lightly. "Everyone is fine. Katerina sends her love . . . Let me see your right palm."

Ian looked at the reddened palm of his hand, and then held it up to show Yannick.

"Is it sensitive, Ian?"

Turning his palm to look at it, Ian said, "Intensely, right after my return. The tenderness has lessened a little." He stared at his palm as he spoke. "I'm grateful for even the pain that remains, as a reminder of Katerina." Slowly he closed his eyes and then his hand. "I can feel her here."

"She *is* here," Yannick said. "Her palm is red as well. Katerina feels your touch, and she always will."

Ian let his hand open again. Opening his eyes and staring into his palm, he felt Katerina squeeze in reply. He smiled and lowered his hand.

"I can't wait to see her again, to see Nola."

"Look," Yannick said, raising a hand to point to a grove of trees on the left side of the room. Katerina and Nola stood there talking to each other.

Ian walked toward them absentmindedly. But he never seemed

to get any closer. Eventually he stopped and just basked in the joy of their images. When he again turned to speak to Yannick, it was as if his steps had not moved him forward at all.

"Give them my love."

"I will, Ian. And it won't be long before you'll be visiting us again."

"The Crone Mother won't like that," Ian said.

"You'll come to the farm. The Sisterhood has no say there. Besides, I think the Mother turns a blind eye to what happens on our farm."

Ian smiled, looking back at Katerina as her image faded. "The old lady might not be so bad after all, just as Katerina said."

"The expectations of the office," Yannick added. "It's time for me to go, Ian."

Ian moved back to Yannick and embraced him.

"I'll be visiting you periodically, Ian."

"And I, you . . . and your family," Ian replied.

The next thing Ian realized, he was walking down the hallway again. He fully remembered his visit with Yannick, but couldn't remember Yannick's departure.

Looking into additional rooms, he noticed that none of the rooms any longer restricted themselves to interior spaces. Ian could tell that they also stretched out into parallel realities. Within each room, there were people—obvious alternate selves of each other—carrying on their individual lives completely unaware of their other selves or the finely choreographed interaction between them all.

Ian never did go back to the work, or to the life he had before Katerina came to his tea that first time. The time leading up to the Menchune taught him too much of life's real importance to be able to go back to focusing on corporate pursuits and material possessions.

No longer did Ian have the driving urge to acquire specific items—the purpose of his acquisitions was accomplished. He felt that pull toward ownership only rarely. Once in a while he was drawn to some small item, most often something found in nature, but the connection was never quite as strong as he had felt before. Djalma's speculation was that Ian continued to manifest the ability to create other portals as he desired. Ian was inclined to agree, though he did not really care to adventure to other destinations.

Ian continued to live in Liz's basement after the Menchune. He helped with her guests and gardens. He and Djalma continued to be close friends.

Katerina remained the understudy, sifting through the archives for lost arts that would allow her and Ian to spend more time together. When Ian met Katerina at her parents' farm, she and Nola performed a limited Cleansing Ceremony in an attempt to allow Ian to stay longer. It helped a little, but not enough.

With the rediscovered tools from the archives, and Yannick's Tolen connections—as well as the continued "physical" connection they managed—Ian and Katerina never encountered any real threat of madness from the forced separation after their Union. The building physical wear of the travel, however, continued to reduce the time they could share together.

Now and again Ian would come out of a visit feeling an intense disassociation with his home reality. It was a peculiar sort of weakness. He seemed to have strength enough in his muscles, but there was faintness deep inside of his body and mind. Sometimes Ian worried that he just might end up disappearing from both worlds. Yannick, however, taught Djalma ways to help Ian recuperate after his increasingly infrequent visits.

Katerina learned many things from her secret studies that probably extended their lives and visits together, but the negative impacts of their early visits could never be fully overcome. And visits took as much out of her as they did out of Ian. Worse yet, when Katerina came to his world, the visits returned to their early soundless state.

Over the years, Yannick gave Djalma much information he would never have found otherwise. One day, Ian happened to find Djalma on the rock by the river where they had first met. He looked downcast.

"He's gone, Ian. Yannick—my teacher, my friend—is gone," Djalma said dolefully.

Struck to the heart at the loss of his father-in-law, and sympathetic to the loss Katerina must be feeling, Ian fought to resist the urge to sink to the ground. Slowly, he moved over to the rock, rested a hand on Djalma's shoulder, and lowered himself to sit beside his friend.

"Such a loss," Ian said mournfully. "We will all suffer for it." Then, for some hope against hope, Ian asked, "Are you certain? Surely not Yannick!"

"Yes, Ian. I'm certain. I felt the connection break the instant he passed away. He had taught me to experience his presence as I do my own."

Poor Katerina, Ian thought. Now she is without family—she had not yet gotten over Nola's death several years before.

The old friends just sat together for a time, grieving while silently listening to the river flow by, the birds singing overhead.

"There is something else I need to tell you, Ian."

Ian's breath was weak as he looked up to meet Djalma's eyes. "Please, no more bad news."

Djalma forced a very slight smile. "Nothing more like that, but you may think of it as bad news.

"Yannick knew his time was short, and near the end he made me promise to charge you with a task. He apologized for not compelling you himself, but he said he understood your resistance, and thought it would be less disturbing to all involved if he took the responsibility on himself. It seems he always thought there would be time for you to take over."

Ian had an uncomfortable feeling about what was coming

next. He felt his face tighten and his brow lower. "What are you talking about Djalma? Out with it. Take over what?"

"You were always meant to be my teacher," Djalma said. "That's why we came together."

Ian leaned quickly back and braced himself with one arm, as if he were trying to get far enough away to better focus his eyes on Djalma. "That's insane, Djalma! Me? Be a teacher? *Your* teacher?"

Hurriedly, Ian got to his feet and started across the top of the rock, around behind Djalma. Before his foot met the path, he turned around and looked down at his friend. "Who came to whom for help?"

Djalma, having previously had time to consider the improbable situation, was calm. "I know what you're thinking. But Yannick said you always had more information than you were willing to take responsibility for. He said to tell you he's sorry for not being here to tell you himself. But you have within you all the information you will ever need."

Ian gave Djalma a blistering look. Sunbeams through the trees warmed his back, and defensively, he withdrew from the conversation, paying attention instead to the sensations of his body.

"Ian," Djalma said to regain his attention. "Yannick told me to come to you for the rest of my training."

Ian felt like storming off, cursing at the sky as if at some perverse deity. "And did Yannick say just how I was to get access to this information that has thus far evaded me?"

"Acceptance."

"What are you saying, Djalma?"

"Yannick said you should accept the responsibility of being the possessor of such knowledge."

Ian's frustration quickly burned itself out. He shook his head and a smile broke, followed by a quiet laugh. "This is lunacy."

He turned to look down the path, toward the road. "I need to go home." Looking back at Djalma, he asked, "Will you be all right?"

"I'll be fine."

"Okay, then. Let's talk another time," Ian said. "Come visit."

Ian started down the path. A few steps into his exit, he started talking to himself, objecting to what he had just heard.

Djalma called to him, "Ian?"

"Yes, Djalma," Ian shouted, without breaking his gait.

"When can I expect my first lesson?"

Ian's only response was an increase in the speed of his footstep and the volume of his protestations. Over all that, he still heard Djalma's laughter, and his parting words. "Good night, my friend."

Despite his consternation, Ian felt the warmth of his friendship with Djalma, and the support, beyond death, from Yannick. It made him smile for a moment. But he did not feel like taking on such a responsibility as Yannick felt he was prepared for! In fact, he felt like being angry, so he continued to step heavily and object to this blessed plight under his breath.

Too near to the loss of Yannick, Liz became ill. Ian cared for her until the end of her days. On her last night, he was meditating outside her bedroom when she called him in.

"I love you, Ian."

"And I am blessed for it. I love you, too, Liz."

"I've got to take a trip, Ian," she said, looking into his eyes.

Her voice was clear, but Ian could see that her eyes were hazy. He patted her hand and smiled.

"Do you need any help?"

"No, friend. I'll be all right. I won't be going by myself. I have to pick up a little wisdom that's waiting for me."

Ian struggled to avoid sobbing. He didn't want to disturb the peace Liz seemed to have. "Pick up wisdom? You've always been one of the wisest people I have known. You always knew what was important."

Liz tried to squeeze his hand, but she barely had strength to hold it.

"I want you to stay here after I'm gone. You don't have to run the place the same way I did, nor even have guests. I want you to stay as a favor to me."

For his own composure, Ian tried to stop her. "I'd be glad to do what you ask, Liz, but there's no need to talk about that now."

Liz was unyielding in her intent. "Guests aren't so bad, though, and every now and again you might have one who proves to be the very reason you've been taking people under your roof all along." She smiled, but only momentarily, as if it took too much time and strength.

"But you don't *have* to have any guests, except one. Sometimes I hope to be able to come back and rest a period here between destinations, visit with you and Djalma. Not too often, because I'll be busy. Just every now and then."

Ian rose up and kissed her on the cheek. "You come as often, and stay as long as you like . . . when that time comes."

He lowered himself down in the dining chair beside her bed.

"Will you stay?" she asked.

"Yes, Liz, until I go to live with Katerina forever. There's no place I would rather be."

Liz was quiet for a long time after that, with her eyes closed. Ian just looked at her slight smile, and the glow that seemed to emanate from her face.

After the better part of an hour, Liz slowly opened her eyes, looked over at Ian and said, "Take care of Djalma for me." With that, she closed her eyes and Ian never heard her make another sound. It took a while before he had the strength to rise up and check her breathing.

Liz had begun her own travels.

"Come stay anytime, dear friend," Ian said. "You know a way of honoring the gift of life that few people, including Djalma and me, will ever learn. We will be lost without you . . . for a long time."

Being apart from Katerina—except for the touch of her hand and the rare visit allowed them—and being without Liz, Ian tried to devote himself fully to Liz's way of serving people. But it could not be the same. Most of his spirit went into the gardens, as he dreamed of the gardens that surrounded Katerina in the understudy's cottage.

Despite his lack of enthusiasm for drumming up business, the B&B prospered almost more than Ian could tolerate. The breakfast part had to go, because he hated cooking, but people were always coming to study with Djalma and some of them needed a place to stay. For those who needed some financial assistance, Ian had them agree to cook breakfast and clean up afterward, in return for a reduced rate.

In fact, the people traffic was a good thing for both Djalma and Ian. It kept them somewhat social, feeling useful and focused.

One day when neither was busy with guests, the friends were taking a walk. All of a sudden, Ian said, "I have an excellent idea. We should trade houses, Djalma. You move into the big house with your visitors, and I'll stay in your cabin."

"Forget it, Ian. I have to entertain them all day. At least you should look after them at night."

"They're coming to see *you*," Ian insisted.

"Only as long as they don't know who the *real* teacher is," Djalma teased.

Ian threw up his hands in surrender. "Point taken. I never said a thing about it; I love my guests. Wouldn't have it any other way . . . I must go home now." Ian turned and walked toward the "big house."

After months of initial resistance, and then the periodic protest of disbelief, Ian had begun to open up to what Yannick had said was his responsibility, to accept that he possessed a body of knowledge that he could impart. For a long time, he had resisted, feeling that he was as much in the dark as he had always been. He couldn't abide the idea of being a "false teacher," unable to instruct even himself.

But he let the Powers That Be know he was willing to accept

the knowledge—in his mediations, his walks alone. As far as he could tell, the only result was a decreasing fear of possessing knowledge. He appreciated that Djalma was not pushing to provide this supposed information he could not find within himself.

One day, Ian and Djalma went on one of their frequent walks through the woods together. It became obvious to Ian that despite his friend's attempted participation in the conversation, Djalma was preoccupied. Some of his responses were completely nonsensical.

"What's wrong, Djalma?" Ian asked. "You're attention is definitely elsewhere."

"Nothing. Um, something Yannick was trying to teach me, but didn't complete before he passed. It's nothing to trouble yourself with. I'll get the information as soon as I am ready for it."

Ian finally convinced Djalma to talk it out. "Perhaps hearing yourself express the issue out loud will help you realize the answer."

Reluctantly, Djalma started on a discourse of an elaborate concept Yannick had been expounding on. For about thirty minutes he rambled on explaining concept and method, until he reached the end of Yannick's instructions.

"I haven't been able to get past this point on my own, no matter how hard I try," he said.

Ian hadn't precisely heard all that Djalma had said, because so much of it seemed too far over his head to even make any attempt to understand. The rhythm of Djalma's voice had been matching their footfall as they walked and Ian had become completely detached, relaxed.

When Djalma was finished with his exposition, there were a few minutes of silence, save footsteps that continued their steady beat. Then, absentmindedly, Ian spoke as almost an unconscious continuation of the rhythm of conversation and step that mesmerized him.

Djalma's abrupt halt broke Ian's inattention.

"What?" Djalma demanded.

Ian was barely able to recall what he had just said, or recall that he had spoken at all. With a bit of effort, he found the first word, heard himself say it, and then mechanically added additional words, one after another until the last—as if recalling something he had learned by rote.

"Discovery . . . of a truth initiates its own inevitable obsolescence . . . the ever-progressing horizon."

Djalma stamped the ground with one foot. "That's exactly the issue!" Then he broke into a little jig. "Yes!"

Barely out of his meditative trance, Ian was a little confused about all the excitement.

Realizing the implication of what had just happened, Djalma went completely still, staring at Ian. "That was not an idle speculation. How do you know that, Ian?"

Ian's first response was completely reactionary. "I don't!"

Stopping to consider the information he had offered Djalma a moment before, Ian had to admit that it made perfect sense to him now. But he was certain that he hadn't had access to that information the instant before he'd said it!

"Or . . . I didn't," he added, not really sure how to express what had just happened.

Djalma took a couple of steps toward Ian and grabbed him by the shoulders.

"You've done it, Ian! Yannick was right!" Djalma exclaimed.

Ian pulled away. "Don't be ridiculous! It's a matter of grace; a fluke."

"Aaaaah, you've got yourself in it now, my friend," Djalma teased, his eyes wide with excitement. "My teacher."

Unwilling to stand for any more of Djalma's playfulness, Ian turned and continued on his walk. Djalma called out a couple of times, and then rushed to catch up. It took considerable restraint on his part, but Djalma was silent. So was Ian—for the rest of the walk.

The progression was slow, but little by little, merely by opening himself to an expanded awareness a little more all the time, and not restricting what it brought him, Ian found that he came to be aware of things he didn't think he could know. He never did imagine himself as Djalma's teacher. It was more as if each of them was teacher and student. He often needed his "student" to help him realize that what he had mined was gold and not pyrite, fool's gold.

As time passed, Ian would take on a student from time to time. It was always someone who had inspired him, and the tutelage would last only a short time. He was accepting the responsibility more than he had ever desired to. But most often, Ian used his new capabilities to pass the information to Djalma, who would disseminate among the wider audience.

In time, Katerina became the Crone Mother. Even though she could then require the Council of Crones to perform the Cleansing Ceremony, it only took one attempt to realize the process was too little too late. By that time, the consequence of the psychically demanding ceremony was about as bad as doing nothing at all.

Even though it was too late for Ian and Katerina to benefit directly, Katerina's reign as the Crone Mother would be beneficial to many in the years to come. Lost wisdoms were revived due to her years of study. The Aronkar and the Tolen renewed their unity as one people living two paths. Their assistance to each other benefited both peoples.

Best of all, the full conditions of the Harmony Ceremony were discovered, documented, and made known to the entire body of the Sisterhood. With the Tolen and Aronkar operating as partners, Katerina searched and found within the Tolen archives some long disregarded texts—unrelated to any of the rituals performed by her father's people, but actually lost parts of the tradition of the Union Ceremony. Quickening of the bond between the Union couple was—as the Aronkar had always known—vital to healing the Collective Consciousness. Just as Katerina had suspected, however, the process had never needed to be as restrictive as the Aronkar had practiced it throughout their history. In fact, they had been missing the possibility of a remarkable development.

Specifically, works within the Tolen archives made it clear that it was advantageous to all the infinite realities if the Union couple could further overcome their isolation in separate realities. This achievement into a shared—expanded—reality by a bonded couple from disparate realities began to provide a potential opening for others, thus providing many more people the possibility to learn of and contact their own Spirit Mates. Henceforth, if the Collective Consciousness called to any two, the Sisterhood saw it as their honor to assist both members of the pair in any means they could to locate each other and to achieve their life together in whatever way the couple might choose.

Ian accepted the long periods of time between visits to Katerina, but he didn't come to like the separation any better. As he grew older, he found it increasingly harder to cross the chasm between Katerina and himself. The ever-widening gaps in time between possible reunions became a source of great frustration and sadness.

When he started to get lost between locations—essentially becoming comatose, in his world—Ian was forced to ask Djalma to move into the "big house." Djalma agreed reluctantly.

The comas began the end of Ian's journeys to Katerina. There was little he could do but await the time to rejoin Katerina, in a place they could both inhabit.

With the Tolen and Aronkar cooperating as one, eventually Katerina was able to learn her father's art of dream-calling. She was too weak to make much use of it by the time she mastered the talent. She tried, however, to compensate with dream connections when Ian lost his ability to materialize in her world.

One night, Ian realized he was in a dream, about to receive a visitor. He had learned to recognize the subtle sensations provoked by a visitation. He was elated because it had been a long time since Katerina's own failing energetic signature allowed her to visit.

As soon as he saw her in his dream, Ian's heart broke, for he knew why she had come. Her image and energy were very different from any of her other visits. This was not an ordinary dream projection.

"My time has passed, Ian. I will wait for you in the Mist of the Immortals, dear one."

Ian reached out for Katerina, and found himself jarred from sleep. He just lay there. The worst of his pain was the idea that he must wait until his own time. For the promise he had made to Katerina, never to harm himself, he would wait.

Ian lifted his right hand so that he could see it without lifting his head. Almost afraid to find out if he could still reach her in the Mist, he began to close his hand.

Ian felt Katerina's fingers slide through his.

Afterwords

Epilogue

When Ian finally located her again, Katerina was sitting atop the fine old outcropping in the field on her parents' farm. Her eyes were closed, and she wore a blissful expression. It was wonderful to once again see the place where they had spent so much of their last evening together before the Menchune.

As he approached, Katerina broke the silence, speaking slowly, quietly. "The first recognition of the soul's complement is so potent that even sampling the reminiscence is rapture."

Ian considered her words as he moved closer. The joy radiating from Katerina's face induced him to return to his own first memory of her. Though his eyes rested on her present image, they perceived her in another time and place—until she broke the spell with a sudden burst of movement.

She opened her eyes and sat up straight, looking at him. "I want to have that with you again," she said.

"Okay," he replied, mentally and emotionally scrambling to complete the return from his reverie. "Manifest it and we will indulge ourselves until overwhelmed."

"No, not here in the Mist, Ian. But within physical form . . . in the realm of limitations. I want to find you for the first time . . . *again*!

Author's Note

This novel was intended to be a five thousand-word exercise, preparing me to return to several pre-existing manuscripts after a delay. *Sacred Vow* had more to tell and believed its story was important. Several times the story grew beyond my intended limit. I objected, eager to return to my recently neglected writings. Eventually I was lured into following.

Weeks later, hiking with a friend, I told him of some of the views unfolding in this new book. After listening attentively, he said, "Do you really believe this is the way it works?"

We continued deeper into the woods, and I gave his question thought. I was a little surprised at the answer I finally realized. I said, "Until I saw this information in the story, I can't say that I had any such ideas. But now, yes, I think this is *a* truth."

So I followed *Sacred Vow*, became familiar with the people and their stories, learned from their teachings, and traveled where they led. Just when I was willing to abandon all my earlier tales for this new adventure, *Sacred Vow* gently brought me back to where it had commandeered me . . . at the opening of the book I had been working on before its arrival.